The Inheritance

A Novel

CHRISTINE SLEETER

Sleeter Publishing
Monterey, California

The Inheritance
Christine Sleeter

ISBN-13: 978-1986247498

Cover design Delaney-Designs

Published by
Sleeter Publishing
Monterey, California
christinesleeter.org

The Inheritance

A Novel

CHAPTERS

Chapter One

The First White Child Born in Colorado

IF YOU INHERIT something, do you also inherit responsibility for its history? Even if you have no awareness of that history?

If I hadn't encountered a chance story, I probably would not have become obsessed with this question.

While fixing dinner for my favorite guy and my parents one Saturday afternoon in March 2015, my mind replayed a tale I heard earlier that day. I had been interviewing an elderly woman in an assisted living facility for a master's degree course oral history project. During the interview, she mentioned her grandfather's family who lived in a small town in southern Colorado.

"Grandpa's first wife died when they arrived to homestead," she said. "Eventually he met and married Grandma. She was a lot younger than he was. My mother was their first child. Grandma used to say my mother was the first white child born in Colorado."

As I listened to her, I remembered my own grandmother telling me much the same story about *her* mother being the first white child born in Colorado. "My grandmother was just a teenager when she and Grandpa went there from Tennessee. There she was, in a tiny little town of no more than about six cabins, a morning's horse ride from Steamboat Springs, in the middle of winter, having my mother—her first baby—with no one around to help except a couple other women. She went back home to Tennessee to have the second baby, and by the time she got to the third, they were living in Steamboat Springs proper."

I must have been ten when Gram told me that story. I remember thinking Colorado was big—I had stared at it on a map in school, wondering why Colorado and Wyoming were square when the rest of the states had curvy or jagged boundaries. Was Gram's mother the first white child because hardly anyone else lived in that large state? I hadn't wanted her to think I didn't believe her, so I didn't ask. With time, that story settled under so many others that I forgot about it, like a neglected library book on the bottom shelf. Now suddenly here it was. But with Gram having passed away a year earlier, I couldn't ask her what it meant.

I realized I had lost track of where I was with the dinner recipe. I turned down the burner, refreshed the iPad screen, and studied it. Chicken in tomatillo sauce. The photo I saw on Pinterest was appealing, but I should have stuck with something I already knew how to fix.

As I slathered sauce over the chicken and placed it in the oven, I tried to figure out what bothered me about the two stories. Obviously, there couldn't have been two first white children. Which story was right? Or, was either of them right? Could Gram, always a stickler for accuracy, have gotten the story wrong? Did it even matter?

I dashed into the bathroom for a quick shower before Sean and my parents arrived. My parents liked Sean and he liked them, different as they were from each other. I was still trying to figure out why. I sensed he liked the idea of family, although he rarely spoke about his own. Even early in our relationship, while he enjoyed my family stories, he shied away from telling any of his own. As near as I could tell, he never saw anyone in his family.

My parents had made their home north of San Francisco in the same small town where they raised me, their only child. Although neither grew up in a small town, they were both born with small-town blood. They never tired of going to the same few restaurants, and were perfectly content seeing one movie about every six months. Dad, who worked in the post office, knew almost everyone by their mail, and Mom, a medical technologist, knew them by their health. Dad might say, "Bill Mikkelsen's been getting medical supply catalogues lately," and Mom would reply, "I'm not surprised, given his diabetes."

Sean, on the other hand, thrived in the city. He started out a schoolteacher, like me, living and working in Cypress View southeast of the San Francisco Bay. But he only lasted three years in the classroom before he joined Tomorrow's Curriculum, a small but profitable company in San Francisco. Although he had relocated, my home in Cypress View was, as he put it, "only a bridge away."

My parents probably thought Sean would be good marriage material, although they knew better than to say so. At first, Mom was put off by his knock-out good looks. With wavy black hair, blue eyes, thick lashes, and an aquiline nose, he looked like he could be a movie star. Early in our relationship, when I texted my parents a couple of photos of us, she warned me that handsome men usually had boatloads of women circling around. Then she met him and did a complete one-eighty.

"He makes you happy," she remarked. He did, indeed. Ours was a relaxed friendship with occasional sex but no particular expectations. This was exactly what I needed, the perfect antidote to my earlier plunge from an emotional cliff when an intense relationship ended. My parents figured Sean and I were in love. We weren't. But there was no point trying to spell out what we were to each other.

Dinner that night was a success. The three of them complimented my cooking as they cleaned their plates. Even Mom, often critical of something I did, requested the recipe.

Over dessert, I asked Dad what he knew about his mother's "first white child" story. I told him what I had heard from the elderly lady earlier that day. "How much do you know about Gram's grandparents' arrival in Colorado?" I asked.

"Their arrival?" he said, surprised. "You mean how they got there? I suppose by train and stage coach, I don't think they used those covered wagons."

"No, I mean that story about Gram's mother being the first white child born in Colorado. You've heard it. The story makes it sound like no one else lived in the whole state when Gram's grandparents arrived."

Dad frowned. "Of course I've heard it, Denise. I know they went there for the free land. They probably homesteaded. Nana used to tell your Gram stories about how hard things were when she was a little girl. Why?"

Dad didn't seem bothered by the implausibility of his mother's story. I persisted. "It just seems weird that two elderly women would tell the same story about their own ancestors. I mean, they can't both be right."

The three of them gave me puzzled expressions. Then Sean threw back his head and laughed. "Denise, this reminds me of my own grandmother," he said, surprising me by mentioning her for the first time. "She always told the same stories at least twice, usually more than that. Never remembered she had already told them."

"That's not what I—" I began.

"My father did that before he passed," Mom said, shaking her head. "Please warn me if I start repeating myself."

"What did you just say?" Dad looked at Mom slyly.

"Oh, Bob!" She batted his hand with a laugh.

3

I studied the three of them. Why was I the only one at the table who found it odd that two unrelated elderly women would tell the same story from their family's pasts? And why had that question, like a song heard on the radio, lodged itself in my head?

My parents left not long after dessert, preferring the trek up Interstate 880 to sleeping in Gram's old bed.

Sean thought they had an old-fashioned attitude about unmarried sex. He even thought it was kind of cute. "You're still their little girl, Denise. I know they like me, but they also like to think they're protecting your virtue."

"I'm thirty," I pointed out. "A lot older than they were before they started having sex."

"And a sexy thirty you are," he said. "But since your parents aren't here now to protect your virtue . . ." His hand slid down under my waistband.

Sean seemed to imagine my family as the one he wished he had. His eyes looked wistful whenever I mentioned seeing or talking with my parents. To him, they represented television's quirky but loveable *Modern Family*. Or at least that was how he characterized my relationship with them. I inferred that his relationship with his own parents wasn't lovable. Maybe not even quirky.

But because he over-romanticized my parents and their home, warm hearth and all, he seemed oblivious to the rough spots, particularly how hard I worked to please Mom. As long as I could remember, I felt I had to earn Mom's love. I constantly competed with other things in her life, mainly her work, which seemed core to her identity.

I remember my first day of school in third grade. As my classmates arrived, all freshly polished for a new year, I realized my old backpack, resplendent with its cartoon cats, felt childish compared to their sleek new ones. When Mom picked me up that afternoon, I pleaded with her to take me to Target so I could get a new one. Without responding, she drove me home and dropped me off.

"Denise," she said when I protested, "you should have thought of this last week. I've gotta get back to work. Ask Dad to take you to Target." With that, she drove off.

The next morning, she kissed me on the top of my head and offered to take me shopping for a new backpack after school. However, since Dad had already done so the previous evening, I proudly displayed my new yellow backpack trimmed in bright lime green. Mom just nodded, looking hurt, which made me feel like I had done something wrong.

Dad was different from Mom. He liked his job supervising in the post office, but when I needed him, he was there for me. I didn't have to work to earn his love. I could count on it surrounding me, warm and comfy like a security blanket.

Then there was Dad's mother, Gram, who had been City Clerk of Cypress View much of my life. We frequently visited her and my grandfather, who died my senior year of high school. Sometimes they drove up north to visit us, but for Dad, her home represented warm childhood memories, so we usually did the visiting.

Gram and I seemed cut from the same piece of cloth. I never needed to explain myself to her like I did to Mom. When I started playing with Dad's old basketball, Gram was the one who put the hoop back up over the garage. For my twelfth birthday, Gram gave me a ticket to a Golden State Warriors game with Dad. I jumped and twirled around the living room, momentarily forgetting the new jacket Mom and Dad had just given me until Dad draped it over my shoulders. Mom stared as though I were a strange creature that had dropped down from space.

By the time I was in my early twenties studying for my teaching credential, then teaching fourth grade, I had my own bedroom at Gram's, even though I was sharing a small apartment with friends. The apartment was where I tried on adult life, but Gram's home was my refuge. Dad applauded the arrangement; Mom seemed jealous, even when I pointed out that they lived two whole hours away. I didn't bother mentioning that I saw them often enough, and talked with them on a regular basis.

To minimize Mom feeling miffed, I did little things for her. I passed on magazines I thought she'd enjoy, and took her to Starbucks and the mall when she and Dad visited. But there had always been something jagged between us. Gram once told me that was simply the nature of our relationship.

"Your mother does love you," Gram said, "but she never loved motherhood."

"Then why did she have me?" I felt exasperated.

"When she and your dad married, it was your mother who wanted a baby. Your mother has a very strong sense of family continuity, you know, which I've always suspected was prompted by her own parents' divorce when she was young. Your dad would have been happy to wait

5

for a child, but your mother really wanted you. She just didn't realize how much work it is to be a parent. Taking care of a baby isn't like having a baby doll, or even raising a puppy. It's emotionally demanding in ways she never anticipated."

"But Dad never made me feel like I was in the way," I replied.

"No, as soon as you were born, your dad found a well of love in his heart that he hadn't known was there. Loving you has always energized him. Being a supervisor at the post office never defined who he is like being your father does."

"And being a medical technologist did define Mom," I continued her thought.

Gram sighed. "It isn't as emotionally intense as parenting. I think she's used her work as a rudder when she couldn't figure out how else to navigate her life. But she does love you, Denise."

As I grew up, I came to appreciate Gram treating me as an adult. When my grandfather died, Gram didn't hide behind the platitude of "We'll be okay." Her life was shattered for a time. She let me see her pain, then invited me into her gradual process of healing.

Gram managed to live in her home independently (more or less, with increased help of services like Meals on Wheels) until age ninety-four. One day a year and a half ago, stepping off her front porch, she broke her hip in a fall her doctors thought was triggered by a small stroke. After several days in the hospital, it was obvious she wouldn't return home, at least not anytime soon, so Dad and I moved her into a nursing home. Gram died six months later.

But she always continued to express her love. While in the nursing home, she told me she intended to leave me her house. She was writing it into her will. Initially, I balked. But she insisted, saying that my cousins didn't live nearby and my parents had their own home. If I didn't take it she'd have to sell it, which she would hate to do since we both loved that house.

This was true. Gram's craftsman-style home, built during the 1940s, had always been my cozy quilt in front of the hearth, my chocolate chip cookies with milk. Its gleaming hardwood floors and neatly framed windows reflected Gram's care. Its garden, now overgrown with weeds, had displayed Gram's obsession with color and beauty. The idea of selling it to strangers unnerved me. Sitting there at her bedside in the nursing home, I knew I was losing Gram. Accepting her house would keep her close to me.

First, though, I sought my parents' advice.

Dad was matter-of-fact: "Why are you even asking? You love that house. Of course you'll take it."

Mom looked as though I had betrayed her before saying, "How generous of Gram." Guilt battled with anger inside me. I threw Dad a pleading look. He rolled his eyes as though saying, Here we go again.

"Mom," I said, "If I accept the house, I'll need your help figuring out how to fix it up. I have no clue how to even start."

She thought in silence for what felt like a full five minutes, then said, "Well, it doesn't seem right to talk about this while Gram is still breathing. But when the time comes, I supposed we could start with the kitchen."

So now when I cooked for my parents like I had earlier that evening, Mom's influence permeated the kitchen and dining room. Oddly, even though I now lived in Gram's house, what didn't permeate it was my influence. To me, it was still Gram's home rather than mine.

෯෯෯

MY BEST FRIEND Angela wouldn't blow off the "first white child" stories, so I couldn't wait to talk with her the next afternoon after our Sunday shift at the Red Handle, a soup kitchen for homeless people. I had met Angela there four years ago wen I first started volunteering there. She was recently divorced and also an elementary schoolteacher.

Although I had never laid eyes on her before, I immediately felt a sense of recognition, as if she were my long-lost and longed-for sister, even though we don't look alike at all—I'm tall and thin while she's short and stocky; my blond hair is cropped, hers rarely sees scissors. Being an only child, I loved regarding her as my sister, although she didn't share my view.

"Denise," she had explained, "I have a sister who lives in Michigan, and we never got along all that well. To me, the label 'sister' isn't a compliment."

But then later, when I told her about Gram's dying wish to will me her house, Angela quipped, "So as your sister, does that mean the house is half mine?"

Was she serious? Could she be jealous? She didn't seem so, although I wasn't sure. When my school principal learned I had inherited a house while other young teachers struggled to pay rent on small apartments, she advised me to say nothing.

Anyway, there we were Sunday afternoon after our volunteer shift, sitting in Federico's Cantina, a small family-owned bar and restaurant. Home cooking at its best! Federico, from Mexico, liked to travel to visit relatives in other Spanish-speaking countries. When he did, something new would pop up on the menu. The special that day was a Chilean dish, *cazuela*. Beef, chunks of corn, potatoes, carrots, and other vegetables swam in a broth that tasted like a sun-washed herb garden.

As we munched on taco chips while waiting for our orders, I told her about the previous morning's interview and the odd coincidence it produced. Angela's eyes narrowed. "I'm struck by both of them emphasizing *white*. What did they say about the Indian people who were there?"

Her question surprised me. "Nothing. Why?"

She folded her arms and regarded me. "Denise, use your head. It sounds like both of these mothers were born just as white people were tossing the Indians out of Colorado to get their land, most likely the Utes. It doesn't matter whether they were the first ones born to white people in the state. They probably weren't. And they sure weren't the first people there, but the idea of 'first' kind of makes the Indians invisible, huh? What the story tells me is that white families had settled in and were starting to have babies, which means the Indian people had been forced off their homeland."

I was stumped. I hadn't thought about the white-Indian thing. Nor was it clear to me why Angela jumped right on it, and why her eyes were needling through me as though I had forgotten to put on my clothes.

Finally I said, "Um, well, I guess I could ask the lady I was interviewing."

"And you don't know your own family's story? You think the first white child was just born onto a blank canvas or something?"

I shrugged. "I hadn't thought about it, and I have no clue about Gram's ancestors. Don't get your nose so out of joint. I was just a kid when Gram told me that story." I couldn't figure out why Angela seemed to smolder. "What's with you?"

Angela exhaled and dropped her eyes. When she looked at me again, the anger that had blazed a minute ago had subsided. "You know my grandmother who lives in Colorado?" she asked.

8

I nodded. Angela had told me a little bit about this grandmother whom she had gone to visit over Christmas break. Apparently when Angela was a child, her father had taken her from California to Colorado to visit his mother a couple of times before he and Angela's mother split up. Shortly after they split, he was shot in a convenience store hold-up, a customer in the wrong place at the wrong time. After that, Angela lived in California with her mother and sister. Her memories of her father were sketchy, and she lost connection with this Colorado Springs grandmother. Until last Christmas, when a letter from her prompted Angela's visit.

"Well, she's Ute. That makes me part Ute."

I blinked. When Angela had told me about her trip to Colorado Springs, she hadn't mentioned her grandmother being Indian. And in our endless conversations, this was a piece she had never mentioned. With her tawny hair, Angela didn't look part Indian to me. But then I realized I just assumed all people of American Indian descent had black hair and brown skin.

Angela didn't miss my surprise. "Yeah, I don't look how a lot of people think Indians are supposed to look. I'm no expert on the Utes since I grew up in California and haven't spent much time in Colorado. When I was a little kid, she was just Grandma to me. She doesn't live on the reservation. It was just like visiting anyone in town."

"So she grew up in Colorado?" I asked, trying to figure out where to start.

"No," Angela replied. "She grew up on the reservation in Utah, but left when she was seventeen."

My face must have looked blank. Angela continued, "She met my grandpa over in Rifle where she and her mother went to sell beadwork. Grandma was an expert at beadwork, a real artist."

"Rifle?" I asked. "That's the name of a town?" I pictured Wyatt Earp and Doc Holliday's shootout at the O.K. Corral.

Angela laughed. "Yeah, it's just a town on Interstate 70 not too far from the Utah border. Anyway, the way Grandma tells it, she used to go down south to Rifle with her mother and aunts periodically to sell beadwork at a large trading post there. Sometimes they spent a few days shopping and just getting away from the reservation. Grandma felt like it was a big deal when they went. She'd wash her hair and fix it up for the occasion. One day, she met this gorgeous white man who was working in the trading post. At least, she thought he was gorgeous." Angela laughed

9

again. "Grandma was even attracted to his strong, white teeth! Kind of like buying a horse."

"This was your grandfather, I take it."

"Yep. Bob Walker, the grandfather who died long before I came along. Grandma didn't want to go back to Utah after she laid eyes on him. Her family told her to stay away from that white man, but she was hooked."

"Wow, what a story," I said.

"Yeah. They just ran off together. They moved around for a while, then settled in Colorado Springs when my grandfather found steady work. So that's why Grandma's in Colorado. When I was there last Christmas, she told me a little bit about how she got there, but she and I talked mainly about my personal life. Well, I talked and she listened. She's a good listener. So I only know a little bit. But I do know enough to know it was devastating to the Utes to be forced off their homeland, and I know that white people did that in order to take their land."

"My great-great-grandparents didn't fight the Indians," I blurted out defensively. I could hear my dad saying, *They went there for free land.* But was it actually free? And how did I know my ancestors hadn't fought?

"I'm not accusing them, Denise, and I'm not accusing you," Angela said. "I'm just making the point that these two stories took place at a time when things careened downhill for Grandma's people. Who won and who lost depends on the way the story is told. The way you heard both stories erased Grandma's people with the word 'first,' while acknowledging them in the background with the word 'white.'"

I wasn't sure what to say. Part of me felt I should apologize to Angela and her Indian ancestors for what my white ancestors may or may not have done. Another part of me felt angry for being made to feel guilty.

"Well, beyond the little bit Gram told me," I muttered, "I really don't know the story."

"I'm not trying to upset you," Angela said almost apologetically, her thick brows furrowed.

"No, I know you aren't, you just raised some questions I hadn't thought about."

She put her hand over mine. I squeezed it and shook my head. "On a different note, how about catching a movie Friday evening?"

She withdrew her hand with a sheepish look. "I have a date. A divorced postal worker who likes to surf in his free time." Since her divorce Angela had been on dozens of what I considered disastrous dates, thanks to internet dating. She'd go out with a guy one evening, then spend the next evening telling me what a jerk he was.

"You don't surf," I pointed out, wondering how she managed to select people she had nothing in common with.

"Duh. We aren't going surfing, we're meeting for dinner and a walk. I know you're booked up next weekend with Sean, but maybe we can grab a quick dinner sometime this week?"

"Sure," I said, still wondering why her first reaction was how our grandmothers' stories conflicted. Did she resent something about me, or Gram, that I didn't recognize? Was she trying to avoid getting into it with me, whatever "it" was? I hoped we'd be able to clear the air next time we talked.

Chapter Two

If the Ancestors are Protecting Me, Why do I Feel Trapped?

MONDAY I FLED to my fourth-grade classroom after a depressing afternoon staff meeting. I was grabbing my jacket on the way out the door when I remembered an email Sean sent earlier. Tomorrow's Curriculum had sent him to the Philippines for a couple of weeks. The company specialized in creating, adapting, and selling on-line curriculum modules aligned with curriculum standards used in the U.S. Their global division, where Sean was housed, worked mainly with Third World countries. U.S. specialists like him collaborated with government functionaries and teachers to adapt American-made curriculum for local use. Sean's message included two attachments and a link:

Can't wait to hear what you think of this stuff. Take a look at the attached Eng Curric Guide and a think-piece we use in the States. The link goes to a draft multimedia science module. Have fun exploring!

One of the attachments, a 164-page English *K-12 Basic Curriculum Guide* from the Philippines Department of Education, detailed specific weekly content standards for each grade level. I'd save it for one of those nights when I needed help getting to sleep. The other, only six pages long, sketched a curriculum plan to connect science with English literacy development.

When I logged into the website, I found folders loaded with stories, science content, and interactive exercises, all directed by cartoon characters representing Filipino school children. I chuckled as I recognized Sean's intellect and humor throughout. The materials were smart, fun, and challenging. I dove in, playing around with activities and jotting notes for what I could use.

Abruptly I stopped, anger flaring. I wouldn't be able to use any of this stuff. Not after having spent the last hour listening to the school district's assessment coordinator Cynthia Jorgenson talk at us teachers as though we were fugitives from her remedial class.

"Since the tests will start a week after spring break, there isn't much time to double down on prepping your kids," she said as though we hadn't been preparing them for testing since Christmas. "Let's look at where we are." PowerPoint slides whizzed by as she plowed through five years of test results in reading and math for the district, then for our school.

"As you can see, Milford didn't hit its growth targets for either subject area last year, and reading the year before," she said, waving the remote at us like a paddle. "This year as you know will be even more challenging since we've switched to an online test battery. Now, I know you have a lot of English-language learners here, but you need to do whatever it takes to get those English reading scores up." Most of our kids are from blue-collar families, many of them generationally impoverished through low-wage work. About half are Mexican American. Many families speak Spanish at home.

Sarah Peel, our principal, stood. "Thank you, Cynthia. All of our teachers will be meeting with reading coaches before spring break. After break, we'll dispense with social studies and science so we can concentrate on reading, math, and computerized test formats."

We teachers quietly seethed. I couldn't see how dropping everything to drill for tests was educative. I recalled an incident two years earlier when I was in the second day of a two-week ecology unit I designed linking social studies and science. The unit considered how ecologies formed geologically, work biologically, and support particular economies and lifestyles. I had carefully embedded reading and writing throughout. The kids were starting to ask great questions, like under what conditions buckskin was good to use for clothing.

Suddenly the associate superintendent wandered in, just "visiting classrooms," he said. When the bell rang and I dismissed the kids for lunch, he cornered me to ask how I was using the adopted textbooks.

"I'm using them along with other things. We're actually reading some primary historical sources," I replied, believing this was a good thing. "Let me show you."

"And which standards does this unit work with, exactly?" he asked, ignoring what I said.

I began reeling them off, but he stopped me. "Miss Fisher, if you were teaching in a high-achieving school, this unit would probably be fine.

But you aren't. These kids are going to be tested on material that's aligned to the textbooks, so I'd advise you not to stray very far from them."

Now, sitting at the computer on my desk, my mind replayed the conclusion of Ms. Jorgenson's speech: "I don't care what you've been doing. You've got to get these scores up. The reading coaches you're working with know exactly which skills each of you should zero in on, especially with your bubble kids."

Bubble kids. I hated that term. It refers to kids who don't quite test at the proficient level, but are close. If enough move from below proficient to proficient, the school can be reclassified from not meeting, to meeting, its target. Or, more bluntly, we can go from Failing with a capital F to succeeding in our mission to educate.

What was I doing here? Bringing up bubble kid test scores wasn't why I became a teacher.

I had majored in geology. California's geological history and its widely diverse geological forms always fascinated me. In the north are mountains formed by volcanic activity. In the east and along the coast are other mountain ranges formed by tectonic uplift and glacial erosion. Landforms and minerals in different regions have huge implications for the ecosystems that develop, which in turn shape the kinds of economies people create.

But I graduated with only the murkiest sense of what I would do with my degree. So, I lived with my parents for a couple of years while I worked as a barista to begin tackling my student loan. My parents thought my job was a terrible waste of my education, so I looked into teaching. I was pleasantly surprised to find how much I enjoyed working with kids. Six years ago, I was hired to teach fourth grade at Milford. Most of the time, it had been a good fit for me. While I couldn't spend more than a half hour or so every couple days on science, I'm good at weaving science into other subjects. It's fun, actually, to figure out how to connect basic arithmetic or writing with science—fun for me, and fun for the kids. I think they learn reading, writing, and math better when they're doing something interesting rather than slogging through canned activities.

So fiddling around with Sean's online science module made me jealous. He could think creatively, while I was supposed to obsess about test scores.

I felt stuck. I couldn't just stop teaching in order to explore other options. I was still paying down my student loan, even though inheriting

Gram's house had eliminated the need to pay rent. I couldn't return to barista work, and I wouldn't sell insurance like my friend Maura after discovering she hated teaching. I loathed the idea of becoming a school administrator because then I'd be one of the ones telling teachers what they could and couldn't do.

I texted Angela: *4:00 quick beer Jake's?* Her reply was almost instantaneous: *Yep, might be a tad late.*

Jake's is a brewpub about halfway between our schools. By late afternoon, the same few people are usually seated on the patio and the rest of the place is only beginning to fill.

I ordered a beer, then sat down to wait for her.

Angela had entered my life not long after the disastrous end of what I had thought would be the romance of my life. I was twenty-seven, and Peter had walked out of my life. I might still be a candidate for a psychiatrist's couch if it weren't for Angela.

I met Peter when a couple of other teachers and I happened to stop in a local café that was featuring live music. I couldn't pry my eyes from the sax player whose blond hair swept across his boyish face like a half-drawn curtain. During the break, he came to our table to chat. I was so nervous I could barely talk, but somehow in those few minutes, he managed to learn my name and where I worked. The next day he surprised me by showing up at Milford just as I was about to leave. Two weeks later, he had practically moved into my bedroom in my cramped, shared apartment.

Over the next few weeks, love reigned. I didn't exist without Peter; life before him had been only a mirage. At his gigs, he seemed to play as though every note was a love song caressing me. He even composed a couple of tunes for me. With him, I felt exciting, enticing, larger-than-life. Because he was larger-than-life to me. I dropped everything I had been doing to be with him, including preparing lessons for school. Not trusting him to love me for who I was, I tried to become who I thought he wanted me to be. How stupid, in retrospect.

One day, I caught a rumor about him and someone named Karin. I don't know if it was true, I never met her. But I confronted him.

"That's it," he said, and began stuffing his things in a bag. "There's no Karin but there might as well be. You've changed, Denise. I think it's time I moved on."

"How have I changed?" I demanded.

"You cling like Saran wrap. And for God's sake, stop turning your bedroom into your classroom!"

"What the hell are you talking about?" I was flummoxed.

"You should hear yourself." In a falsetto intended to mock me, "'Put it here.' 'No, not like that, let me show you.' 'Do it a little slower, yeah, like that.' 'Good boy, I think you've got it.'"

"I didn't say that!" I felt completely humiliated.

"Maybe not 'good boy,' but the rest—all the time. There's a difference between wanting to know what a girl likes, and needing instruction, Denise. You need to learn that difference. Christ, I'm never dating a teacher again."

In Peter's wake, all the worst teacher stereotypes affixed themselves on me. I felt schoolmarmish, bent on correcting everyone else's mistakes and unable to see my own. Utterly boring, completely undesirable, headed straight for spinsterhood—a long-discarded concept that suddenly felt like it fit. I pictured myself thirty years hence – grey hair in a bun (never mind that I wear mine short), blouse buttoned up to my throat, old-fashioned glasses my only adornment.

At school, I went through the motions, but my normal passion and energy had evaporated. My social life, which had atrophied to Peter, no longer existed.

But Peter was right. I had become needy. I clung, I drove him away. It took a while for me to realize that.

Gram tried to listen. But having never experienced rejection, she simply couldn't understand what it felt like to be treated like yesterday's trash. She did succeed, however, in convincing me to seek out productive ways of filling my time. "Look for ways you can give to others," she had advised. "You'll be surprised at how much others give back."

So I volunteered to read to elderly residents of an assisted living facility, and to take a once-per-month shift serving the homeless at the Red Handle. My first morning there, as Angela and I headed for the door at the end of our shift, she grabbed my arm. "Want to get a quick bite? You look like a fellow member of the Dump Club."

I stared at her.

"C'mon, do you have time?" she asked, steering me out of the building. "There's a diner two blocks that way." She pointed. "Where's your car?"

It turned out that my car was parked right in front of hers. We drove to the diner in tandem. After getting seats and menus, then placing our orders, Angela looked directly at me and said, "I hope I'm not being too blunt and I don't want to offend you, but you have the look of a dog that's been kicked too many times. It's a look I know well, by the way. I see it a lot when I look in the mirror."

"What happened to you?" I asked, not yet willing to open up my own pain to this stranger.

"My ex-husband dumped me. That was over a year ago, and it still hurts." She looked away, then wiped her eyes with the back of one hand. "Sorry, I wasn't expecting that."

"You don't have to talk about if you don't want to," I replied.

"No, that's okay. I hardly ever do talk about it, but since you seem to be in the same boat, maybe you'll be able to empathize. See, the thing is, we're both injured birds. I'll tell you what happened to me, and if you want to, you can tell me what happened to you. You have this protective look about you, like you aren't sure who you can trust and you might not even know whether you can trust yourself. No prob. We just met, why would you trust me? But if we're dealing with the same thing, we might be able to help each other."

We stayed in the diner for about three hours. Angela told me the story of her three-year marriage, which ended when her husband left her.

"I shoulda seen it coming," she said. "The signs were all there, but I didn't read them. Not until I came home from work one day and he was gone. His clothes, his books, his golf clubs. The apartment looked like a windstorm had blown through, leaving my stuff scattered." Angela's ex had moved in with another woman, and subsequently married her. "They've even got a kid, who as near as I can tell was conceived while he was still living with me." She had turned to cigarettes and one-night stands for comfort until she realized she didn't enjoy either.

"I just kind of backed away from the whole dating scene for a while until I got my courage up to try again. I joined a dating website a couple months ago. I go out now and then, but I haven't found anyone serious." She emptied her glass of beer. "So tell me about what happened to you."

I did. I described how intoxicated I felt when I met Peter. The glamour I associated with his life, his music, his being on stage. His lovemaking, how he seemed to know where to touch me and when, how to play the rhythms of my body as skillfully as his saxophone. And not because I was instructing him what to do! Then that high began to show tatters, resulting in him leaving.

"I hadn't been so full-on in love with someone before, and I was scared of losing what seemed like the perfect relationship. I didn't trust him, is what it boiled down to. And I have this image in my head of teachers being boring, so I kept trying to be someone else when I was around him. God, I feel like a dork."

"You're a charter member of the Loser Ladies League," Angela quipped.

I burst out laughing. Angela joined in. Unable to stop, we both doubled over until our insides ached. After that day three years ago, we turned to each other when we needed someone.

The door to Jake's opened and Angela entered. I had intended asking her point-blank if she was upset at me about something, but as soon as I saw her, I realized I needed a lift rather than an argument. She tossed her bag next to mine, gave me a quick hug, and went to the bar. Returning with her beer, she asked, "What's up?"

I plunged in. "Has your school had its Cynthia Jorgenson meeting yet?" She rolled her eyes and nodded yes. "What bothers me most, not just about that meeting, but about the whole education package it represents, is that teachers aren't being taken seriously as professionals. We aren't expected to think or treat our kids as thinkers. My principal recognizes the problem, but feels powerless to do anything about it. It's demoralizing."

"Yep," she agreed with me. "Thankfully summer isn't that far off."

"Angela, I don't think I can keep doing this. Here I am, into my sixth year of teaching, working on a master's degree, and being told to fixate on test scores?"

This was not a new topic of conversation between us. "I need another plan, Angela. I can't just keep going through this same routine, then jump back in."

"And you think I like it any better than you do?" she asked. "What keeps me sane are the kids. I just compartmentalize the adults in my school into this little box in my brain. When adults' nonsense breaks out, I shove it back in, which is what we're doing right now."

"Yeah, but it doesn't stay there, and the district's fixation on testing has real consequences for what we do. I've just gotta come up with something else. Maybe look around for another job in education." I stared into my beer, then smirked as I said, "I can just see it on my headstone: *Here lies Denise Fisher, master of raising bubble kid test scores.*"

Angela laughed. "You could do worse. Folks might think you're in the champagne industry."

"Bubble master, that's what I'll have on my headstone. Let's hear it for champagne!"

᪠᪠᪠

I WAS CLEANING house on the last day of spring break when I glanced out the window and noticed my neighbor Mr. Jackson retrieving his mail. Gram had become fast friends with the Jacksons, particularly him, as they commiserated over their gardens, weighing the pros and cons of this plant versus that. She also pitched in occasionally when he needed a volunteer to help out with this or that community issue. He lived alone now, Mrs. Jackson having passed a year before Gram, and their two grown children having married and moved away.

Mr. Jackson reminded me of Yuri Kochiyama, a Japanese American human rights activist I wrote a research paper about in high school. As a teenager her family was sent to an internment camp with other Japanese-American families, then she lived in New York advocating for impoverished Puerto Rican and African American families later on. Her courage had stuck with me. Mr. Jackson, currently president of the local chapter of the NAACP, was always intervening in local disputes related to race, leading voter registration drives, and seeking support for youth community initiatives. I regarded him as a local hero as well as an occasional stand-in for Gram when I needed an older person to talk to.

Mr. Jackson seemed to think he could coach me into becoming a gardener like Gram. The other day, he had arrived at my door with fertilizer and an offer to help me clear weeds, check the health of perennials, and make any needed repairs to the watering system. As we studied the bed Gram used to fill with colorful annuals and vegetables, now overgrown with weeds, he asked how I saw bringing it back to life.

"I know you know a thing or two about plants," he said. "Your grandmother told me about the botany classes you used to take in college."

"I majored in geology," I said as if to excuse my ineptitude with flora. "I only took two botany classes, and that was eons ago."

He just stood there, apparently not buying my excuse.

20

"Besides," I continued, "I feel like this is still Gram's garden, so I should keep it up the way she did, although obviously I haven't been doing that. I know it's theoretically my home now, but I keep seeing it has hers. Besides, I never had a garden before and frankly don't know what I want."

"You need to see what's here first," he had replied as he set down the fertilizer. We located Gram's garden tools and proceeded to dig up fistfuls of weeds, dismayed to find vestiges of invasive iceplant Mr. Jackson had been trying to eradicate.

Now, as I watched him retreat, I thought of Gram. Both she and Mr. Jackson embodied integrity. At least, so I had thought. But then, why did Gram tell that first white child story that seemed not quite true? If it was only half true, or not even true at all, what else might she have told me that was suspect?

What about Dad's comment about free land and Angela's speculation that my ancestors were complicit in stealing from her ancestors? Honest as I assumed Dad, Gram, and everyone else in my family was, what about the fact that I now had this huge asset—a house—that most people my age could only dream about?

Angela had gasped when I told her about my inheritance. "Must be nice," she mumbled.

I felt guilty. Until then, we had both been apartment renters. Suddenly I was a homeowner through the accident of birth.

"I supposed I could have told Gram to forget it," I had suggested. Actually, at first I had, but it didn't take much for her to change my mind.

She threw me a look. "Don't be silly. If I were in your shoes, I'd jump at it."

Since then, she hadn't mentioned the unfairness of it, although she seemed to avoid coming over to my house, often sidestepping my invitations with "Let's go see a movie instead," or "I'm beat, see you next week?"

I tossed the vacuum into its closet and entered my bedroom, still the same little back room Gram had given me when she was alive. I hadn't yet been able to bring myself to move into her bedroom, which still looked as though Gram had stepped out to run an errand and would return shortly.

What did I actually know about Gram's parents and grandparents? Quite little, actually. I knew her maiden name was Margery Foster, but had no clue who the Fosters were, or which of her grandparents had relocated to Colorado from Tennessee.

Curious, I pulled open the bottom drawer of my desk where I had stuffed a jumble of family records—photos, letters, my birth certificate and passport, old clipped-out newspaper stories, things like that. I dumped the contents out on the bed. Sifting through, I found Gram's obituary, with her parents' names and dates of birth and death.

Gram's mother, Iris MacGregor—the supposed first white child born in Colorado—entered the world in 1886. MacGregor. There was the name I couldn't recall. The MacGregors must have been the ones from Tennessee.

So, which Indians were in the Steamboat Springs area right before Gram's mother was born? A quick online search confirmed Angela's guess that they were Ute. I learned that the Utes had lived for hundreds of years throughout what is now Colorado, southern Wyoming, northern New Mexico, and much of Utah. The band closest to Steamboat Springs hunted and gathered along the Yampa River and considered the hot springs sacred. Beginning in the late 1500s, Utes traded with the Spanish for horses, which greatly increased their mobility. French and English trappers appeared in the 1700s, but it wasn't until 1862 that white people in search of gold began to pitch tents near Steamboat Springs. That was twenty-four years before Gram's mother was born.

During the 1870s, the U.S. government pressured the Utes to sign various treaties and agreements ceding land so the arriving white people could settle on it. Colorado was made a state in 1876. But by then, as far as the U.S. government was concerned, there was no Ute nation. In fact, the U.S. stopped treating Indian tribes as nations in 1871 when Congress included a proviso in its Indian appropriation bill that no more treaties would be negotiated. In 1879, the Utes of northern Colorado, who had by then been subjected to several years of starvation, rebelled, killing eleven white people at the White River Indian Agency. Two years later—five years before Gram's mother's birth—the U.S. forced the Utes from their homelands of northern Colorado onto arid land in what became Utah.

What a sorry history. But since my great-grandmother wasn't even born until the mid-1880s, she probably didn't know any of it, although her parents might have had an inkling. When did they first arrive in Colorado? And why? Looking at Steamboat Springs on a map, it's obviously not the most accessible place to go. People coming from the west could follow the Yampa River to get there, but people coming from the east, like my ancestors, would have had to cross massive mountains. Obviously people did it, but why? Gram's grandparents must have had a fierce motivation to put themselves through that trek, although I may never figure out what it was.

I was stuck. Or maybe I had as much of an answer as there was to be had. Maybe there was nothing to chase down, maybe I was wasting my time obsessing over that story. I needed to shove it from my mind.

⊰⊱⊰

ENTERING THE TEACHERS' lounge for lunch on Monday, I spotted fifth-grade teacher Jessica, sitting alone. Her usual companion Cath was out sick, so I plopped down where Cath usually sat, asking, "Mind if I join you?"

"I'd like that," she replied.

Some of the older teachers regarded Jessica as "too PC" because of work she started the previous year with Mexican-American teachers in the district. Jessica isn't Mexican American, she's white like I am, but she had joined a lobbying effort to get "Raza Studies" into the schools, and she used a lot of Mexican-American books in her classes. I didn't know her very well personally, however, mainly because she was married until about a year ago, and I hang out with singles. She's also private as a possum; it was ages before I learned she and her husband had split.

Jessica said quietly, "I can't wait until we can start actually teaching again!"

"Me too," I agreed. Oddly, a few of our colleagues actually liked the test period because it gave them a break from class preparation. Even the majority who normally put a lot into their teaching, by the time May rolled around, didn't have much gas left in the tank. Some just let themselves go with the testing flow.

"I hate all this Robinson-Woodrich stuff we have to use because it's aligned to the tests they publish," she continued. "The other day I read about them hooking up with small agencies in Third World countries to produce curriculum preparing kids for jobs our corporations export, like in call centers."

"Call centers?" I asked.

"And other minimum-wage jobs we send overseas, I believe. I think they're also setting up private chain schools in Africa and India to train kids there for similar kinds of grunt-work jobs."

This sounded a little too much like a conspiracy theory. I wasn't fond of Robinson-Woodrich, either, but mainly because I connected it with Cynthia Jorgenson-style teaching and testing.

When I didn't reply, she shifted topics. "Anyway, I've been playing around with my social studies curriculum this year, linking it with children's literature and bringing Native Americans right up into the present. Have you ever noticed how, after being the subject of a rousing unit in early September, they just kind of drop by the wayside?"

I hadn't. The fourth-grade social studies curriculum teaches California history, and the fifth grade teaches U.S. history. Both start with first peoples but then, as Jessica was pointing out, shove them aside after the opening chapters.

"There's more now than when I was a kid," I said as the first white child story slid back into my consciousness.

"Yeah, but ask your kids if they think Indians still exist. I didn't think about it either until last year when Cath pointed out that Indians disappearing from the curriculum teaches kids that Indians are all gone. So I asked my kids what they know about Indians, and it was all teepees and tomahawks a long time ago. So I've been figuring out how to include them in history all along the way. After testing, I want to do something with reservations today and maybe bring in a speaker."

Was this what Jessica and Cath spent lunches huddled together discussing? "Gosh," I said, "I'm not sure who you might invite."

"Or I could contact someone at, there's this museum up Interstate 880 that works with schools around Indian education. You aren't familiar with it, are you?" she continued.

I wasn't. Since social studies is not my forte, I usually start the year off with geology. Then I give the textbook's nod to early Chumash, Yurok, Miwok, Maidu, and Cahuilla people before moving on to Spanish exploration and the missions. My class never does a full-blown mission project like a lot of teachers do, but we visit one every year. We briefly cover the Mexican period, then the Gold Rush, always a favorite with the kids. After that we get into the waves of immigrant groups, and development of the economy, which I love tying back into science. So, I suppose Indians do get lost along the way.

My eyebrows must have wrinkled in puzzlement because she quickly said, "Oh, I didn't mean to put you on the spot, I was just thinking out loud."

"Well, now that you mention it," I said, "even what we teach about the past leaves out a lot." I briefly told her about the two versions of the first-white-child story, and Angela's interpretation of an unnamed Indian presence designated by the term *white.* "I mean, I had to look up which tribes were in Colorado, since I had never learned that."

Jessica stared at me as though I had uttered something profound. "What?" I asked.

"My god, I never even thought to ask whose land my German ancestors took. How could I have missed that question?"

"What on earth are you talking about?" I asked.

"Last year I did all this research on my German ancestors in Illinois and Iowa. You might have heard about it. Some of the teachers here read a letter I wrote to the newspaper editor about it."

I was clueless. She continued, "Okay. Well, I realized I didn't know anything about my family beyond my grandparents, so I dove into this gigantic family history research project. Maybe one of my biggest takeaways was how English-speakers during the world wars were so afraid German-speakers were plotting to help Germany take over the U.S. that they pressured them to get rid of everything German, including their stories. So people like me grew up with a big blind spot about who we come from."

I nodded, my mind racing to keep up. She continued, "And now you're pointing out another blind spot. Who was there before the Germans? Whose land was it, and how did my ancestors get it? Why didn't I even think to ask that question?"

The bell announced the end of lunchtime. Jessica looked at her half-eaten sandwich still poised in her hand. "Guess this'll be a snack later on," she said, jamming it into her bag.

"Dang," I said, feeling as though I had just discovered an interesting bookshop right before closing time. "I want to pick back up on this conversation later."

"Sure," she jumped up, then reached across the table and gave me a little hug.

ക്ക്ക്

AFTER A WEEK of intensive preparation for the state's tests, Angela and I dragged ourselves like slugs into our favorite Caribbean fish restaurant. Testing season depresses me. This year the kids had to take every standardized test on a computer. Many of our kids don't have computers at home, and while we use them at school, we don't use them so regularly that everyone is comfortable with them, especially when they are supposed to be concentrating on something other than the keyboard. There are always kids in tears by the end of the day.

This restaurant was tiny with a few tables jammed into a room about the size of my parents' living room. But they did fantastic things with fresh fish and vegetables. If you weren't there early, you'd end up waiting in a long line outside. We were seated a few minutes before 5:00.

Angela was just warming up: ". . . and by the time the bill came for dinner, I think he was drunk. He had spent the whole fuckin' evening telling me about his ex-wife and how much he misses her, guzzling as he went. No wonder she walked out on him! He's a self-centered lush."

"Angela," I broke in, "Why do you do this? You say these dates are fun, but this doesn't sound like fun to me at all."

She chewed on a hangnail. "Honestly? I'm afraid of growing old alone. Whew, that's the first time I've actually said that out loud. I just keep looking."

I was dumbfounded. "Growing old? You're only thirty-two."

"Yeah, and my biological clock is ticking away. I want a family, Denise. I want kids and a partner to raise them with." I could hear tears creeping into her voice. "At least you have Sean. And a house you could raise kids in."

True. I had a house and I had Sean. Angela seemed to think I was within striking distance of the future she wanted for herself. But that wasn't actually the case, mainly because I wasn't thinking about marrying Sean. I said, "Sean is fun. He's great for my battered ego. But I don't see building a life or a family with him. I've told you that."

"You have, and I still don't get it."

Sean Grayson had been a classmate in my teacher credential program. At the time, I had a Pacific Ocean-sized crush on him, which of course he knew. Whenever I saw him, my whole body radiated energy in his direction. But he had been recently married, and the credential program began on the heels of his honeymoon. We became friends, but that was all.

After finishing the program, I returned to Cypress View to take a job at Milford, while Sean found work in a school somewhere else. I didn't see him after that. My radar, always attuned to news about him, picked up on his divorce after his third year of teaching. But by then, I was full on into my ill-fated relationship with Peter. It had been Angela who suggested I reconnect with Sean. I found him on Facebook, where I learned he wasn't in a relationship—that is, if you trust what people post on Facebook. I friended him, and we began to chat. Chatting led to coffee, which led to, well, whatever it was we now had.

I took a deep breath, then expelled it loudly. "When I reconnected with Sean, I was still feeling the bruises Peter left me with. I don't feel them anymore, and Sean has a lot to do with that. I have a great time hanging out with him whenever he can manage to come this way. He makes me laugh, sometimes he takes me nice places, and he's not bad to look at, either."

"And your parents like him."

"There's that," I said. My parents not only liked him, they assumed he was their future son-in-law. And they treated him as though he were.

I studied my drink, then said, "I'm not ready for marriage. I'm thirty, but I still have a few years left on the old biological clock. I can't go through what I experienced with Peter again, and the good thing about Sean is that our relationship doesn't have that emotional intensity. Sean lifts me up. When I first met him, I thought he was the hottest guy on the planet, but now I think he's one of the nicest, with one flaw: his world is centered on Sean. That isn't a bad thing, it just means that he only tunes into my thoughts and feelings up to a point. I was thinking about this the other day, actually, when I was talking with my neighbor. Mr. Jackson takes the time to listen to me. He asks questions, then really listens. Sean doesn't do that. I can't take a personal problem and probe it with Sean like I can with you, or with Mr. Jackson. I'll get part way into it, and he'll start suggesting solutions so we can move on to something else. As a result, the kind of intimacy I would like in a relationship hasn't developed. But he's a friend and I'm enjoying the ride."

"Does he know how you feel?" she asked.

"We never talk marriage and kids. My parents try hinting at it, but neither of us picks up their bait. Truth be told, he may not be thinking about getting married again."

Angela stared at her glass. "What?" I asked.

"I'm pondering the unfairness of the universe," she finally said. "I want a family and can't seem to find someone to build it with. You don't seem to want a family, or at least not in the immediate future, but the universe gave you someone anyway."

My mouth dropped open but my brain couldn't figure out what to say. Was she jealous? Could this be why she had torn into me days earlier? Assuring her she would find someone seemed too facile; offering to give her Sean was too glib.

"Sorry," she said, "I don't mean to dump my bad luck on you. How about if we order?"

Had I done something that was eating at Angela, or was her comment just something in passing? As I tried to think how to ask her, she flagged down a server to take our orders.

I decided to let her comment ride for the moment. I shared my conversation with Jessica.

"Is she the one with short dark hair and turquoise glasses, about our age? I've met her at a workshop or something," Angela said.

"Yeah, that's probably her."

"I hear she's seeing this gorgeous guy with killer blue eyes, Joe something. I forget which school he teaches at. He's hot, and he has the cutest Australian shepherd," she continued.

I stared at her. "You and your one-track mind. So back to what I was saying, Jessica was talking about how little the Indians appear in the curriculum, and I happened to mention the white child story and the Utes. She suddenly got this 'oh-my-god' look on her face and started explaining how she hadn't thought about which Indians were there before her German ancestors. It was weird because we just sat there, like, we both have similar questions but neither has a clue where to go with them."

"Speaking of," Angela said, "I've emailed my grandmother about the white child stories. She doesn't think much of them and isn't sure why they would get passed down as part of family lore unless it's to glorify settler colonialism. But she invited me to spend a few days with her when school is out, and said I could bring you along."

"Cool. Hey, that gives me an idea," I said. "When school's out, let's you and me go to Colorado for a week or so. We can nose around first in Steamboat Springs to see what kind of information is available, if any, and put that story to bed. Then we can go visit your grandmother in Colorado Springs, and do a little hiking along the way. What do you think?"

She smiled broadly for the first time all evening. And so did I. If Angela were pissed with me, I was sure she wouldn't have invited me to visit her grandmother. Everything was okay.

Reverently that night, for the first time since her death, I climbed into the bed that had been Gram's. This room, her bedroom with its rose-print wallpaper and lace curtains, its intricately carved old dresser and chest of drawers, its lounge chair by the window and writing table in the corner, this was now my bedroom. The house would need a makeover, á la HGTV. But this was now my home, my hearth.

Of course, Gram had wanted me to claim her home as mine all along. She didn't want me to continue sleeping in the small back bedroom, or to place my things carefully around hers as though she had only gone out to tea with a friend and would be returning momentarily. No, she willed me her house so I could make it my home.

After Gram died, when I gazed at my reflection in the bathroom mirror I half expected to see her walk up behind me, sometimes with a compliment, often with a question, and always with a smile. Tonight, having moved my toiletries into what had been her bathroom, I looked into the mirror. It seemed as though a younger Gram looked back at me. Gram, alive in me, me alive in her.

I wondered if Gram's grandparents lived in her, those who left Tennessee for Colorado as well as those who stayed behind. If so, did they live in me as well? I pictured armies of people behind me from whom I descended. I could recognize my parents and my grandparents; the rest were faceless and nameless, but they were there nonetheless. Did I carry all these people forward anyway, simply not realizing their presence in my being? Were they my protectors, surrounding me even though I couldn't see them?

I didn't know. But I did know that Gram was not completely gone. She continued to live, within me and within the house. But not as a ghost. Not as something scary, not as a poltergeist playing tricks on the living, not as a spy watching my every move. No, she lived in all she had taught me, the love she had given me, and yes, my body that carried her DNA.

And I was finally an adult. Not a renter anymore, not someone camped out in the back room of someone else's house, but mistress of my own domicile. More than that, I was Gram's legacy. While she left me much to live up to, she also nurtured a foundation I always assumed I could trust. As I claimed Gram's house as my own, I knew I was also claiming her history, her strength, her values, and her unconditional love.

Chapter Three

Discovery that Cost Everything

I FELT LIKE a little kid on Christmas as we walked along Denver's 16th Street Mall. On this balmy late June evening, people were out in droves sampling the cafés, shops, coffee houses, and bars that seemed to spread in all directions. Where to start?

"Holy shit," Angela breathed as she looked around. "I think the average age is twenty-five."

Although we had almost bumped into a family with three children in tow, she was right. Jeans-clad eighteen-year-olds on skateboards rolled past a clump of young professional couples, the men's jackets tossed over their shoulders, the women teetering on four-inch heels. Two young women holding hands, one with spiked pink hair and the other with a long greenish black mane, passed us in animated conversation.

I whipped out my phone. "Selfie time." I looped my arm around Angela's shoulder as I said, "Look at the camera and say cheese."

I snapped a picture, then checked it. I had cut off the top of my head. Looking up, I noticed a young man propelling a small child out of our way. I asked him to take a couple of pictures of us.

Much better! I texted them to Angela, then to my parents with the note, "Made it safely!" Another one to Sean: "Smooches from Denver!" And a post on Instagram.

Angela was also texting. "Grandma will like this photo," she said. "I'm also posting it on Facebook."

"I think we covered our bases. Look at all the shops," I breathed as I gazed around. Then I noticed a cluster of older people who appeared homeless, judging from their blankets scattered over cardboard on the sidewalk. I looked away, feeling embarrassed as though, without wanting to, I had glimpsed the raw underbelly of Disneyland. I wondered if I should offer them a few dollars.

"This pedestrian mall seems to go on for miles. Let's eat over there." Angela was pointing to a small café across the street. Lacking a better response, I put the homeless people out of my head.

Fifteen minutes later, after plowing into our yakitori bowls, Angela turned the conversation to one of our main reasons for being in Colorado. "So, you said you haven't mentioned Steamboat Springs to your parents, right?"

"Not that part of our trip," I said. "I didn't want to get them worked up about what I might find out. Dad was funny in a weird way. When I first told him we were coming to Colorado, he said, 'Oh, you're going to find the first white child, aren't you?' Then he laughed like it was a joke, so I just went, 'Right, Dad.'"

"Why would he have said that?" Angela wondered.

"I thought he forgot all about it. I was surprised, but since he was treating it as silly, then I did, too. Maybe he thinks I might actually dig up something he'd rather I didn't." I twirled the straw in my drink idly as I pondered. "I also didn't mention to them that your grandmother is Ute. I mean, it doesn't matter one way or the other. But since my parents wanted to just blow off my question about the white child story, I wasn't sure what they'd make of me being here with someone whose ancestors were here before theirs."

Angela cocked her head. "I'm surprised to hear you say that."

"Surprised to hear me say what?"

"Well, it almost sounds like her being Ute is an issue somehow. What you just said comes across that way."

I blinked. "She's your grandmother, for heaven's sake. Maybe I was just overreacting to my own parents." But at least part of Angela's accusation rang true. I wasn't sure I had ever met a hundred-percent Indian person, and I had certainly never stayed in the home of one. And, too, the thought that my ancestors might have stolen from hers was unsettling.

Angela was studying my face. "Grandmother won't hate you, Denise, I hope you realize that. She's looking forward to meeting you, actually."

I felt as though she were reading my thoughts. I wiped away whatever expression I'd been wearing. "And I'm looking forward to meeting her. After Steamboat Springs."

"Right. So what's your plan when we get there tomorrow?"

I felt myself relax as the topic shifted. "The first thing we'll do is go to the Family History Center."

I put down my fork and dug through my shoulder bag, retrieving a bulging envelope. "Here's what I have so far," I pulled out a newspaper article and placed it on the table. "This is Gram's mother's obituary."

"Where'd you get it?" she asked as she studied it. The brief obituary featured a blurry picture of an elderly white-haired woman wearing glasses. Her full name was Iris Wilson Foster, born in 1886 to Sally and Orville Wilson of Steamboat Springs, Colorado, and survived by a son and a daughter. One of them, Margery Foster Fisher, was Gram.

"It was in the bottom of Gram's jewelry box. I found it when I moved myself into her old room," I replied. "That weekend, I found even more great stuff that I don't think I'd get very far nosing around in Steamboat Springs without." I pulled out a couple of folded envelopes, then smoothed the crease and opened one of them.

"These letters were written to Gram's grandparents, Sally and Orville, after they moved from Colorado to California. I don't know who this John somebody is who wrote them. But he refers to land Orville had purchased in Steamboat Springs. Apparently after they got to California, he went back to Colorado for a visit and while he was there, for some reason he transferred the land titles into his wife Sally's name. It was their daughter, Gram's mother, who was the first white child in the story Gram told me."

"So you'll go to the Family History Museum and do what?"

"Center, not museum. They have a historical museum too, we could check that out as well." I scooped a forkful of rice and chicken into my mouth. "Do you remember me talking about Jessica at my school?"

Angela nodded.

"Well, a few days ago, I told her what we're doing. She said it's possible to find a lot of information in census records and old newspapers and things like that, but to do it from home, you have to pay a fee. Or, you can visit a Latter-day Saints Family History Center in the town where you have ancestors, and look at what they have. They have old records, and they also have computers that get into the census and stuff. I think you can use them for free."

"OK," Angela said as she nodded again. She reached into her shoulder bag and pulled out a rumpled piece of paper. "Now, here's a list of hiking trails in the Steamboat Springs area that I liked from their descriptions online. I downloaded a trail app that uses GPS so we can find them."

I glanced at the list. Six trails, two starred. She pointed. "Here's an easy one. I also want to see Fish Creek Falls, that's easy, too, unless we decide to keep going to the upper falls. Some of these others are pretty steep; it'll depend on what we're up for."

I had been so absorbed turning in students' grades and organizing what family records I could find, that I hadn't even considered researching hikes. I was grateful she'd done the work, although hiking wasn't the main activity I envisioned for myself.

"Maybe you can hike while I'm researching," I offered. "I mean, you don't have to spend hours with me in the Family History Center or the historical museums."

"You can't be serious." She waved her arm in the general direction of the mountains. It was true that I had been awestruck as we drove from the airport toward Denver. I couldn't believe how massive and grand the Rockies were.

"You're not gonna spend the entire time holed up in dusty files while summer wafts over us and mountain trails beckon. I know you too well," she said. I joined her in laughter.

৯৬৯৬৯৬

AS IT TURNED out, that was exactly how I spent time in Steamboat Springs. Three days later, index cards lay spread over a table in the Tread of Pioneers Museum. Sitting in a back room next to an open window, I wondered what I was doing there on such a fine afternoon. I hoped Angela was enjoying whichever trail she might be hiking.

As I leaned back and stretched I noticed the beginning of a headache. My back felt as though I had been hunched over for three solid days. Which was close to the truth. When I had begun searching for information, I had no idea how much I would find. Piles were splayed out in front of me like a 500-piece jigsaw puzzle.

Orville and Sally, Gram's grandparents, were in the village of Yampa in the state's 1885 census, although what had been Yampa back then was now called Craig. John, who wrote the two letters to Gram, grew up with Orville and seemed to have brought him and Sally to Colorado, marrying Orville's kid sister en route. According to the census, Orville was a rancher, but since he didn't seem to own a ranch, I figured he was a ranch hand keeping track of someone else's longhorns. Ranchers imported Texas Longhorns into the Yampa River Valley. Did they run the cattle north in herds? Put them on trains? I had no idea. Someone named Tom, apparently Orville's cousin, carried mail in Steamboat Springs for a while, then some years later shot himself (accidentally) and two other people in Utah. Having given birth to Gram's mother Iris mid-winter in 1886, Sally (presumably with husband and daughter) returned to Tennessee two years later to have a second child. By 1899, they and their six children were living in California. Their sojourn in Colorado had lasted only about fourteen years.

Was this what I traveled almost halfway across the country to find?

Another pile of index cards attempted to track property Orville had acquired. I hadn't found anything saying he owned a ranch. But I could account for twenty-one lots in Steamboat Springs by skimming old digitized newspapers. I couldn't figure out how Orville managed to buy that much property. And why didn't he sell it when they moved west so they could buy a ranch in California? Why did he transfer the Colorado property into Sally's name?

A stack of photocopied articles beckoned. On top was a chapter entitled "The Removal of the Indians: 1879" from a 1972 book about the history of Steamboat Springs. The chapter opened with:

The Sioux and the Cheyenne had attacked the settlers and had done battle with the U.S. Army. Consequently, it was not difficult to justify decimating the tribes and removing survivors to land so poor no white would settle upon it. The Utes, however, posed a different problem. They accommodated the whites, sometimes to the point of forming alliances with them against other Indian tribes. The Ute problem, *that is the problem of acquiring Ute lands*, became acute in the 1870s.

I was aghast at how bluntly the chapter acknowledged white greed for Indian land. Apparently, the Civil War had ravaged so many farms that thousands of white people, like my ancestors, headed west for a fresh start. I wondered if any of my people had been slave owners. I wasn't sure how I would find that out, or if I even wanted to.

The Yampa River Valley offered rich grazing land, and the only thing standing between it and white people were the Utes, who, I should note, had already been forced to cede over half their land. I learned the sad history of Nathan Meeker, who as a young man had written a novel about a ship captain "civilizing" South Sea natives. In his sixties, he agreed to serve as agent in the nearby White River Indian Agency to pay off debts accumulated from trying to found a utopian community in Greeley. The U.S. government had established the agencies themselves to maintain control over the Indians.

This was like adventure novel meets disaster movie!

But it wasn't fiction. Meeker taunted and browbeat the Utes until a group of them ambushed the agency in 1879. The U.S. government immediately sent in troops, and in 1880 the Colorado State Legislature overwhelmingly passed a resolution demanding expulsion of Utes from the state. Most white rhetoric in newspapers recommended complete extermination. The army coerced the Utes of the Yampa River and White River Valleys into Utah, having forced a peace agreement.

Apparently by the time Orville and Sally arrived, no Utes lived anywhere near Steamboat Springs. Instead, about a dozen white families had built huts along the Yampa River. They set up a post office, a sawmill, a newspaper, a bathhouse, and a school. Obviously, there were white children. Maybe Iris just happened to be the first one born there.

I gathered up the index cards, notes, and articles, stuffing them into my backpack with my laptop. It was almost 1:30 already, and I hadn't eaten since breakfast. As I marched toward the door, Pauline, who worked the museum's afternoon shift, glanced up from newspaper clippings she was sorting.

"Thanks, you've been a great help," I said.

"Don't forget this." She handed me a copy of James Crawford's business letters I had requested, although I couldn't recall why. Crawford, founder of Steamboat Springs, had arrived with his family in the Yampa River Valley in the early 1870s. As I stuffed the document into my shoulder bag, I said, "Thanks again." But she had gone back to her clippings.

As I stepped out into the sunshine, I gazed at the snow-crested peaks in the distance and the nearby slopes, velvety with new green grass. I punched Angela's name in my cell phone, and was surprised when she answered on the second ring.

"Hi, I thought you'd be on a mountain top out of cell phone range," I greeted her.

"You should see the ski resorts around here," she replied. "Some are quite posh. Where are you?"

"On my way back to the inn. Sorry I've been such a terrible travel companion, but I think I'm done."

"Good, maybe I'll pick you up before you get there," she said and clicked off.

About four blocks later, a white Ford Focus slowed down. Angela stuck her head out the window. "Get in."

"Where'd you get the new T-shirt?" I asked as I took in her cute scoop-neck.

"That's where I'm taking you," she said as she turned the car onto Hwy 40 going south.

Minutes later, she pulled into the parking lot of a sporting goods store at the base of Mount Werner. "I got the T-shirt in there," she pointed. "And over there, we're getting gondola tickets up the mountain. Did you eat lunch? We can eat at the top, then hike around for a while."

"I don't have my boots— " I started to say.

"They're in the back, right where you left them two days ago." That was the last time I had joined her for an early morning walk before diving into my research.

Following a jaw-droppingly scenic ride up the mountain, we snagged a table on the Oasis Sundeck and ordered, minutes before the grill would close.

"So are you done?" Angela asked as she took a gulp of water.

"I have no idea," I said, surveying our magnificent view. "I'm not even sure where to start. I can piece together my ancestors' move from Tennessee to Colorado, then to California, and bits about their lives in Colorado. They got here maybe five years after the Utes were driven out. That's such a terrible story, I was embarrassed reading about it. But my ancestors didn't do the driving out themselves."

"They just benefitted from it," Angela said.

"Well, yeah, I suppose so." I shifted in my seat. "When great-grandmother Iris was born, there were maybe twelve families living in the area. Some had kids, but she was probably the first white child actually born in the Yampa River Valley." I gazed off to the west, as though ghosts of those families still hovered along the river.

"And that's it? Three days in the stacks, well, two and a half, and that's what you come away with?" she asked.

"Well, no, I picked up all these little tidbits. Like, one of the first things they built in Steamboat was a bathhouse. I have a picture of it somewhere. That raises interesting questions about personal hygiene. Or this guy John, John Norburt, he seems to have become a local bigwig of sorts. Land speculator, rancher, preacher, alcoholic. But I can't see where that all adds up to anything."

Our sandwiches arrived. "Something bothering me is all this property Orville bought right in Steamboat. Twenty-one parcels that I'm able to document. But as near as I can figure, he didn't bring a whole lot of money with him. I don't think his family in Tennessee was especially wealthy, so how did he do that?"

Angela had put down her sandwich and was staring at her plate, but I barely noticed as I remembered the document from Pauline I had shoved into my shoulder bag. Retrieving it, I flipped through the title and copyright pages. At the table of contents, I almost fell over.

"Holy shit, look at this. A biography of Orville!"

I riffled through the pages until I found it. "Listen," I said as I skimmed. "Orville arrived at the west end of the Yampa River Valley in 1881. Must have been with his friend John. In 1882, he homesteaded near Craig."

I looked up as I continued. "So then he goes back to Tennessee, marries Sally, brings her out here, and they show up in the 1885 census. Pieces are falling into place." Now I was wired.

"Yes, they are," Angela murmured. "Do you know what it meant to homestead?"

I blinked. "What? Let me keep reading, there's more."

She continued as though she hadn't heard me. "It meant he was practically given a chunk of our land. All he had to do was, I think the word is 'improve' the land," her fingers made air quotes. "He put up a shack, stayed there for a given amount of time, and the land was his. He didn't need money, Denise, all he needed was to be white. That had been our land. Two years later, it was his."

While Angela was talking, my eyes quickly skimmed the one-paragraph biography. Orville and family had moved into Steamboat Springs in 1889. Over the next eleven years, he was successively Bath House Manager, Pool Hall Operator, Fireman's Fund Insurance Representative, and Justice of the Peace. I surmised he got into buying real estate with the profit he made selling the homestead. The Utes' land. I finally caught up with Angela.

"Oh. Oh my god," was all I could think to stammer. My great-great-grandfather might not have driven the Utes off their land himself, but he stood ready to cash in on the deed.

As we stared at each other, unsure what to say next, the waiter brought the check. After we paid, I mumbled, "But that was so long ago."

Angela looked at me sharply as she said, "Let's get out of here. I need to think."

For the next couple of hours, we just walked on a trail, speaking little. I could tell Angela was agitated, and she seemed to avoid eye contact with me. Should I feel guilty for what my great-great grandfather had done? It was awful history, to be sure, but it had happened so long ago. It was even quite possible that Orville and Sally had no knowledge of the Utes. And only one of Angela's grandparents was Ute, so it wasn't exactly "our" land. Although it had been Ute land.

But in any case, why take it out on me? I was a hundred years away from even being born, and I wasn't like that. Angela more than anyone else should know that, having volunteered with me to serve homeless people every month. Or listening to my stories about the elderly people I read to. I thrived on helping people, not on stealing from them. I wasn't that kind of person, and Angela knew that, didn't she?

Somehow this past in which I had no hand was driving a wedge between us. I feared for our friendship.

Finally, Angela turned to me. "I'm bushed, let's head back to the car," she said, looking me squarely in the face.

The cold lump of fear that had been growing inside me suddenly melted. I searched her face, which now showed none of the confused agitation I had seen earlier. "Good idea," I agreed, knees wobbling with relief.

⚜ ⚜ ⚜

THE NEXT DAY as we exited Interstate 25 into Colorado Springs, my stomach clenched. Why was I nervous about meeting Angela's grandmother? Maybe it was because of the undercurrent that had already started roiling between me and Angela.

The previous day, I felt as though something had shifted like tectonic plates during a temblor. She didn't say anything about how she processed my revelation, and I was afraid to ask. By today, the ground stopped shaking, but new rifts had appeared. Our banter no longer seemed easy. I edited my words before I spoke. I was terrified of losing her friendship by saying the wrong thing, and terrified of losing it by not saying anything at all.

Or perhaps I feared confronting an American Indian whose ancestors my own had displaced. What would Mrs. Walker think of me? Would her eyes shoot daggers? Would she throw me out of the house over Angela's objections?

We came bearing gifts. Before we left California, Angela told me her grandmother would feed us as though food had been scarce in Steamboat Springs. "She'll make a big stew and expect us to polish it off while she tells stories, and then for breakfast she'll fix eggs and sausages to go along with more stories. She won't let me fill the fridge, so I bring treats she likes."

Treats? "So what should I bring?" I had no idea what would be appropriate.

Angela thought. "What about that granola you like?"

"Miller's?"

"Yeah, bring her some of that. Oh, and nuts. Grandma Carol loves to nibble on them but never buys them for herself. A bag of mixed nuts."

So here we were, rolling into Colorado Springs in mid-afternoon with a box of Miller's granola, a bag of mixed nuts, a tin of shortbread, and a large bag of fresh oranges. Angela turned onto a side street, passed some boxy brick apartments, slowed, then stopped in front of a small sand-colored house. Patchy grass dotted the front yard and a vegetable garden grew along the side. Angela shut off the ignition and popped the trunk.

As I got out, I noticed the neighborhood's small, older single-family homes on tiny lots, tucked amongst assorted evergreen and broadleaf trees. Most of the yards looked neat and newly mowed, but a few eschewed grass for native plants. Angela's grandmother's yard seemed to be the only one growing food rather than ornamentation.

Mrs. Walker's front door opened, and out shuffled a short, stocky woman leaning on a cane. As her brown face broke into a smile, I recognized traces of Angela's face in hers. I hung back as Angela bounded up to her, enveloping her grandmother in a firm hug. "Grandma, this is my friend Denise." Angela reached for my arm to draw me in.

"I'm very pleased to meet you, Mrs. Walker. Thank you for inviting us to stay with you," I said, unsure of the appropriate greeting.

Her face crinkled into a warm smile. "Any friend of my granddaughter is welcome in my home." I hoped she meant it. We gathered our gear and went in.

Mrs. Walker's homey interior reminded me of a mountain cabin. Two couches draped with woven blankets faced a TV set. There was a pot-belly stove and plenty of framed artwork of varying quality, made by local Native teens I later learned. A vibrant painting of a wolf and an eagle contrasted with a stilted drawing of two babies. Another drawing captured hands in motion at a potter's wheel.

Angela led me into a cramped bedroom. "I'll take the top, you can have the bottom," she waved toward a set of bunk beds.

"Is this your room?" I asked, looking around at the chest of drawers, metal folding chair, and woven wall hangings.

"It's anybody's room who needs a place to stay," she replied.

We retrieved our gifts, then joined Mrs. Walker in the kitchen where she was fixing lemonade. Angela said rather loudly, "Grandma, we brought you some of your favorite goodies so you'll think of us when we're gone." I was gratified to see Mrs. Walker's face light up when I handed her the granola. Maybe our visit would turn out well after all.

Angela cocked her head to display her finely beaded floral-design leather barrette. "I told you about Grandma's brilliant beadwork. This is one of her creations."

"It's awesome," I breathed. Mrs. Walker, grey hair pulled back into a long braid, also wore beautiful beaded barrettes of geometric patterns.

"I haven't been able to do that kind of beadwork for a long time." Mrs. Walker looked at her arthritic hands. "I want to teach this one, but she doesn't stay around here long enough for me to teach her anything." Angela giggled.

"Let's sit," said Angela, steering me to the small round dining table between the living room and the kitchen. A moment later, Mrs. Walker set a plate of baloney sandwiches in front of us.

"Can I help do something?" I asked. I hadn't expected her to serve us lunch.

"You can help me eat these," replied Angela. "I told you my grandmother would make sure we don't starve while we're here."

"Will she join us?" I whispered. I could hear her in the kitchen.

Angela shrugged. "She might have already eaten. Don't worry about it. A good hostess provides food and a good guest eats gratefully."

After lunch, I had imagined we would spend the afternoon visiting with Mrs. Walker, but Angela had a different idea. She wanted to show me the magnificent Garden of the Gods Park. She explained, "Grandma will be fixing a pot of stew, then she'll take a nap. She still gets around pretty well, but she's over eighty. You've probably noticed her hearing is going."

"I noticed you shouting," I replied with a laugh.

Later, as early evening shadows lengthened, Mrs. Walker asked about my parents' wellbeing while urging us to refill our plates.

"Mrs. Walker, this stew is amazing," I said, helping myself. "I thought beef stew on a hot day would have felt like burning coals in my stomach, but this doesn't."

"I'm glad you enjoy it," Mrs. Walker replied. "Call me Grandma, there's no need to be formal. And next time you come, I'll fix bison. Have you ever tasted it?"

I hadn't. I asked, "Do they sell it in the grocery store around here?"

"My son Thomas brings it to me," she said. "He lives over in Utah, near Ft. Duchesne on the reservation with his family. He likes to go hunting over there."

"Didn't you tell me the tribe has a big herd of buffalo?" Angela asked.

"Yes, *Gkah-gkoo-chee*, I believe about five hundred head," Mrs. Walker replied.

"*Gkah-gkoo-chee* is Ute for granddaughter," Angela explained to me. Turning to her grandmother, she asked, "Grandma, didn't you tell me that Thomas's wife is Uncompahgre?"

"Good, you were listening," her grandmother beamed.

"I'm trying to learn," Angela replied, then explained to me, "Uncompahgre is one of the Northern Ute bands. The other two on the reservation in Utah are White River and Uintah. Grandmother is a member of the White River band."

"We were called carrot eaters," Mrs. Walker said, eyes twinkling. "*Yamparika*. That's the origin of the name of the Yampa River. I think my ancestors got that name because they ate vegetables but didn't care for the river fish. Some other band gave them that name. There are several Ute bands. Most of the others are part of the Southern Ute Nation in the southwest corner of Colorado. Now, tell me, Denise, what did you think of Steamboat Springs?"

"It's beautiful," I replied. "I can't get over the magnificence of the mountains."

"Don't believe her," Angela laughed. "She spent the whole time digging in archives. I didn't drag her onto a mountain until yesterday afternoon."

Mrs. Walker said, "My granddaughter tells me you were finding out more about your family there."

"Yes, well, my great-grandmother was born there and I just wanted to find out a little bit more, you know." I described some of the kinds of information available in the Family History Center and the museum, but sidestepped details of my family's history of homesteading. After Angela's reaction yesterday, I didn't want to stir anything up.

We finished eating, my head spinning. Just yesterday, I had read about the White River Utes being removed to an arid patch of land in Utah, and here I was sitting across the table from one of their descendants. Questions flooded my head, but I wasn't sure which one to ask. I figured Mrs. Walker's grandparents were among the people who were forced out. Had a bunch of her ancestors died in the process? What had it been like for her growing up on the reservation? How often did she go back there?

Angela returned from the kitchen with a pot of steaming coffee, mugs and sugar. As she heaped sugar into her coffee, her grandmother shot her a warning glance. Seeing me notice their nonverbal communication, Angela explained, "She worries about me getting diabetes. It's common on the reservation."

"It's common here, too," added Mrs. Walker. "I try to get the young people to eat healthy, but some of them just think I'm trying to return them to the old ways. Maybe I am; the old ways were much healthier for our people."

She had a good point. I thought about all the junk food young people eat. I wasn't sure my own students took seriously my attempts to teach healthy eating.

Angela said, "White people's schools have never been healthy for Grandma's people. I've heard that the schools try to kill Indian peoples' spirits. That's what you told me, right Grandma? Grandma went to a boarding school for a while, didn't you?" Angela's head swiveled back and forth as she addressed each of us in turn.

Mrs. Walker said, "Only for a while. That school wasn't for me. That's where people started to call me Carol all the time. Nobody remembers my childhood name anymore."

"Tell her about the name jokes Ute people used to play on teachers," Angela prompted with a grin.

Mrs. Walker's face crinkled in amusement. "My mother told me this story. For a long time, most of our people kept their children away from white men's schools because they were not healthy places. My mother's parents refused to send my mother. The teachers there didn't speak our language, and couldn't even say our names, so they gave us English names, like mine. But the older people retaliated by giving the teachers Ute names that meant things like 'farts a lot' and 'face like a weasel.' Older people would tell stories about the teachers and laugh, but since the teachers couldn't understand our language, they just thought our people were happy."

As we sipped coffee in silence, I wondered if she regarded me as one of those teachers. But we didn't have Indian students at our school. None, at least, that I was aware of. Maybe white education is okay for white children. Or maybe not? And what about the Mexican students at my school?

Angela's voice broke into my mental agitation. "Tell us about the reservation land. I know your ancestors in Colorado were forced onto the reservation in Utah. You've mentioned that land kept shrinking as white people figured out ways to take more of it. Didn't the government try to turn your ancestors into farmers or something, and then give away the land that wasn't being farmed, something like that?"

Mrs. Walker gazed at her granddaughter as though trying to figure out how much to tell. Finally she said, "Yes, that is so, *Gkah-gkoo-chee*. My grandparents told me that men in the U.S. government would draw lines on paper maps, and we were supposed to stay inside the lines they drew. But that never made any sense. My grandparents knew where there was plenty of food, and it wasn't inside the lines. At first the lines were just around the reservation, but then they made much smaller boxes for each family. Allotments, they called them. Families were supposed to stay in their own little box and become farmers like white people. But the land my ancestors got was dry and rocky, bad for growing food. The land left over, the government gave away to more white people."

Angela remained silent while I squirmed.

She continued. "Our way is to share what the land has to offer, and in return, we take care of the land, our mother. When they put each family into a little box, I don't think the government wanted us to share with each other. I think that's one of the ways they tried to weaken us."

I squirmed again. She looked at me and smiled. "You've seen a little bit of the Yampa River Valley. You can imagine the animals, the berry bushes, the sweet roots and grasses that grew there. That's where my ancestors are, that's where our home is. The Yampa River knows us. What we have in Utah, it isn't really our home. This place, Colorado Springs, isn't really home, either, even though I've lived here for many years. But this place isn't where our stories and our ancestors are."

I thought about Gram's home, now my home. Somehow, my conception of home seemed shallow compared to Mrs. Walker's, for whom home seemed less rooted in an individual attachment to a structure, and more in an intergenerational communal relationship between people and place.

Mrs. Walker continued, "Since the land in Utah is dry, most people didn't want it, but the white people who wanted to farm it diverted water for their own use. So rather than starve, some of our people went into Colorado to hunt when they needed to. One of my grandfathers told me stories about going there with a hunting party when he was a boy. They had a right to do that, it was in the treaty, but even still, some in the U.S. government treated them as trespassers."

I wondered what Angela was thinking. She was looking off into a corner now.

"That's terrible," I said, unsure what to say but feeling as though I should say something.

"Yes, it was. The more people came to Colorado, killing animals our people relied on and plowing up land to make their farms, the harder it was even to hunt there. The government gave my grandparents rations, but the rations were bad. People starved. But we are also survivors. My grandparents survived a few miserable winters and dry summers. So did their children."

Angela asked, "Grandma, why did you marry a white man? And why did you stay here in Colorado Springs that's full of white people, rather than going back to Utah?"

Her grandmother regarded her gently. "I've told you, *Gkah-gkoo-chee*, I was only seventeen. I had no wisdom back then." She sighed. "But I would do it all over again. Your grandfather was good to me."

Angela asked, "Why didn't you go back to the reservation when he died?"

"I live here now," Mrs. Walker replied. "And besides, things have changed. We cannot just go back to how things used to be, or recreate a past that no longer exists. We need to take our wisdom from the past into the future with us. Here in Colorado Springs, there are not many Utes, but there are many Indian people trying to figure out our future together. I took you to our Indian Center last time you were here, but I don't think you paid much attention."

Angela shook her head and looked down. "I was busy worrying about my own problems," she mumbled.

Her grandmother placed a broad hand on one of Angela's, nodding. "As an elder of the Indian community here, I have a responsibility to the young people who don't know who they are. We work with them to connect them to their roots. Part of our history is tribal and part of it comes together with others. We've always formed alliances. I learned that from my grandfather. When I became a grandmother here, I remembered what he taught me. That is the work I do now with the young people here."

We sat in silence for what felt like several minutes. I was trying to process the fact that Mrs. Walker and I both looked to elders for wisdom and protection, yet what her ancestors needed most protection from was my ancestors. My head spinning, I felt exhausted. Finally, I stretched. "It's been a long day, I think I'll tuck in. Mrs. Walker, thank you for sharing so much with us."

A few minutes later, after washing my face and donning the old T-shirt I sleep in, I was settling into the bottom bunk when I heard low murmurs from the kitchen. Then Angela's raised voice seeped in through the closed door: "Grandma, it's hard for me to listen . . ." She said something more I couldn't hear. "Her ancestors stole the land your grandparents were pushed off of."

"Yes, but she's only learning that now. And so are you."

My body ran cold. They were discussing me! I concentrated in an effort to make out what they were saying.

There was more low talk, then Angela's voice rose. "So you think she'll actually sell her house and turn the money over to the tribe?"

Her grandmother gave a reply I couldn't make out. Angela continued, "Yeah, and you know what else? When her grandmother willed her the house, at first she didn't want it because she didn't earn it herself, but then she changed her mind. She gets a free house by just existing, and I'm still in a tiny apartment. That house should be yours!"

"Hush. You're blowing things out of proportion. She's your friend. Her grandmother was just watching over her. Besides, I have a house right here where I live. What would I do with another one in California?"

"Oh, you know— " her voice trailed off.

How could Angela say that about me? I felt as though I'd been stabbed. She was even more jealous than I had realized. And I hadn't even asked Gram for the house.

Presently, I heard the door open. Angela tiptoed in and rummaged through her suitcase. Then she tiptoed out and into the bathroom. She must have thought I was asleep. I knew I couldn't just pretend I hadn't heard anything. I couldn't picture sitting across the table from her at breakfast the next morning as though nothing had happened.

She tiptoed back into the bedroom, then climbed the stairs to the top bunk. I lay there listening to her roll around in her bed, then gradually become still.

I wanted to cry, but knew I had to remain quiet. I had lost my best friend. I hadn't realized how deeply she resented me. Why had we ever agreed to take this trip? Why couldn't I have let that story about the first white child go? And what did she expect me to do, give away all my possessions and move to Europe?

Chapter Four

Hanging Upside Down

THE CURTAIN GLOWED with morning light. I had been dreaming I was arguing with my ancestor Orville, then with other white teachers who insisted on changing children's names.

I needed to use the bathroom. But I wasn't ready to face Angela, not just yet. I remained quiet as I listened to my surroundings. Was she awake?

I heard noise coming from the vegetable garden outside. I rolled out of my bed, then cautiously looked at the upper bunk. Empty. According to the clock, it was only 6:30. I scurried past Mrs. Walker's closed bedroom door, into the bathroom.

When I returned to the bedroom, I peeked through the curtains to locate the source of the noise. There was Angela, dressed in yesterday's shorts and T-shirt, ripping weeds from the garden. Anger seemed to radiate from her body. I decided to confront her.

I threw on my clothes, then went outside. As soon as she saw me, she stopped moving. She said shortly, "You're up."

I plunged in. "Angela, I heard you last night making awful accusations about me to your grandmother."

She straightened up. "How else do the dots connect? I started seeing the picture the day before yesterday when you were telling me what you found out about your family. Then last night listening to Grandma, it just came together. My ancestors were rounded up and pushed off to some god-forsaken patch of sand in Utah so white people like you can have their land. Your people took full advantage. Your grandmother inherited a chunk of money from selling the land that she used to buy a house. Then she gave it to you. It's all so unfair, and you don't even see that." Her lower lip quivered.

Her logic seemed to leave out a lot. As far as I knew, none of my ancestors intentionally set out to take things from anyone. They benefited from government policies dispossessing the Utes, sure, but they didn't *make* those policies, and by the time they got there, the Utes would have been gone. Gram surely didn't know about any of this, nor did I until this week. And my family had left the Utes' land a long time ago. Even Mrs. Walker last night said she had no use for my house in California.

"Angela," I said, "Your reasoning seems so skewed."

"Skewed?" She threw her hands into the air. "Oh, you are too much. You're gonna try and weasel out of this just like white people always do. You have these privileges you don't seem to want to admit to. Well, I see them and I'm tired of it."

"Privileges?" Privileges plural? "What are you talking about? You know damned well that my life is a lot like yours."

"That's what I mean, you don't see it." She started ticking points off with her fingers. "One, Indian people are impoverished because white people got their land, and I don't see plans to give it back. Two, unlike the rest of us, you get to live someplace nice and comfy without even having to pay rent or a mortgage. Three, you bitch and moan about not being in love with Sean as if everything you get has to be perfect. Well guess what, life isn't like that for most of us."

Obviously this had all been building up in her. Why drag in Sean? I didn't know what to say.

"And four," she continued, "much as you complain about how hard it is to get along with your mother, you have two living parents who are both still married to each other, had good jobs to support you, and love you. I'm barely on speaking terms with my mom and haven't had a dad since I was a kid. You have no idea what it's like to grow up with a single parent who isn't sure how to put food on the table from one month to the next."

My mouth dropped open. Where had this come from? "Look, Angela," I began.

Angela turned away from me. "Just leave, why don't you?"

I tried again. "Angela, can we just talk?"

She reached into her pocket and tossed me the car keys. "No point. I'm gonna spend the rest of the summer here with my grandmother. At least if it's okay with her."

I looked at the keys in my hand. What was I supposed to do now? Stunned, I turned and stumbled back toward the door, where I found Mrs. Walker emerging, an old green robe draped around her.

"What's going on?" she asked me. "I heard shouting."

"We had a fight. I'm leaving," I said.

I recognized sorrow in her face, but didn't know whether she was sorry to see us fight, sorry Angela had such a lame friend, or sorry to be awakened so early. I stomped into the guest room and gathered my scattered possessions, stuffing them into my bag, then marched out the door with my gear.

On the porch Mrs. Walker was holding Angela, who cried into her shoulder. There didn't seem to be a place for me in their tableau, so I unlocked the car, tossed my bag on the back seat, got in, and drove off. Angela, the sister I had always wanted, was gone from my life.

Three hours later, I was slouched in a corner of the Denver International Airport. After staring at my cell phone as though expecting it to say something, I rang up Sean. He answered while apparently engaged in another conversation.

"Sean?" I said to the jumbled voices on the other end.

"Denise? I didn't look to see who was calling. Can I call you back in a few minutes?"

"I—I suppose so." I started weeping into the phone.

"Denise, is something wrong? . . . Bradley, let's finish this up later. This call sounds urgent." He came back on the line. "Okay, I'm alone now. Tell me what's going on."

"I had a big fight with Angela, and I'm coming home early."

"Where are you?" he asked.

"I'm in the Denver airport. I'll get into Oakland at 3:50."

While I tried to think how to convey what all had gone wrong, he said, "I'll pick you up and drive you home. Now, tell me what happened."

"I never should have tried to track down that stupid story about the first white child in Colorado, that's what started it all," I said as I struggled to keep my voice steady.

"I thought you were hiking in the mountains. That's what the pictures you texted looked like."

"Yeah, we were, but I spent most of the time tracing my family's history in Steamboat Springs. I found way more than I'd anticipated." I exhaled as though I had been holding my breath since leaving Angela's grandmother in Colorado Springs. "What it comes down to is that Gram's grandparents were homesteaders outside Steamboat Springs. They got there just as the Utes were being kicked out, and got a chunk of their land, probably for free more or less. That must be what Dad meant when he mentioned the free land. The Homestead Act gave any head of household 160 acres of public land. All you had to do was apply, spend at least five years turning it into a farm, and it was yours. Basically for free. But what they called public land had been taken from the Indian tribes. Angela's Ute ancestors on her grandmother's side were the ones that got kicked off the land my ancestors got." I paused to wipe my nose.

"Uh huh," said Sean sounding puzzled. "Okay, I'm following you I think, but that was, what, well over a hundred years ago."

"Yeah. Well, Gram's grandparents seem to have sold their homestead and bought up land parcels in Steamboat Springs. I suppose with more white people coming, property values shot up. After they sold the land in Steamboat Springs, Gram must have inherited some of the money and used it to buy her and Grandpa's house." Then I told him about Mrs. Walker's stories about her life. "I don't know what Mrs. Walker thinks of me. She looked sad when I left, probably because her granddaughter was upset and yelling at me."

"But what would any of that have to do with Angela? Why take it out on you?"

"That's just it, I didn't do anything. Except exist." Once again I felt the onset of tears. "So I drove the rental car back here to the airport. Angela can find her own way when she gets ready to leave. She said she wasn't coming back anytime soon."

"Okay," Sean said, "I'll be there at 3:50. If you don't see me immediately, just wait. You know what traffic is like. I'll be there as soon as I can."

"Thank you, Sean," I said. I felt relief unloading this story to someone who not only didn't hurl blame at me, but would be waiting for me on the other end. I wasn't sure, though, that Sean would understand why I felt so wretched, especially since I was struggling to understand it myself. Obviously I was hurt by Angela's anger. But there seemed to be more to it.

I thought back to that evening a year or so ago when I went to Angela's apartment because she sounded so depressed on the phone. When she answered the door and saw me standing there with two decaf lattes, the corners of her mouth turned up briefly even though her body had wilted. Her mother had gone to visit Angela's younger sister and her family in Michigan again and had made snide comments about Angela not yet giving her grandchildren. Come to think of it, she rarely talked about her mother, while I blabbed on about mine. And yes, a lot of the blabbing was me letting off steam about one thing or another Mom had done or said. Maybe I hadn't actually listened to Angela's silences about her mom.

And now, now I wasn't sure our friendship would be salvageable.

It was true that white people benefited from having claimed Indian people's land. I knew poverty was a huge problem in Indian communities, and as I had listened to Mrs. Walker, I could trace that poverty to their loss of land. What had Mrs. Walker said? The land is our mother, our home. It isn't a thing to buy and sell. White people turned land into a thing, a commodity.

If Orville and Sally had stayed put in Tennessee—that would have been after the Civil War when I imagine the economy was still in a shambles—it's possible Gram never would have inherited whatever money she used to buy the house. If that's how she bought it. I racked my brain trying to remember. I thought she told me once that she bought it with an inheritance, but I could be wrong. Or what if she inherited it from a different branch of the family?

Would it make a difference if I found out otherwise? Really, even if I didn't have the paperwork to directly link up purchase of my house with Orville's homestead, that didn't change the general picture. I did get a house for free, so to speak.

But even if Angela connected the dots correctly, was she right to blame me personally? She seemed to think we actually inherit responsibility for what our ancestors did. Of course it was common back then for white people to regard Indians as not quite human. But since that belief had faded away—it had, hadn't it?—was I somehow still responsible for actions such a belief was used to justify way back then? Did Angela actually think I should do something about a chain of actions I wasn't sure had happened the way she thought they had?

Was the heavy weight I felt on my shoulders my deep suspicion that Angela was right, and my utter cluelessness about how to remedy it? Or perhaps my guilt about how unfair it seemed that I was simply given a home while everyone else we knew scrimped to pay for theirs?

As Sean pulled the car up to my house a few hours later, I regarded it warily. Somehow that house had cost me my best friend.

Sean helped me take my things inside. I felt I should invite him in, but needed to be alone. He seemed to sense that. He put his hands gently on my shoulders as he said, "You get a good night's sleep, lady. I'd be willing to bet Angela will call you tomorrow to beg apologies when it sinks in how much she overreacted."

I didn't think so, but didn't contradict him. Instead I said, "I'm sorry I'm such awful company. And that you have to turn around and drive back . . ."

"I have a meeting early in the morning, so even if you were great company, I'd be heading back to the city anyway. Just maybe not as fast." He winked. "You call me tomorrow. Okay? And call your parents. I know your dad can always cheer you up."

I nodded and he left. Inside, I sank down on the couch, staring at the floor. The last people I wanted to talk to right now were my parents. How would I explain to them the significance of what I had found in Steamboat Springs? Even if there were gaps in the paper trail I had assembled, I knew they would feel upset that I was even questioning the legitimacy of my family's ownership of this house. Questioning my family's honesty, its integrity. Even Mom, always resentful of my close relationship with Gram, had figured out how to make peace with my inheritance.

At some point I would need to tell them what happened in Colorado—what I found out about Dad's ancestors, how Angela reacted, our broken friendship. But not yet. Not until I knew how I was going to make sense of things myself.

Shadows outside were lengthening. I stumbled into the bedroom, tossing my suitcase on the bed. Then I threw myself down next to it and allowed the tears to come, tears that had been bottled up since I boarded the plane hours earlier. Long heaving sobs rolled through me.

I must have fallen asleep because the next thing I knew, the bedside clock said it was after midnight. As I headed into the bathroom, I glanced in the mirror. A raw, puffy face looked back, eyes swollen like tomatoes. I pressed a cool wet washcloth over them.

Angela hated me now because of this house. What did she expect me to do, give it to the Ute Nation? And what would they do with a house in California? I looked around the bathroom, previously so familiar and now somehow strange, threatening. Was it mocking me because I didn't actually belong here?

I returned to the bedroom and went to bed, not entirely sure I would survive the night.

I woke up feeling as though an elephant had been sitting on my head. Light seeped through the curtains. Morning. The house hadn't eaten me. It wasn't a monster, it was just a wooden structure.

A shower and coffee cleared my head somewhat. My eyes, still swollen, looked even worse when I tried to camouflage the damage with makeup.

I realized the person I most wanted to see was Mr. Jackson. He might know something about the circumstances that led Gram and Grandpa to buy the house. He would also know what I should do.

Mr. Jackson looked surprised when he saw me at the door. "I didn't expect you back for another couple of days. Come in, how was your trip?" He peered at my face. "You don't look too good."

I entered and slumped onto the couch. "Yeah, I'm home early. Angela and I had a major fight and I need your help sorting it out."

"Let me get you a glass of water." Mr. Jackson turned toward the kitchen.

Although I had been inside the Jackson home numerous times before, I found myself studying the framed family photos on two side tables. There were a few of him and his late wife, the rest showed his two grown children and their families.

"They grow fast, don't they?" Mr. Jackson returned to the living room.

"Will you see any of them this summer?" I asked.

He set the water in front of me, sat in an adjacent armchair, and replied, "I'm driving down to Santa Barbara in a few days to see Autumn and her crew. I wish Edward and his family didn't live so dang far away. The flight to Boston seems to get longer every time I make it."

"They could come here to visit," I pointed out, recalling them doing that maybe three years earlier.

"Yes, but it's complicated with kids and all their gear. And expensive. There's five of them and only one of me. Now then, do you want to tell me what happened?" He leaned forward, hands clasped between his knees.

I took a sip of water and plunged in. I described what I had learned about Gram's family in Colorado and Angela's reaction when I told her. "You see, her grandmother is Ute, but that hadn't seemed like a big deal to her before. I knew she spent last Christmas with her grandmother, and

I recently learned she had Indian ancestry, but none of this seemed significant to how she saw things."

"Yet she knew about the relationship between homesteading and the government's policies to claim Indian land," Mr. Jackson said.

"Yeah. I mean, I just grew up with this idea that homesteading was what a lot of my ancestors did, you know, part of the hardships they endured to pave the way for me. I never thought about them taking something that wasn't theirs."

"Your ancestors probably didn't think of the land's original inhabitants as fully human, and just went along with policies of the U.S. government," Mr. Jackson said, one eyebrow lifted. "What happened next?"

I plowed ahead, telling him about our drive to Colorado Springs, meeting Angela's grandmother, and conversing with her. "It was like, the more stories she told about her own life, the quieter Angela became. I thought Angela had heard those stories before, but I think some were new to her, especially when her grandmother began talking about the land and how Indian people responded to being pushed onto a reservation."

"Ah, yes indeed," Mr. Jackson said. "Much the same trauma, I imagine, that's in our stories of slavery and Jim Crow. White people stole land from Indian people. They stole labor and freedom from us. Stories of the past need to be told in order to understand the present, but they evoke powerful feelings. If Angela hadn't heard them before, maybe she experienced the searing anger you feel when you learn for the first time what was done to your people."

He studied me. "I think you've plunged into a gradual discovery of something that feels threatening to you, while Angela experienced an instantaneous recognition that explains some part of her life. The picture she sees may not have all the supporting details, and she may have made some leaps that don't quite fit, but she's pulled threads together that have given her a powerful new perspective."

I looked at him. "But she's blaming me, and she's accusing me of having this cushy and privileged life as a result. It's as though I were the one who drew those lines on maps creating reservations, or I hauled her ancestors into schools designed to make them forget who they were. I wasn't even born then. And it isn't my fault that I have two parents and a boyfriend. More or less." Fresh tears pooled in my eyes.

"Well, you do have a lot. And you're a living symbol of all that happened in the past, as well as a beneficiary. Although I must say, I don't see you having a boyfriend as having anything to do with colonial history. But if I heard you right, your ancestors did claim land some of her ancestors lost, and no one ever gave it back."

"But I can't change that," I protested. "I don't know what to do."

"Where is Angela now?"

"She's still in Colorado Springs. She decided to stay there the rest of the summer with her grandmother. I couldn't stand to stay another minute, so I left. That's why I'm home early."

"And how did her grandmother react to you?" he asked.

"Well, that's the funny thing. She seemed indignant about the past, but not angry at me. I would have thought Mrs. Walker would be the one to want me out of there, but no, she seemed okay with telling me stories. It was like, as long as I was okay listening, she was okay talking." I dabbed at my eyes with a fresh tissue from a box he handed me.

"I would imagine she's experienced a boatload of anger, but learned to channel it into something constructive," he replied.

"Like working with the local Indian youth?"

"Like that, yes. Why do you think I let myself get talked into running for president of the NAACP? It's not like I don't have anything else to do."

If I weren't in such a funk, I would have laughed. Mr. Jackson thrived on his work with the NAACP. This wasn't something he had to be talked into taking on. It was work that sprang from who he was.

He continued, "You need to give Angela time. She has a lot to digest that it seems she hasn't thought about before. And you need to deal with the possibility that she won't want to pick back up with you when she returns, at least not right away. Now, I suspect Angela is only part of your concern. You seem to have opened up something even closer to home, am I right?"

"Mr. Jackson," I said, "I have no idea how to process all this, or what to tell my parents about Gram's history. It's like, no sooner do I allow myself to feel that house is my very own home, and suddenly it stinks. I don't even know the circumstances in which Gram and Grandpa bought it. Do you? Were you living here when they bought it?"

He laughed. "I was probably fifteen when they bought it. No, your grandparents predated me in this neighborhood by many years. But your grandfather did mention to me once that it was your grandmother's family money that bought the house."

"Okay, so I remembered that part right," I said. "See, one of the things I've been trying to remember is whether Gram bought it with an inheritance from her grandmother. Because if that's what she used, then that's the money her grandmother got from selling the property in Colorado."

"I can't help you there," he said. "You seem to be asking questions your grandparents didn't think to ask. While you're deciding what to do with this information, you will, of course, talk with your parents about something. Perhaps not just yet what you're trying to sort out. But at the very least, they'll wonder how your trip went."

"I know, and I don't know what to say," I said, burying my face in my hands.

"I could make a suggestion, but I think you're able to work out what to do. Now, if I remember right, you're about to start summer school next week?"

"Yeah, I'm taking a master's class at the university," I said. "I didn't go through one of those programs that combines a master's degree with a teaching credential."

"So you're going to be busy for the foreseeable future, which will buy you some time to make sense of what happened. And that fella you're seeing, Sean?"

"Sean brought me home from the airport last night. He thinks Angela overreacted. He's like, this is all ancient history, why worry about it now?"

Mr. Jackson said, "Well, you have some thinking to do, and no real pressure to get your thoughts in order fast."

When I got home, I texted my parents more photos as if I were still in Colorado.

The next afternoon, I called them. Mom answered the phone.

"Hi, Mom," I greeted her.

"Are you home now?" she asked.

"Yeah," I replied.

"It looks like you had a lovely trip. I can't wait to see the rest of your photos when I see you next. Aren't the Colorado Rockies grand?

California's Sierras are nice, but nothing like the Rockies. What was Angela's grandmother like? She didn't look at all like I had pictured her."

I sighed. "She's Indian, Mom."

"Really? Oh, so that makes Angela part Indian? Oh. How interesting." I could tell Mom was fumbling for a response.

"And she was very hospitable. She cooked like we hadn't eaten for weeks. I'm going to have to go on a diet," I continued.

"You probably hiked it all off, and you must have a bit of a tan now," Mom said, recovering. I looked at my arm, as pale now as it had been when I left.

"Not really, I used plenty of sunscreen," I said. "What are you and Dad up to?"

"He went to the Weed and Feed to pick up mulch for the garden," Mom said. "You can try his cell."

"That's okay, we'll talk later next week," I said. "I just wanted to give you a quick holler and let you know I'm back. Angela decided to stay on with her grandmother a while. I'll be busy with summer school starting tomorrow, so I guess she figured I wouldn't be very good company."

"Okay, sweetie, well, come see us as soon as you can. Bring Sean along. Is he there, by the way? Can I say hello to him?"

I rolled my eyes. "He'll be over in a while, Mom. I'll give him your regards."

When I hung up, I felt better. We hadn't said much, but Mom's voice was reassuring. I could get through this. I glanced at my watch, then dashed to the bathroom to dab on some lip gloss and straighten my hair before Sean arrived.

Chapter Five

Errant Student

"KEY ODA."

Puzzled, I looked up from the book I was thumbing through. A man about my age was writing on the whiteboard. I recognized him from when I first walked in, but I had assumed he was another student since he was chatting with one. His short brown hair almost looked military, but his stubble beard decidedly did not.

On the board he was writing, *Kia ora, Ian McAlister, Karakia* and *Aotearoa.* He turned and addressed us. "Welcome to Topics in Literacy. I would like to begin by honoring the Ohlone people on whose land we stand, and the many ancestors who have gone before. We are grateful for their stewardship of the land. Peace and goodwill to all. *Tēnā koutou, tēnā koutou, tēnā tātou katoa.*"

He made a little bow with his head, then said, "My name is Ian McAlister. As you might guess from my accent, I come to you from Aotearoa New Zealand. We began with a very short *karakia*," pointing to the term on the board, "which is a traditional blessing. How many of you are familiar with the term *Aotearoa?*"

Cheryl, sitting in front of me, raised her hand. "Isn't that the Indigenous name for New Zealand?" Cheryl was one of those people who always had the right answer for every question. I didn't particularly enjoy being in class with her, as she made me feel like a dolt who never read the news.

"Yes," he said in a way that sounded like *yees.* "Our power-sharing system between European New Zealanders and the Indigenous Māori is reflected in how we refer to our country. The first people to arrive gave the islands a name that translates to English as *land of the long white cloud.*" I wondered if we would be spending the next three weeks learning a foreign vocabulary that would be useless in California. Maybe I should have signed up for Advanced Studies in Teaching History, instead.

"*Kia ora* is our most common greeting," he continued. "Everyone uses it, it doesn't matter if you're European like me, or Māori. So. *Kia ora.*" He looked at us as though expecting a response. Hearing only a few murmurs, he repeated, "*Kia ora,*" waving a hand like a choir director. This time, all of us stumbled through its pronunciation.

"Good. Now you know a little bit of what your struggling readers sometimes feel. These words," pointing to *Kia ora, Aotearoa,* and *karakia,* "don't mean much to you, and may not sound like you think they should, given their spelling and your American ears. Here's another one." He wrote *Māori* on the board. "How would you say this?"

I wasn't about to make myself look silly, but apparently a couple of my classmates were, as their hands shot up. He called on Joyce, a kindergarten teacher from another school.

"May-OH-ree?" she ventured. "At least, that's how I've always said it."

If I wasn't mistaken, he had already used the word and it didn't sound like that.

"I hear that a lot when I'm in the states. We say, Mao, Mao-di."

I tried to position my tongue to make "r" sound more like "d" or "l."

"Why is there an *r*?" I didn't mean to ask this, it just slipped out.

"American English-speakers pronounce the 'r' sound differently from New Zealanders." He looked directly at me. "Your name is?"

"Denise Fisher," I said, wishing I had kept my mouth shut. Not five minutes into the course and I was already a troublemaker.

"Thank you, Denise. All of you bring what you know to the text I've written here in order to make sense of it. When it doesn't make sense, you feel frustrated. You may even wish you were somewhere else. If you don't get anything else out of the next three weeks, remember that feeling of frustration, and your desire for someone to give you a key that will unlock the gibberish that isn't forming itself into something meaningful."

Then he flashed me the quickest grin. It was gone in an instant, like sunlight poking through thick tree branches on a windy day. Maybe I only imagined it, because now he was passing out the course syllabus, brow wrinkled in concentration.

Four hours later as I walked to my car, I wished I could process the class with Angela. She wouldn't have been taking it, of course, since she already had her master's degree. But we would turn it into a drama to play with the rest of the summer. Even though I knew about half the other students because I had been with them in other classes, I didn't know any of them like I knew Angela.

We would start with Ian McAlister. Why was he here in California, and how did he happen to get this summer job? The university was too cheap to import someone from New Zealand, even someone with the Reading Recovery background Ian had shared with us. He must have been in California already, although he didn't tell us much about himself.

Angela would want to know what he looked like, and by her question, she'd know that I knew she was asking if he was cute. How would I respond? He looked, well, Scottish. Not bad looking, but not someone you'd look at twice. Ordinary. Except that fleeting grin. Did anyone else see it, or was it just for me?

I would tell her that he was "personable." Friendly but not flirty. Professional but not stuffy. Approachable. He gave us his email address but not his phone number. You can send me a message I'll read when it suits me, but don't call me.

"Not much drama there," Angela would conclude. "Unless he's hiding something, like having an affair with your advisor." A wicked grin would light up her face.

"Fat chance," I would reply. My advisor, in her sixties, was a grandmother married to the same man for about four decades, and shaped like SpongeBob SquarePants.

We would then move on to the rest of the students in class. To my description of Cheryl, Angela would reply, "I bet she doesn't have a life."

"She has a rock the size of Gibraltar on her left hand," I would point out.

"It'll be gone before she hands in her thesis," Angela would predict.

About half the class members were teachers enrolled for professional development credit. Angela rarely mocked teachers, but she would ask what schools they were from. "We did introductions, but I don't remember," I would reply. "Someone from McKinley, and a couple from Mission Vista. A kindergarten teacher who was at Bayside, but she's trying to get into a different school."

"Bayside," Angela would remark, wrinkling her nose. "Their principal is terrible. She's so stuck on the Open Court reading program that I'm surprised she'd let one of her teachers study Reading Recovery." Bayside's principal had been a classroom teacher for only three years, then scurried off into administration as fast as possible, we figured in order to escape the complex demands of working with kids.

The other class members were graduate students, most also teachers like me. A couple of the grad students were enrolled in the doctoral program. The graduate students seemed perpetually stressed out. Like me, they worried about their papers, their master's project, their grades, and whether they could get everything done to some degree of satisfaction while teaching full time.

"So you got a B on the paper, so what?" Angela had said the first time I complained. "They're not going to flunk you, and it won't affect you on the pay scale," our main motivation for earning the degree.
She was right.

God, how I missed her!

I wondered what she would say about the writing assignment due next Monday. McAlister wanted us to write a short essay about something we struggled to learn. "I want you to crawl back into that experience. What did it feel like? What did it taste like? How did you work with it? I don't want any academic citations in this essay, just your memories of the experience itself."

I had always been a boringly good student. What on earth was I going to write about? Well, it wasn't due until next Monday, so I'd worry about it later.

All week, I kept hoping Angela might call me, text me, send me an email. Should I call her? What was she doing? What was she thinking about? I checked her Facebook page, but there was nothing new since a selfie in Steamboat Springs.

I wanted to know what she would say about Ian. (He preferred being called by his first name.) I needed Angela to help me make sense of him. He was becoming a puzzle I couldn't quite put away after class.

The second day I got into a one-on-one with him about teacher autonomy. He believed very strongly in teaching young people to write from their experiences and passions. I did too, but I kept picturing Cynthia Jorgenson hammering away on the district's expectation that we use the standards-aligned textbooks.

"Maybe you can do that in New Zealand, but we can't." I had caught him during a small group discussion. "Believe me, I've pushed as far as I can, and it seems like whenever I come in with an idea of my own, I get shut down."

He pulled up a chair and sat. "Who are you working for?" he asked, looking directly into my eyes. I noticed his were grey like the ocean on a rainy day.

"Umm. I work for the school district here, Milford Elementary in particular."

Then he began drawing circles on paper. He labeled them District Administration, School Board, Parents, Students, Principal, Fellow Teachers. He was a lefty, I noticed. No ring, and no un-tanned ring line on his ring finger. But so what?

"Try rank-ordering these. Who you are working the hardest to please gets a one. Least hardest gets a seven. See what you come up with."

Then he moved on to someone else. I looked down at the paper in front of me. I would like to say my kids ranked number one, but they weren't the ones paying my salary. I wondered how my classmate Patricia would respond, but she was engaged in a discussion on the other side of the room. I stared at the paper again. Of course, everyone would say the kids come first, but the reality didn't feel that way. Or maybe some kids, the ones who had been primed since they were born to do well on tests, maybe they came first and others didn't. I folded the paper and stuck in it my bag.

When I got home I retrieved it and flattened it out. I decided to call Angela. After all, one of us would have to be the first to break the silence. The ball was fifty percent in my court.

She answered after the second ring. "I don't want to talk to you."

"Wait!" I said, waving an arm as though it would stop her from hanging up. "You're not still mad at me, are you?"

"You just don't get it, do you?" Her voice was icy. "Are you at home?"

Where else would I be at 9:00 on a Friday evening? "Yes," I replied.

"Have you thought any more about blood on the money that bought your house?"

I exploded. "What do you want me to do? I've gotta live some-where!" In truth, I had thought a lot about it, but kept running into a dead end trying to figure out what I should do. Then I remembered the time difference between California and Colorado.

"I woke you up, didn't I?" I said.

"I wasn't asleep yet. Grandma's been telling me stuff about her and about my dad that I'm having a hard time digesting."

"What stuff?"

She exhaled loudly. "Nothing I can talk to you about. Just leave me alone, Denise."

With that, the connection went dead.

I had imagined Angela and her grandmother spending their time going to powwows, working with Indian teens, Angela learning a little of the Ute language and meeting some of the elders. But her voice didn't sound like someone immersed in a cultural love affair. She still sounded angry with me, but also unnerved as though she had been flipped upside down. What could her grandmother have told her?

The next day, Saturday, was Dad's sixty-fifth birthday. Sean and I drove to my parents' house after picking up the cake I had ordered. As Sean emerged from the bakery into the sunlight, I noticed how his sharp white cotton shirt set off his dark hair and blue eyes like white ceramic sets off French roast coffee. Then why wasn't I full-throttle in love with him? I trusted him, I enjoyed being around him, I liked him (in bed as well as out). I should be mad about him, but no. After my devastating experience with Peter, I didn't trust myself to be mad about anyone. Then shouldn't what Sean and I had be enough? Angela could be right. Maybe I thought I was entitled to more than life gave me.

"My dad will be pumped," I said as he started the car. "Thanks for being part of this milestone."

"You don't need to thank me, Denise," he said. "I enjoy being around your folks. You're lucky to have them. You're even lucky to have the friction with your mom."

"Huh?"

"What I mean is, in spite of the friction, you still care about each other. The other day I pictured what it must have been like for your mom to suddenly have a baby to take care of. You know how your mom always likes things to be just so. She likes to be in control of what's around her. Then suddenly, there's this baby, and I bet you were a handful."

"Moms always adjust to their kids," I replied.

"No, they don't, Denise," he said firmly. "I bet your presence in your mother's life was hard for her to deal with. Not because she didn't love you, but because having a baby around upset the ordered world she was used to. She would have dealt with it as best she could."

"She took it out on me, is that what you're saying?" I thought for a minute. "Actually, you might have a point." I imagined myself as a baby,

Mom at her wits' end because I wouldn't go to sleep when she wanted me to. Or because I demanded to be fed before she was ready. I'd be on the receiving end of a boatload of her frustration. I hadn't quite thought about it that way before.

I said, "You may be right. So now that you're analyzing my family, I get to do the same. You know I don't like to pry, but you hardly ever mention yours and you switch topics when I ask. What's the story?"

His hands tightened on the steering wheel as he stared ahead. Finally, he said, "That's because I haven't seen them for years. I think I told you I grew up outside Weed, over near Mount Shasta. My family was dirt poor, which would have been okay if it didn't seem like they wanted to stay that way. But as far as I could tell, they did. My dad used to get drunk, then come home and take his frustrations out on my mom. She finally kicked him out and got the locks on the house changed. He just disappeared. Never saw him after that. I have no idea if he's even still alive."

"Wow, I'm sorry to hear that," I said.

"There's more. Sure you want to hear this?" He glanced over at me.

"Yeah, of course!"

Sean continued. "Okay. Well, Mom tried to make ends meet by working as a waitress, but as soon as I finished high school, she wanted me to get a job. I think I've already told you that I'm the oldest. Anyway, my younger sister got pregnant in high school and dropped out. My younger brother eventually graduated, although he had started doing drugs by then. I worked a couple years, but when I enrolled at the community college, Mom hit the ceiling. She said we didn't have the money for me to keep going to school; I needed to help her support the family. Which by then included not only my sister Sheila, but also her bawling brat. I thought, fuck, how am I ever going to become anything in this dump? So I took off."

He was silent for a few seconds, then said, "I sent them some money every now and then for a while, but I don't think Mom ever got over being pissed that I had left. Even though she cashed my checks, she never thanked me. I used to call her sometimes, but finally I quit trying because it seemed like the only thing she was interested in was when I was coming back. And I wasn't. I imagine there are still Graysons living in Weed, but I haven't looked any of them up and don't intend to."

"Wow. And your siblings never tried to track you down?" I asked.

"No, and I hope they don't. My brother would need to get clean before I'd want to see him, and my sister Sheila—well. All I can imagine is that they'd want money from me. I managed to escape. I'm sorry they didn't, but I couldn't see what else to do. That's why I keep telling you you're lucky, Denise. You might think your parents are annoying at times. But they care about you, they're always in your corner. I guess that's why I've kind of adopted them."

Pieces fell into place. It wasn't my imagination that Sean seemed to slide right into my family as if it were his own. He really did value my parents, but not because he had much in common with them. He didn't. But they were the image of the family he wished he had been born into.

Sean gave me a few minutes to digest his story, then shifted the topic by asking about my summer course.

"It's being taught by this visiting professor from New Zealand," I said. "It's turning out to be more interesting than I thought it would be. He makes us think a lot about why kids would want to read. Yesterday we did a discussion all on Twitter, which was hard because we had to keep messages so short. Which was the point: you have to choose your words carefully."

As I described the activity, my mind replayed our laughter as we composed tweets and replied to each other's tweets. Ian had done this activity with kids several times. "Most kids figure it out pretty fast," he had said. "I was still trying to compose regular sentences while kids used creative shortcuts right way."

Ian seemed to "get" kids. But he didn't have any of his own. Someone asked him. "I have two nephews over in Tauranga," he had said. "It's about an hour's drive from my mum's house in New Zealand. I'll see them at Christmastime." I thought I caught a glimpse of wistfulness crossing his face, but it disappeared so quickly I couldn't be sure.

Sean was talking. ". . . literacy practices there, Sylvia Ashton Warner and all. Are you learning things you can try out in your classroom?"

"Sure, unless we have to go page by page through the textbook next year," I said. "I mean, I'd need to think about how to actually incorporate what we're learning. But the biggest thing I'm getting is a better idea of how to tune into the work kids do trying to learn to read and write. I thought I was good at watching them and listening to them, but Ian takes it to a whole other level."

How had ordinary-looking Ian wandered into my mind while I was sitting right next to a friend who also happened to be gorgeous? I shifted to my more immediate problem. "Sean, while we're at my parents, I need you to help steer me away from talking about Angela and the homesteading stuff."

"Sure," he said. "You're still worrying about the Utes?"

"It's the ethics of stealing land that bothers me," I said.

"Well, in that case, I suppose you could worry about the whole continent having been stolen from all the Indian tribes that were here," he said. "Our generation is a little late for that, though, I think. But yeah, I'll help. Whatever you need, Denise. I'm surprised you haven't heard from Angela yet."

"I called her Tuesday night," I said. "It was a very brief conversation, I guess that's why I didn't mention it. She's still in Colorado Springs and still angry with me, but her grandmother seems to be giving her more things to get upset about, so it isn't just me now that she's pissed at. By the way, the tribes are still here."

"Huh?"

"You said tribes that *were* here, in the past tense. They're still here in the present tense," I said.

He shrugged. "Whatever."

We arrived at my parents' just in time for lunch. It's funny, although I grew up in this house and regarded it as home when I was younger, it never imprinted itself on me the way Gram's house did. As soon as I got my teaching job and my own apartment, mentally and then verbally, I stopped referring to this house as home. Surely my parents had noticed, but they didn't mention it.

The take-out Mom had ordered from a local restaurant was spread across the kitchen table. Dad had specified no gifts, but I set a package down in front of him anyway as I gave him a kiss.

"Happy birthday, Dad." I said.

"What's this?" he asked as though surprised.

"Open it," I said. He ripped off the wrapping paper and pulled out a blue Colorado sweatshirt. He held it up as though to check the size.

"Perfect, thank you, sweetie," he said.

"I figured since you're retiring soon, you'll need more of these and less of the shirts you usually wear," I said.

He kissed my cheek. "Angela help you pick it out?"

"Yeah, she did," I said.

Sean, taking mention of Angela as his cue, asked, "So when's the official retirement date?"

For the rest of the afternoon, without them noticing as far as I could tell, Sean deftly steered my parents away from Angela and our trip to Colorado. At times, I sat back and simply watched how easily he let them fill a void in his own life, seeing him in a different light now, after what he had told me about his own family. I tried to imagine Sean's father, long vanished and possibly dead. How could that man just abandon his own family, his three children who had depended on him? I imagined Sean's mother, worn out by now from trying to hold the family together. Had his sister married? Did she have more kids? What about his brother? Did he ever straighten out? Or might he be doing time now?

I wondered why I didn't feel the same intense passion for Sean that I had felt for Peter. Maybe my botched experience with Peter had destroyed my capacity to endure those feelings again. Maybe the warm affection I felt for Sean was as good as it would get for me. I could certainly do worse.

❧❧❧

I WOKE UP Sunday morning with the essay Ian had assigned for Monday hanging over my head. We were supposed to write about something we had struggled to learn, and I hadn't started yet. What was I going to write about?

I reflected on my own process of learning to read and write. When I was a kid, even before entering kindergarten, I liked to create little books. Initially I would draw pictures, then dictate a story to Mom, who would write it down. One day, figuring I knew what writing looked like, I wrote down my own story. But I didn't know how to read yet, so I asked our next-door neighbor Mrs. Hagan, who was out in her yard, to read it to me. Having raised three children, she smiled when she saw my gibberish and fell right in. I was so proud of myself! Shortly after that, I entered kindergarten, where I quickly learned the alphabet. It wasn't until years later that I realized Mrs. Hagan had made up my story based on the pictures that accompanied it. By then, I was writing stories using real letters and real words.

No, learning to read and write wasn't a struggle for me. Neither was schoolwork in general.

I looked around my ample kitchen with its walk-in pantry. Since returning from Colorado Springs, I couldn't shake the guilt I felt at owning twice the square footage Mrs. Walker owned. My three bedrooms were more spacious than her two. I had two full bathrooms, double her one. I had a separate dining room, while she put her dining table in the same space as her living room. She had worked all her life for what she had. Me? I had been handed mine.

I supposed Angela had reason to be angry, although I still couldn't figure out what I was supposed to do to about it. Did she want me to wallow in guilt? Give her my house as a kind of recompense for historical injustice? Give my house to the Ute Nation and move to Europe? To which country?

But she wouldn't even talk to me. Would I ever be able to trust her again? Angela was the friend I thought I could rely on no matter what. Had that trust been just an illusion? Why did old people, like Gram and Mr. Jackson accept me exactly as I was, while so many who were my age wanted me to be different?

I sat down and began to write. I wrote about the pain of having been dumped by the man I thought was love of my life. I wrote about my life-long desire for a sister, then Angela's entry into my life. I wrote about our friendship, the jokes we shared, our bond of understanding. I wrote about my imperfect relationship with my parents, especially Mom, who probably wanted me to feel closer to her than I actually felt, and my resulting guilt. I wrote about Gram, and my sense that she continued to live in me. I wrote about my successful struggle to turn Gram's house into my own home. I wrote about the "first white child" story, and the curiosity it provoked in me. I wrote about Angela's idea that we go to Colorado, then the horribly unsettling things I learned there when my research findings collided with Angela's grandmother's stories. I wrote of loss, hurt, confusion, guilt, and anger.

When I finished pouring myself out, I looked at the essay I had written. It was fourteen pages long, single-spaced. No citations. I knew it wasn't exactly what Ian wanted, but it was an honest account of personal struggle. I had no idea how writing it would improve my ability to develop my fourth graders' literacy. But I had put pen to paper (or, font to screen), immersing myself in my own struggles, as Ian had asked.

I composed a short email to him, attached the document and hit send.

I didn't think about it again until the next day when I walked into class. Ian looked at me as though I had forgotten to put on my clothing.

Chapter Six

Colonial Histories Everywhere

WHY HAD I sent Ian that emotional outpouring? Ian was my professor, not my therapist! I wanted to crawl under a chair. No, I wanted to disappear entirely. Beam myself somewhere else, anywhere else.

Writing the essay had been therapeutic. But sending it to Ian? What was I thinking? I should have just made up something to write about, or, I don't know, I must have struggled with something when I was a kid in school. Like singing, for instance. I hated music class. I should have written about that. But no, I had to write about what was hurting me most right now.

Trying to look invisible, I slid into a seat in the back of the room behind Jerry, the size and shape of a football player. Then I opened a book and faked reading. I pictured the book expanding to the size of a sinkhole that would swallow me up, covers snapping shut behind me.

Ian started class, then divided us into small groups to discuss what we wrote about our learning struggles.

"I wrote about how hard it was to get fractions," said Nancy, a forty-something middle school teacher and fellow master's degree student. "Even the pie thing they do with kids didn't work for me at first. What did the rest of you write about?"

"Putting ideas into my own words," Jerry said. "You know, when the teacher tells you not to copy what's in the book but to use your own words? I used to copy down a sentence, then substitute a word here and there. I didn't know what else to do until my dad told me to put the paper away and just talk."

It sounded like everyone did the assignment correctly except me. When my turn came, I mumbled that school had always been pretty easy for me, and since I couldn't think of something I struggled with in school, I wrote about something else.

"What?" asked Daphne, a second-grade teacher who radiated perpetual enthusiasm. She looked at me as though I were a wayward child needing a nudge to straighten out.

"Just an issue with another teacher I'm struggling with. It's kind of private, so I'd rather not talk about it." Technically, that was true: Angela was a teacher, and I desperately did not want to share what I wrote.

"Well, maybe she can talk about what she learned from it," Jerry suggested, looking at Daphne rather than me. I couldn't tell whether he was defending me, or dismissing me.

As my groupmates talked around me, it struck me as ironic that the main thing I was struggling with in school was this damned essay. I heard myself snicker. Daphne looked at me oddly.

Fifteen minutes later, we had a few bullet points to share with the rest of the class. I had chipped in vague phrases here and there, like "not knowing where to go with curiosity," without directly mentioning my own essay.

As groups shared their discussions, Ian managed to link points with theory and research about struggling readers. Soon he had mapped out a framework on the whiteboard, pinpointing the kinds of problems many children experience acquiring literacy, and strategies for each problem. I was amazed. How could he take our scattered ideas and construct something so coherent? Then he used the framework to give us directions for the project we were to complete, due a week from Friday.

"Three weeks doesn't give a lot of time for a course," he said, "but I think you can start on something you'll actually be able to use. Any questions? Right. Let's take a short break."

I considered leaving the building, the campus, the planet. But before I could even stand up, Ian materialized in front of me. "We have something in common I might be able to help you with, Denise. Can you stay after a wee while?"

"Yeah, uh, well, I'm sorry but I shouldn't have sent all that to you," I stammered.

"No worries. It looks like you used my assignment for something you needed to think about."

"Well, now I feel kind of stupid. I mean, I could have written about how hard music was for me. I blew it, didn't I?"

"You wrote what you needed to write," he said. "We'll talk after class, yes?"

I dashed to the ladies' room to compose myself.

After class, I hung back as the rest of the students left. When the last one was gone, Ian said, "They didn't give me a very usable office here. D'you fancy a cup of coffee?"

"Sure," I said.

We headed for a small coffee shop across the street. As we walked, Ian talked about New Zealand's treaty that established power-sharing between the Māori and everyone else. "The Treaty of Waitangi was made in 1840 between Queen Victoria and the Māori. Basically, in exchange for agreeing to become a British colony, the Māori gained the right to control their own lands, the Queen's protection, and rights of British citizenship. While you Americans made hundreds of treaties with the Indigenous nations here, we have just one."

He seemed to be filling space before broaching whatever it was we had in common, but I decided to go with it. I asked, "Was it broken much like ours were?"

"Repeatedly. Right after it was signed, the Māori lost heaps of land. Most Pākehā—that's what we call European colonizers and their descendants—either didn't know about the treaty or didn't want to know. Or, they thought the Māori were the ones breaking it. But the Māori didn't just let the treaty die. They fought long and hard to get it taken seriously. Now it's a recognized part of our legal framework. What can I get you?"

We had arrived at the coffee shop, which I was glad to see was empty with the exception of a student hunched over a laptop.

"Just a latte," I replied. "But let me get it."

"No, I invited you," he replied. I claimed a table while Ian got the coffees.

As he set them on the table, he commented, "I can't get used to American coffee, ours is much better. No offense." He flashed a mischievous grin, then sat.

"So," he said. "You're one of the few white Americans I've met who's seriously grappling with what it means to descend from colonizers. I think you're where I was, maybe five or six years ago."

Ah. So his chatter about the treaty hadn't been filling air space. I sipped my latte and asked, "What happened?"

"I was finishing up my master's degree and decided to sign up for a paper in Māori history. I thought of myself as an open-minded, liberal sort of chap. I knew some of the history, but not in much depth and was curious. When I got in there, it turned out that most of the other students were Māori or Pasifika, only a handful of Pākehā like me."

"Pasifika?" I wondered what ethnic group that was.

"Sorry. An umbrella term for people from Pacific Island nations, like Tonga or Samoa. Anyway, I didn't leave that paper the same person I had been when I entered."

He sipped his latte as his eyes took on a faraway look. "I had to rethink most everything I know. You haven't been to New Zealand, have you?" he asked.

"No, obviously," I replied, thinking of my complete lack of familiarity with New Zealand terminology, even his use of the word "paper," which seemed to refer to a course.

"Y'see, I had mentally detached my family from the whole colonization process by virtue of location. My ancestors, they came at different times, but settled in the South Island, mostly around Dunedin but some in the Christchurch area. Most came from Scotland, but some Brits and Irish were in there as well. Anyway, the Māori were concentrated in the North Island. So the story we grew up with was that our ancestors didn't take anyone's land, it was empty when they arrived except for some other Scots. That was the first falsehood I had to confront."

"You're from the South Island?" I asked, knowing as little about New Zealand's geography as I did of its vocabulary.

"I was born in Cambridge, in the Waikato region of the North Island, but only because my mum and dad moved there to manage a hotel. Hang on." He retrieved his laptop and opened a map of New Zealand.

Pointing to the South Island, he explained, "Here's Dunedin, and here's Christchurch. And here are the mountains where tourists usually go tramping. A lot of *Lord of the Rings* was filmed there. Did you see it?"

I hadn't. I shook my head.

"Well, anyway. You'd know the Scots settled Dunedin because it looks like Edinburgh. Here's the Waikato region, and here's Cambridge." He pointed to the middle of the North Island. "Over here's Auckland. And over here on the coast is Tauranga where my sister's family lives."

I studied the map. "Okay, so the Māori are mostly on the North Island and the Europeans came mostly to the South Island?"

"Well, no," he replied. "Europeans, including my ancestors, displaced Māori who were living on the South Island. And Europeans, who started showing up in the 1600s, made their first settlements up here." He pointed to a northern spot on the North Island. "Y'see, the story passed down in my family, I think it was like the story passed down in your family, was that no one was there when the ancestors arrived. Sure, I knew Māori on the North Island had been pushed around, but I didn't associate any of that with me, or with the well-being of my people as compared to Māori people today."

"So what happened? You said you didn't come out the same as when you entered," I asked. Out of the corner of my eye, I noticed a couple of women setting coffees on an adjacent table. I had been listening so intently to Ian that I hadn't even heard them enter.

He continued. "The Māori students, my classmates, they simply didn't take our shit. We'd be reading primary documents, and I'd still be thinking, well, my people didn't have anything to do with that. But my Māori classmates, they'd say, 'Look at these dates, man. When did you say your people arrived? Who do you think they got their land from?'" He threw up his hands. "I didn't want them to be right. So I dug into the records about my own ancestors, as far back as I could, and, well, they were right. Once I was able to say, 'My people made a living by taking your people's land away,' then we could actually talk. And then I started to learn."

I thought about how hard it was for me to admit to that statement, and the ways I had learned to dance around it. Well, by the time my people came along, the Indians were gone. Or, well, that was so long ago, and anyway, I didn't have anything to do with it. Just like Sean referring to the tribes in the past rather than present tense. Or me avoiding Angela's anger by stating that I hadn't done anything. Maybe my avoidance, in fact, actually magnified her anger over past injustices.

"So then what?" I prompted, hoping he could give me a clue as to what I might do.

"So then I learned about the gold rush, and the land grabs and land wars, and the treaty being ignored time after time, and schools trying to turn Māori children into brown English people. Y'know, colonization involves a combination of physical violence and control over how people think. We Pākehā grew up learning to see the Māori as the problem, so at first, I thought the Māori and Pasifika students would want us Pākehā to disappear. But then, I realized they weren't trying to boot us out. What they actually wanted was for us Pākehā to listen to them."

I recalled how readily Mrs. Walker had talked. Maybe the fact that I had listened actually mattered. Maybe she wanted me to hear her side of things.

Ian was saying, "I'd been afraid they'd want to take back the land my mum's house in Cambridge is on, but when I said that out loud, Hemi, he's a bloke I later worked with, he just laughed. 'No one's gonna chuck your mum out into the motorway.'" He grinned. "That was an ice-breaker, that. I realized right then that what I'd been most fearful of was that the Māori intended doing to us what our ancestors did to them, and we'd be sent packing."

Retribution. The same fear had crossed my mind.

Ian continued, "What Hemi said next was a turning point for me. He said, 'We know the colonizers aren't gonna leave. Sometimes we wish you would, but we're realistic. You're still here. But at least you could stop acting like colonizers.'"

He grinned again, eyes flickering. "Well, I was gobsmacked. Now, that might sound simple, but it's huge. We Pākehā are used to defining things, being in control. We pay attention to Māori only when it suits us. Being in control is embedded so deeply in our psyche that we don't even see it. So learning to share power and learning to support land claim initiatives, well, that's been a steep learning curve for me."

Two young women who had just claimed another table burst out laughing, obviously having a very different kind of conversation. The young man who had been hunched over his laptop glared at them.

I was struggling to visualize what any of this would mean for me, in practical terms. How could I share power with people I didn't even know? I asked, "That blessing you started class with on the first day, is that somehow related?"

"Yes," he replied. "Well, adopting Māori protocols isn't, by itself, sharing power, although acknowledging the culture is a form of respect. But the *karakia* I began with recognized the Indigenous people of this area, the Ohlone people. I can't simply walk into a place without considering whose land I'm on."

When he said that, I realized I never thought about whose land I was on. Even though my fourth-grade social studies curriculum briefly mentions the Ohlone, it doesn't acknowledge this place as their homeland. We teach about different pre-Columbian Indian tribes in California, all in the past tense, then move on to the Spanish explorers and the missions. I remembered Jessica's comment about the social studies curriculum gradually erasing Indians, teaching students that Indians had vanished.

"I don't even know any Ohlone people," I admitted.

His eyebrows lifted. "There's a group of 'em working on getting back a bit of ancestral land in the San Francisco area. On this side of the Bay, too. Actually there are projects all over your country to reclaim land. You're not familiar with them?"

I wasn't. It was embarrassing that a foreigner would be teaching me things I should know about my own country. I looked down at my hands, still holding my empty cup. I shook my head.

Ian shrugged. "No worries, that would be a good starting place." He paused, then said, "I have an idea. Since you've already reshaped one of my assignments to fit your needs, why don't you think about what you could do with the literacy project? You don't have to do it the way I laid it out. Take what we've talked about and shape it into something meaningful for you."

I studied his face for signs of mocking but he appeared serious. I replied, "Well, okay, let me give it some thought."

"Right." He stood and gathered his bag, then looked directly at me. "I know you might be feeling rather awful right now, but I think you have guts."

I wasn't sure how to respond, but I said, "Thanks for all of this. It helps."

"Good."

At the door we turned in opposite directions. I wondered, not for the first time, how he came to be in California. Obviously he hadn't just arrived here. Although I had no idea what my next step might be, at least I now knew there could be a next step.

⊰⊰⊰

HEMI APPEARED IN a dream as a Ute telling Orville and Sally to go back to Tennessee. There, they encountered him again, this time as a Cherokee telling them to go back to Europe. Then Ian appeared, writing down what everyone was saying. He handed me the transcript he wrote, telling me I had eleven days to resolve everything;

otherwise I would fail his class and Angela would never speak to me again. Sean laughed, offering to whisk me away to the Philippines.

I woke up exhausted, and I hadn't even started on my project yet. But over breakfast, an idea percolated. It seemed that my subconscious had been grappling with my fourth-grade social studies curriculum, while my conscious mind worried about Angela.

I could see at least two problems with my curriculum. One, it was generic to the whole state rather than having a local focus. Two, Indian people disappeared in its immigration story, just like Jessica had pointed out. What if I gave my social studies curriculum a local focus, starting with the Ohlone people? And rather than dropping them as we moved on to waves of immigrants, what if I kept their story central?

Given the enormous footprints history had stamped onto Indian–white relationships, this idea of refocusing a fourth-grade curriculum seemed paltry. What good would that do? I thought about the amazing work of the young Pakistani activist Malala Yousafzai who I saw featured on TV the other day. She was busy advocating for huge changes on behalf of girls around the world. Would someone like her dismiss my elementary school curriculum idea as too small to matter? On the other hand, what we learn in school affects how we think, how we see the world. Whatever I did in my own little classroom was imprinting itself on future generations in one way or another. So maybe my patch of the world—my classroom and my curriculum—maybe that wasn't too insignificant to consider.

If I wanted to tackle what it meant to act like a colonizer, I might as well start by examining how my teaching had maintained a colonial perspective, and what an alternative perspective might look like. I would need to do a lot of reading. There might be a workshop I could sign up for; I hadn't paid attention to any such thing before. I'd also need to meet some local Ohlone people. I wished I could talk with Angela! She'd have ideas for what to do next.

Ian would have to do. When I arrived to class, he was writing on the whiteboard. I asked, "Can I interrupt you for a sec?"

"Sure." He stopped writing, but kept his arm poised to resume.

"I, uh, have an idea for my project, but I could use a little help in getting started. You, uh, seemed to know something about the Ohlone people, and I wondered if you have contacts or anything you can share with me." I realized my palms were sweating.

"Sure, catch me during break," he replied, then continued writing. That seemed abrupt. I took a seat and pouted.

A couple hours later, Ian announced break time. I had to stand in line to talk with him, as I wasn't the only student with a question. When it was my turn, I told him about my idea.

"Good, good," he replied. "You said something about contacts?"

"Well, yeah, I'm not sure where to start, and it seemed like you know people and events and things that might help me get going."

"I think you're jumping ahead of yourself," he said. "Before you talk with anyone, you need to do some homework. I suspect there are good Ohlone histories available to read. Actual books, I mean, not just what's on the Internet. I haven't looked, myself. Check the library here, or see what's on Amazon. And start with Ohlone nation websites, see what information is there and what they recommend reading."

I felt foolish. These were steps I could have figured out myself. Had I known Ian would brush me off rather than opening up as he had the day before, I wouldn't have approached him.

He continued, "What you want are sources Ohlone people themselves regard as credible. Do a little cross-checking."

The Ian I had coffee with yesterday felt warm, but this one felt cold. Impersonal. I thanked him, then stepped out to take advantage of what was left of break.

Later, I pondered Ian's comment about wanting his ancestors to be innocent of having stolen Māori land. If your own family didn't know about an earlier theft that benefited them, were they accountable? More importantly, were you? Whenever we studied the Indians in school, I heard, and maybe even said, "Don't blame me, I wasn't there and my ancestors didn't know what was happening." Was I just hoping they didn't know? Might I want to use their presumed innocence to prop up my own?

Ian said that any claim to his own family's innocence vanished when he looked into the records. Māori were there when his ancestors arrived. The land had not been empty of human habitation. The Scots took it for their own gains, and Ian's ancestors participated in the taking. They knew full well what they were doing. My ancestors in Colorado had acquired a homestead right after the Utes were expelled. Did they know they were getting someone else's land? Did they think about what it meant to participate in a process of legalized theft? Did they regard the people whose land they were taking as people, or as less than human? Obviously I couldn't ask them, and I didn't have diaries or letters they may have written. But perhaps I could find clues as to how white people were thinking in the *Steamboat Pilot*, a newspaper published since 1885. While I wouldn't find my ancestors' thoughts there, I would at least get some idea how people like my ancestors thought about the Utes.

When I got home, I opened my laptop to search for mention of the Utes in digitized issues of the *Steamboat Pilot*, up through 1898 when Orville and Sally appeared to have left the Steamboat Springs area. I found three articles.

A spread on December 30, 1896 detailed the geography of Steamboat Springs, particularly its beauty, mineral resources, and potential as a railroad stop. The first paragraph concluded: "Civilization, in its westward march, passed around and left of this place unmolested to the dominion of the savage." The next paragraph called the area the "holy of holies of the Ute kingdom," then stated plainly: "Upon what was once the primeval home of the red man the town of Steamboat Springs is platted."

So anyone reading the local newspaper would know that the white town of Steamboat Springs supplanted so-called "savages."

A piece on the front page of an August 1897 issue described a battle between Utes and the militia in Meeker, about ninety miles southwest of Steamboat Springs. The battle broke out because "the Indians were raiding ranches down the river." It described details of the conflict, including how many on each side were wounded and killed, and white settlers' fear of the Indians. One paragraph described the Utes' elaborate communication system using signal fires atop peaks visible from the Uintah Reservation. Apparently the Utes were well-coordinated. Colorado's governor said he would negotiate a process to get them to retreat peacefully to the reservation on the condition of never again entering Colorado. The Utes did not see it that way, however. A shorter article five months later reported on Utes raiding cattle. When the Indians told the Colorado game warden they needed hides for tanning, the warden said payment for the cattle would be deducted from their government allowance.

These articles appeared almost twenty years after the Utes had been forced from their homeland in Colorado. I remembered Mrs. Walker mentioning that one of her grandparents had participated in the hunting trips when their families were starving because their land in Utah was bone dry. In her voice, I could hear her ancestors' anguish at losing the homeland that supported them as white settlers destroyed it by plowing it up and setting fences. Out of necessity, hunting must have morphed into raiding farm animals. Mrs. Walker's story told of survival and loss of home. The white man's story told of fear and indignation that the Indians ignored their boundaries. Two very different tellings.

Gram's grandparents must have been aware of the Utes' hunting expeditions. But like other white people at the time, they probably justified expulsion of the Utes by seeing themselves as superior and the Utes as "savage." Otherwise, how could they live with the knowledge that their fortune came at someone else's expense?

After Ian could no longer deny his family's implication in the colonization of Māori people and the taking of their land, Hemi had directed him to pay attention to how he (and other white people) continued to act like colonizers today. Ian found that challenging, but at least he had been surrounded by Māori classmates who would have pointed things out to him.

What might I do? How was I continuing to act like a colonizer, and how might I learn a different way of relating to the people whose land I occupied? And how might I turn any of this into a class project within eleven days?

My fellow students' reactions to my project underscored my own uncertainty. During a break later that week, a cluster of us was griping about how little time we had to finish our projects.

"This is the last time I'm taking one of these three-week summer courses," grumbled George, another master's student and teacher. "It's like getting no summer break at all."

"We'll still have almost a month before going back to work," another pointed out. "Or at least teachers who work in my district will, yours might be different."

"Lucky you," said George.

"At least you're not trying to finish writing a dissertation proposal at the same time," added Patricia, one of the doctoral students in the class.

Our grumbling led to asking each other about our projects. One teacher was creating a literature-based unit around the concept of identity, and another around adolescents dealing with family conflicts.

"What are you doing, Denise?" asked Nancy.

"I'm reworking part of my social studies curriculum to make the Ohlone people more prominent. And of course develop kids' literacy," I replied.

"Oh, don't you love doing the missions?" she exclaimed. Studying the Catholic Church's missions is part of the fourth-grade social studies curriculum, but many teachers go far beyond what is required. To many of my teacher colleagues, "doing the missions" is a large project that involves visiting a mission, building a model of it, and writing a paper about it. The Internet is loaded with directions about how to build a model of a California mission. Many kids use sugar cubes as bricks, giving a new meaning to sugar-coating history, I thought. You can even buy kits to build models of missions. Some teachers spend as much as a month on them, although the current fixation with reading and math test scores has led some schools to drop social studies altogether. Personally, I was never that interested in the missions, so my classes did what was required minimally, skipping the model and the paper.

Plus, I was just beginning to realize that the missions more or less enslaved Indians and eviscerated their cultures.

I replied, "Not really. The mission unit never interested me that much. Besides, they were part of the process of colonization."

"Yeah, but that was a long time ago. And you can also look at their important role in bringing the Church to California, as well as the beginnings of California's Hispanic culture," offered George.

Nancy persisted, "Well, I don't exactly see the point of going into any more detail about past atrocities than the curriculum already presents. I mean, kids of course need to learn that the Indians were treated badly. But that was so long ago— "

"With ongoing impact," I said as I thought about Mrs. Walker's Ute ancestors going back into Colorado to hunt because the land they were moved to in Utah was so arid. "But I'm just getting started working on it. The missions might not even be something I focus on."

The others drifted off, but Nancy seemed upset. "Won't dwelling on the past just stir up feelings about what happened? I mean, we can't change history. Isn't it better to learn to appreciate each other today?"

This wasn't a conversation I was prepared to have. I wondered whether other Milford teachers might react like Nancy. What about parents of my students? I recalled Sean's reaction just the other day when he asked if I was still worrying about the Utes. If he were standing here, would he be asking why I was worrying about the Ohlone, especially since I didn't even know any? And what if my questions led to realizations that would upset not only my students' parents, but my own? Maybe I was sticking my toe into a pond that was bound to become a sinkhole. And, to be truthful, a year ago if I had heard about someone working on a project like the one I was contemplating, how would I have reacted?

I wished I could bounce my uncertainties off Ian, but he was still inexplicably distant. I couldn't figure out why. He was a brilliant instructor, but he was beginning to remind me of one of those plastic blow-up dolls, this one hiding away a real person somewhere inside. I had seen that person. Maybe I was the only one in class who had.

But after treating me like a complex human being and revealing himself, he had boxed me right back into the more distant student role. I couldn't figure out what I might have said or done to cause him to do that. I hadn't even flirted with him! It hurt, but there didn't seem to be anything I could do about it.

By Sunday morning, having dived into Ian's project, I felt overwhelmed. This was turning out to be far more complicated than I had anticipated. I suppose I had imagined reading about Ohlone history, tracing back how white people took their land and reaped the benefits, updating history with current events, and then packaging all that into a tidy curriculum. How naïve! Instead, I found myself trying to untangle how we know anything about colonized peoples' history when the colonizers wrote most of the records, telling history from their own colonizer point of view—the viewpoint I had grown up with.

I begged off seeing Sean over the weekend so I could figure out what I was doing with this project, due a mere five days from now, yikes! But every time I wrote down something that seemed firm, I ended up with more questions. One challenge was the extraordinarily rich diversity of Indian peoples in California. Although my social studies textbook surveyed a few tribes living in different ecosystems, I had severely underestimated how large and diverse California's Indian population was. You couldn't just affix distinct peoples to a map, either, because people had interacted, traded, and intermarried. And I had not considered how tribes actively produced food surpluses, but without becoming farmers in any sense their colonizers understood. I had assumed they just lived off the land without realizing how actively Indians managed natural resources.

Another challenge was realizing the extent to which Spain's approach to colonization had differed from the Anglo approach. I couldn't simply transfer what I had learned about how colonization worked in Colorado to California. While Anglos (England, then the U.S. government) outright killed and forcibly moved Indian people from land they coveted, Spain conscripted Indians as laborers, using many of the same punishments Southern plantation owners used on slaves, like flogging.

My brain swimming, I was back to considering myself Exhibit A in a study of someone struggling to learn (and relearn), when my phone rang. Seeing Angela's name, I quickly answered.

"Angela?"

"Are you still speaking to me?" She sounded defeated.

"Yes! Are you okay? You sound like— " She sounded terrible, but saying that would only make her feel worse.

"Can you pick me up at the airport tomorrow night? Yeah, I'm okay." I heard her sniffle.

"You're crying," I said. "Yes, of course I can pick you up. What time? Which airline?"

"Alaska. It's supposed to get in at 8:35." A giant sigh rolled through the phone.

"Tell me what happened. Is your grandmother okay? Did something happen to her?"

"She's fine. She's out at the Indian Center right now. She's just been making me face up to some hard stuff, that's all."

"Hard stuff, like what?"

Silence, then, "Hey, I'm really sorry I dumped on you so badly. I know you're trying to deal with benefiting from the whole colonial thing and all, and it's really hard, and I just kind of flipped out on you. After you left, Grandma told me I should always remember that the Creator gave us all different gifts, and we shouldn't envy someone else's."

"Apology accepted," I said. "So tell me what hard stuff your grandmother is making you face up to."

"Just a minute." I heard her set down the phone, then loudly blow her nose. "Okay, I'm back. It turns out you aren't the only descendent of colonizers here."

Of course I'm not, I thought to myself. There are millions of us. To prompt her along, I said, "Uh huh, and?"

"Well, that's the thing. It turns out I am, too. After you dug up your history and told me about it, and Grandma told us her story, well, I totally identified with her. I'm part Ute, after all, so her history is my history. Well, after you left, that went on for maybe a week. But Grandma said less and less about it. She wanted to know all about my teaching, and she took me to the Indian Center, and she taught me how to cook a couple of dishes I like. But the history thing, it seemed like she didn't want to go back there."

"And then what?" I asked as Angela paused.

"Well, then she asked about you, and I said I wasn't having anything to do with you, and she asked why, and I said you kept dodging your responsibility for the impact of colonization on us today. And she just put her hands on her hips and looked at me. And then she asked what I thought my mom was doing. Well, I didn't have any idea what she was getting at, so I went, 'Well, maybe she's cooking dinner.' And Grandma said that wasn't what she meant."

As Angela paused I began to get a sense of where her story was going. She continued, "Grandma asked if I was aware that Mom's father's ancestors were Norwegian immigrants who got land in Nebraska through the Homestead Act. Well, I didn't know anything about that. Mom never mentioned it. Grandma said I'd benefit by doing the same kind of research on my own history that you've been doing on yours. She said she loved having me around, and was thrilled by my interest in the Ute side of me, but that I need to deal with all of me, and that includes my white side. Denise, three of my grandparents come from colonizers! Well, okay, one that I know of. I'm not sure about my mom's mother's side, although they were white. And I think my dad's mother's folks came to the U.S. to work in a factory somewhere in Chicago. But somehow I just hadn't thought about the possibility that some of my own ancestors came here to get Indian land. Grandma said I probably didn't want to think about it like most white people don't. But when I said I'm not white, she said, like, you're Indian and white. You remember when you called me a week or so ago? Well, that was right after this discussion."

I still felt the sting of her verbal slap during that phone call. No wonder she had been so upset.

"So you've been dealing with all this with your grandmother for the past week?" I asked.

"Yeah. After we had that discussion, well, later she told me more about her own life and how hard all these questions are. And she made me realize how, deep down inside, I resented you for having this nice house that can probably be traced to your ancestors' colonial histories. Well, I not only resented you, I threw all my anger right in your face, didn't I? Grandma finally got me to see that our relationship is too important to trash. Hey, did I catch you in the middle of anything?"

I closed the book I had been reading as tears welled in my eyes. "No, I'm thrilled to be talking to you again."

"Okay, well, let me tell you about her story."

≪∽≫

ANGELA'S GRANDMOTHER, CAROL Walker, leaned back in her chair and closed her eyes. When she opened them, she gazed into her granddaughter's face. "Always strive to make peace with yourself, Granddaughter. When I was your age, I almost destroyed myself."

Angela's mouth dropped open in surprise, since she had perceived her grandmother as self-assured and very together.

Her grandmother continued, "You once asked me why I married a white man. Well, I'll tell you. I married your grandfather to try to become white, myself." She gave a mirthless laugh. "Oh, I never would have admitted that, not even to myself. But I thought I'd die if I stayed on the reservation. You have to remember that back then, everything on the reservation seemed broken. Broken families, broken equipment, broken health, broken people. The reservation, that's where the Indian people were. So, in my childish mind, Indians were the ones who broke everything, and what does that say about us, huh?"

Never having been to the reservation, Angela couldn't visualize what her grandmother was talking about. Her grandmother continued.

"So when Mother and I started going to Rifle to sell beadwork, I started seeing things that weren't broken, a little bit of money here, a carefree attitude there. And I started to associate that with being white. When Bob Walker came along and paid attention to me, well, he was my ride out."

Carol readjusted herself in her chair as she regarded her granddaughter. Angela asked, "So you just got married?"

"I just got married. Just like that. I ran off before Mother knew what was happening. We went to Leadville first where Bob had a job for a

88

while. I cut my hair off short, wore it like a lot of the white women. I wore white women's dresses, completely stopped doing beadwork, even when Bob said we needed the money I could earn from it. Beadwork was Indian, and I didn't want any part of that life. No part at all.

"When our first daughter was born, your aunt Rose, whom you've never met and probably never will, my mother came to spend a few days. I had always stayed in contact with her. My father, I never saw him again. I would have needed to go back to the reservation, and by the time I finally did, his spirit had passed on. But from time to time, Mother came to see me. It shames me now to admit this, but when she came, we stayed inside the house. I didn't want anyone to see her, to know where I came from. I was trying so hard to be white."

Tears stung Angela's eyes. With her grandmother's dark skin and black hair, Angela could not visualize her as white.

"Of course, no one thought I was white," her grandmother continued. "It didn't matter how I dressed, how I wore my hair, how I talked, not really. People always knew I was Indian, or maybe Mexican. The one person it didn't make any difference to was my husband. I think he genuinely loved me for who I was. If I had said, 'Let's go live on the reservation,' he probably would have agreed, he was that kind of person. I think he shielded me from a lot of what white people said."

Her grandmother closed her eyes again, as though resurrecting Bob Walker behind her eyelids.

"Then what happened?" Angela prompted.

Carol opened her eyes. "You know your grandfather died in an accident. He lost control of the car in a rainstorm, your dad probably told you about that. But suddenly here I was by myself in Colorado Springs with four children, no husband, and no income. I had to find a job. I looked around, and the best I could come up with was working the stockroom in Gilson's Grocery. It isn't here anymore; it folded a few years after Safeway came. But they kept me in the stockroom for years because they didn't want my brown face in front of customers. When your grandfather had been alive, he dealt with the white world. He went looking for houses to rent, he registered the kids in school, he bought the car. Now suddenly, my brown face was the face of the family, and I had to take the insults because I had two girls and two boys to take care of."

Angela took one of her grandmother's hands and squeezed it, as though trying to wring out the pain coursing through her grandmother's body. She asked, "Grandma, what happened to my aunts and uncle? How come I've never seen any of them?" She hadn't even seen pictures of them in her grandmother's house.

"Well, both your aunts live in Denver. They're married and I understand they have children but I'm not sure how many."

To the disbelieving look on Angela's face, she added, "You see, Granddaughter, I figured that even if I couldn't be white, my children could be. After all, they had a white father, and none of them looked as Indian as me. Rose and Sandra, the two oldest, took my efforts to heart. They became whiter than the white ladies, like Mrs. Alder down the street who you've met."

Mrs. Alder, a tall blond with blue eyes, somewhere in her fifties, occasionally dropped by Angela's grandmother's house to say hello, perhaps share a cup of tea.

"They both got married as soon as they finished high school. They fled, just like I did when I was seventeen. I tried to stay in contact with both of them, but they never wrote back, and now I don't even have their current addresses or phone numbers. The post office returned my last letters. Your father didn't flee like they did. Even after he moved to California and married your mother, at least he stayed in contact with me until he was killed in that terrible robbery. He made an effort to connect me with you and your sister."

"What about the uncle I haven't met?" Angela asked, her eyes moistening.

"Thomas, my youngest, took another path. He went to the Uintah Reservation, where he lives with his family. They have three kids, and a couple of grandkids. I see them all a couple of times a year. One day I'll take you there to meet them. I think you'd like your cousins." Her eyes crinkled in a nascent smile.

"I didn't know you'd experienced so much pain. Why are you telling me all this?" Angela asked, embarrassed as she recalled the silly boyfriend problems she had shared with her grandmother during previous visits, completely oblivious to her grandmother's life.

"Because you need to hear it. You need to figure out how to embrace your whole self. A few years before you were born, something happened to me. I was working as a clerk in Gilson's, they had moved me out of the stock room when they realized I was more reliable than most of their other workers. One day I overheard a customer complain that she wasn't going to be waited on by 'that damned Indian.' That's what she called me, a 'damned Indian.' When I was younger, those kinds of comments hurt, and I'd try to make myself invisible. But this was March of 1978, when Indian people were walking from Alcatraz near San Francisco to Washington DC, to bring awareness of our needs and begin the road to sovereignty. The Longest Walk, it was called. They didn't come through Colorado Springs, but I heard about it from other Indian people I knew. And I saw some of it on the news."

Angela saw the sparkle that was normally in her grandmother's eyes return.

"Suddenly, I said to myself, well, I am Indian. These are my people, marching for me. And they seem proud of who they are. So I started letting my hair grow long and I started doing beadwork again. And the more Indian I allowed myself to become, the more I realized this town is full of Indian people who had been hiding, like me. My son, your uncle Thomas who you haven't met yet, he benefited from this change in me."

She reached over to a table and picked up a braid of sweetgrass, one end charred from smudging. "You see things like this around my home now, that pottery over there, that blanket behind you, those drawings on the wall," she said. "Do not take these things for granted, Granddaughter. Before I claimed myself as Indian, there was nothing like this around my home. Granddaughter, I spent half my life hating myself. I would do anything to spare you from the same experience."

৵৵৵

"SO I REALIZED I had managed to romanticize Grandma's side of the family and my own identity," Angela sobbed. "She's been through so much, I love her tons. But now I see these huge rifts in my own family that I had been dodging. And I got to thinking about my dad. I was just a kid when he died and didn't have too many memories of him. But as I listened to Grandma, these buried memories bubbled up about him getting mistreated because of his dark complexion. Like, I suddenly remembered being in the car when he got stopped by cops who thought he was Mexican. Well, that all fed into the anger I was feeling. Grandma kept telling me I should hate injustice, but not people. I'm starting to learn. And I miss you."

I was weeping along with her. "I wish I could give you a hug right now," I said.

"I know, I feel your love," Angela replied. "I didn't mean to make you cry, too."

"Hey, we'll see how much of this we can work on together," I said, sincerely hoping we could. "See you tomorrow evening at the airport."

"See you," she replied. "Oh, and Denise? Grandma likes you. She thinks you're good for me."

"Whatever that means," I laughed, relief washing over me like a warm tropical wave.

Chapter Seven

Chasing Gold

I WALKED INTO Monday's class glowing like the Northern Lights. Angela was coming home! Was she on her way to the airport yet? Was she thinking of me? Was she still crying? Was she angry with her grandmother? Any other day, I might have thrown myself into Ian's class activity. Each of us played "expert" for one approach to literacy in a fictitious school district that happened to resemble the one I worked in—large enough for a variety of schools, but small enough that you could name most of them; an ethnically diverse student population mixed only as much as segregated housing would allow. The district had a fictitious budget for literacy programs. After each "expert" argued for his or her approach, we were to decide how to allocate it.

I had chosen a program developed in the Navajo Nation before curriculum standards came along in the 1990s. Most of the kids spoke Navajo, but the literacy curriculum was in English. Figuring kids would learn to read more quickly in a language they already knew, a group of teachers and consultants developed a curriculum in the Navajo language and culture. With it, the kids' reading abilities improved by quite a bit. But apparently when the schools had to adopt the state standards, they scrapped the Navajo program, and the kids went back to reading poorly.

I doubted that program would get votes since our fictitious district didn't have Navajo kids, but I picked it because I wondered how Carol Walker's life would have turned out if she had access to something like it when she was young. I'd have to ask Angela what she thought. And I actually *would* be able to ask her!

I looked at my watch. She should be on her way to the Denver airport by now. I wondered if her grandmother was driving her, or maybe she was taking the shuttle. What was she thinking about? How would she deal with her white ancestors' histories of taking Indian land? I still didn't know how to deal with my own history. Would Angela spend Christmas with her grandmother again? Why did her grandmother like me? In the short time I was there, I hadn't said much. Maybe just the fact that I was a decent listener counted for something. Yeah, that was probably it. And of course she knew I was Angela's best friend, at least until Angela blew up at me . . .

"Denise. Denise? Anyone home?" Daphne was waving her hand in front of my face.

"What?" I started, realizing everyone was staring at me as though I had grown a horn on my forehead. "I'm sorry, what did you say?"

"We're about to vote on the budget," said Nancy. "Everyone has had their say except you."

I looked at her. "Don't look at me, look at the board." She waved a hand in its direction. Glancing at the board, I saw four literacy programs with a total price tag reflecting the fictitious budget we were given.

"She must've had a good weekend," said Jerry, eyebrows raised meaningfully.

"I wish." I frowned at him. "My best friend is speaking to me again, that's all." Jerry rolled his eyes. Tipping my head toward the board, I said, "That looks okay to me."

"Why?" Ian asked.

"Why?" I repeated. "Well, uh, dual language makes sense, given the number of Spanish-speaking kids in the district. The research supports it. And, uh, Reading Recovery for the primary grade kids who are getting way behind." I knew he was asking why the programs remaining on the board held more promise for kids in our fictitious school district than those bumped off the board, but since I hadn't followed the discussion, all I could do was state the obvious.

Patricia prompted me. "So, you're okay with the program you presented being taken off the list?"

"Well, yeah," I replied. "I picked it because it interested me for reasons other than this activity. Someone I know went through a terrible Indian school on a reservation; it was all about taking away everything Indian. It had a horrible impact on her. By the time she was a teenager she hated being Indian. This program would have been way better."

Ian nodded without saying anything or changing his expression. Then he stood. "Well, that wraps up our work for today. You have the readings for tomorrow. In addition, I want all of you to bring one question related to your project, for input from others. Something you're wrestling with. Right."

As I gathered my gear, I heard a familiar voice behind me. "Denise?" I turned to see Ian. "I'm glad your friend is back in your life. I know you've missed her." The first personal thing he had said to me in days. Why the change, I wondered.

"Thank you. I am too," I said, taking another step toward the door.

"And I appreciate why you chose the Navajo literacy program. You were referring to your friend's grandmother, am I right?"

"Yes."

He continued, "At home, many Māori elders have had the same experience. Well, so do a lot of Māori kids today, still. But over the last twenty years or so, New Zealanders have built a larger and stronger system of Māori language schooling than anything comparable I see here in the U.S."

"Will you be going back to New Zealand soon?" I asked.

"Don't know." He looped the strap of his book bag over his shoulder. "After you?" He indicated the door.

As we walked out, he said, "They'll probably hire me on here for a couple more papers—er, courses, that's your term—a couple of courses next semester. I'll be going to Aotearoa New Zealand at Christmastime. No idea what will happen after that. Well, excuse me, I need to stop off in the main office."

With that, he turned right while I continued to the stairwell straight ahead.

At the airport, as I took up my post outside security, a surge of people coming toward me let me know a flight had arrived. No Angela, though. A few minutes later, another surge rolled in my direction. I scanned people as they approached, but again, no Angela. I was reaching into my bag for my cell phone, when I glanced up and saw her straggling in my direction, eyes cast down. I waved frantically, trying to catch her attention. She glanced up, saw me, and rushed toward me.

"Angela, you're home!" I gathered her into my arms, joy flooding my body. She hugged me back in silence. When I released her, I looked into eyes that were red and swollen.

Then she cracked a grin. "Now that I'm home, we're gonna have to help put each other back together, huh?"

"For sure." I hugged Angela's shoulders as we headed toward baggage claim.

Minutes later, we left the parking structure for the freeway. Angela threw back her head and breathed a long sigh. I glanced at her and said, "I'm just so glad you're home."

"Me too. I'm sorry about laying into you about you having two parents and a boyfriend. That wasn't fair," she said.

"Maybe I don't always appreciate what I have," I replied. "You drew my attention to my tendency to gripe unnecessarily."

"Well, in any case, I can't believe how much Grandma gave me to think about."

"So tell me. We have a half hour or so before we're home."

"Well. I guess the first thing I'll need to do is call Mom and find out what she knows about her dad's—my grandfather's—relationship to their land. And what she knows about their history of homesteading. Then my other white ancestors. I might have to do the same kind of research you've been doing."

"It's a lot of work," I commented. "And I couldn't have dug up as much as I did if we hadn't gone to Steamboat Springs. You might need to travel."

"Yeah." I could hear wheels turning sluggishly in her head. "Grandma said it's important to confront that history and recognize its impact on me as well as the people who lost land. But she also said something I hadn't thought about at all."

"What's that?" I asked as I passed a Hyundai Sonata being driven at a turtle's pace by a white-haired person hunched over the steering wheel.

"Well, at first she just dropped comments I didn't get. Like, when we went to the Indian Center where she was working with teens, she told me things like, 'That one there, she's mostly Cheyenne, and that one's Arapahoe mixed with white, and that girl over there, she's Navajo but pretends she's Mexican.' And I was like, well, are any of these kids Ute? And she would just say, 'They're all our wounded kids.' It was like she was leaving these blanks for me to fill in."

Silence, then she continued. "And then stuff like, 'You need to reckon with history but you can't go back and change it.' What the heck's that supposed to mean? Or, here's another one. 'Hate doesn't heal anything.' I'd ask her, what are you getting at, and she'd just tell me I'd figure it out."

"That's deep," I said, thinking how much her grandmother sounded like Mr. Jackson. "I can guess about that last one."

Angela turned to look at me. I glanced at her, then gave my attention back to the road. She said, "Well, Grandma was right, I think I did figure it out. I think what she was getting at was that yes, I do need to know my history. But where to go with it depends on who's in my backyard. Like, you want to reckon with what happened to my grandma's people because of what your people did. But you probably can't do a whole lot because you don't live in Colorado or Utah, you live in the Bay Area of California, and so do I. And maybe it wasn't our specific ancestors who did the same thing to the Bay Area's Indian people, but we're here because they lost their land. And their descendants are still around, probably wondering when we're going to wake up, although I have no clue what they might want us to do. I don't even know any of them."

"Ohlone." I said. "That's who lived here before the Spanish set up missions to, quote unquote, civilize them. They didn't call themselves Ohlone, and they didn't see themselves as all one group. They lived in a bunch of different villages. Other Indian peoples were in the area as well. But the people who are now called the Ohlone were the main ones around here."

"Ohlone, yeah. Kids study the missions in fourth grade," she commented. "You teach about them, so you're steps ahead of me."

"Not really. I skim over the missions," I said as I tried to concentrate on the traffic. Rush hour had passed, but vehicles barreling along at about 75 miles an hour still surrounded me. "But I hadn't thought that much about them from the Indians' point of view, and my curriculum isn't written from their point of view either. Like, our textbook mentions Indians converting to Christianity and working in the missions, almost as though they were hired rather than captured to work. But that's about it. Actually, teachers can get caught up in the mission part of California's Hispanic heritage, and end up celebrating them in a way that downplays their role in conquest and killing."

I pictured Mike, another fourth-grade teacher in my building until he decided to open a restaurant. He had grown up in North Dakota but came to California when he'd had enough snow "for a lifetime," as he put it. He had wanted to "honor the Mexican culture" of our school, but didn't know how until he discovered the mission unit. Never mind that the missions were Spanish far longer than they were Mexican. Mike expanded that unit, cobbling together a smattering of Mexican folk music, stories of Spanish explorers, a lesson on making tortillas, and some Spanish vocabulary for the English-speaking kids in the class. I wondered if he had actually opened a restaurant, and if so, whether his menu, like his curriculum, mashed up things that didn't exactly go together.

"Good point," Angela was saying. "Here I am with a master's degree, and feeling embarrassingly ignorant about the history of where I live."

I flicked on my left turn signal and moved into the passing lane to get around a Winnebago in front of me, then replied, "Me too. But I've been doing some reading. One thing I've learned is how different the colonization process was in California from Colorado. The Spanish didn't systematically kill off the Indians, although they brought diseases that wiped out thousands. But they turned them into mission laborers, in the process destroying as much Indian culture as they could. The impact on people was a lot like what your grandmother told you white schooling was to her. But then when Mexico declared independence from Spain, the Mexican government took over the missions, and the Mexican government set up a land grant process to give mission lands to favored Mexican residents."

"So that's why all over California, you have Rancho this and Rancho that?"

"Yeah. So the Indians went from being laborers in the missions to laborers on the Mexican ranchos. Well, that went on until the U.S. colonized northern Mexico. The treaty ending the war with Mexico affirmed Californios' ownership of their ranchos—that's what Mexicans in California were called. But a U.S. land board required all kinds of proof of ownership. The process was so onerous and expensive that most Californios lost much of their land. They couldn't produce the required paperwork, or had to sell their land to pay off legal fees. The U.S. government then turned around and gave the land to the white people who were flocking in. Just like it did across the rest of the U.S."

I eased back into the center lane. From the corner of my eye, I saw Angela's shoulders sag. She said, "Well, what else do I have to do for the rest of the summer except learn stuff? Speaking of, you aren't missing the class you're taking right now, are you?" She turned to me, brow wrinkled in concern.

"No, it's an afternoon class. But I'd miss it to come get you."

She grunted, then said, "What's the class like?"

I wondered where to start. I began with an overview of course topics, but she stopped me. "I don't want to hear the syllabus, I want to know what the class means to you."

"Well." I took a deep breath as I refocused. "I thought it was going to be about strategies I can use to improve my students' reading. And it is, but I think I've learned more about myself than I have about particular teaching strategies. Ian, he's the professor, he keeps focusing us back on ourselves as learners. He thinks a lot of what teachers do is based on their own experience as learners, so whenever we launch into a different approach to literacy, he turns our attention back on us, and how we might have fared with that approach."

This was the first time I had articulated the purpose of the course in this way, and it made me realize why Ian could be a stickler about some things, but still flexible about others, like how we did assignments.

"So who's Ian?" she asked.

"He's this guy from New Zealand. I'm still not sure what he's doing here, but he's interesting. He makes us think."

"Is he cute?"

"You have a one-track mind!" I laughed. "And I knew you were going to ask that question. Ian could walk across a room and you wouldn't notice him." Until he looked you in the eye, I thought to myself, and then you wouldn't stop noticing him.

"How does he compare to Sean?"

"What? He doesn't. I mean, they're two entirely different people. They aren't people you'd think about in the same sentence. Or the same paragraph, for that matter. Ian is mostly aloof. He keeps us at arm's length." Most of the time, I thought to myself. I probably hadn't done anything to alienate him, he just wasn't a very warm person. Except occasionally and unpredictably.

Angela sighed. "So Sean can relax, he isn't being challenged by a new potential heart-throb." She was getting back to normal.

"I almost hate to bring this up," I said, "but can we talk about my house? The fact that I have one?" I felt my hands tighten on the steering wheel in anticipation of what she might say.

"Just . . . just don't act like you deserve it, that's all," she said quietly.

I was taken aback. "Act like I deserve it?"

"Yeah, well, sometimes you get into talking about what you're going to do with the yard, or the furniture, or, I don't know, it's like you have choices that I and most other teachers I know don't have." She fumbled with the hem of her jacket, then continued. "Maybe not so much like you deserve it, but like it's normal for you, Denise, age thirty, to have this nice place you own free and clear, forgetting that it isn't like that for most people."

"Okay," I replied. "I appreciate your honesty. I'll try to . . ." My voice trailed off. I wasn't sure what I would be trying to do, only that I'd make an effort somehow.

We drove in silence a few minutes. When I saw the one-mile sign for our exit, I signaled to move into the right lane, but a large delivery truck had rumbled up next to me. "Move, jerk-head," I shouted, then grumbled, "Most truck drivers are really careful, but this guy doesn't seem to be paying attention." I slowed to let him pass me on the right, much to the chagrin of the car behind me, most likely.

"Hang on," I said to Angela as I darted into the right lane and onto the exit. When we reached a stoplight at the bottom of the exit ramp, I asked if she had eaten anything for dinner.

"No, but I'm beat," she replied. "I'd fall asleep on my plate. Are you hungry?"

"No," I replied, "just looking out for you. Let's get you home then."

For the first time since I had spied Angela earlier in the airport, I saw her face relax into the contentment of a sleeping baby. My "sister" was home.

৵৵৵

I DIDN'T EVEN have time to enjoy Angela being back in my life before another crisis hit. The next morning when I tried to flush the toilet, it flooded. I mopped up the mess as best I could, hoping toilet paper had caught somewhere in the pipes and was now disintegrating. But another flush brought on a veritable fountain. Thankfully the house had a second small bathroom.

The Roto-Rooter technician I called showed up within the hour. He tried to flush my other toilet—and the same thing happened.

"Ma'am, I'm afraid it's your sewer line. This isn't something we can fix." He produced a card. "This is the best plumber in the area, they specialize in sewer problems. I recommend that you give them a call."

I paid the Roto-Rooter guy, then called the plumber he recommended, frustrated that I was losing precious time working on my project due Friday. The next plumber arrived promptly and was able to diagnose the problem right away. Tree roots had damaged the ancient pipes connecting my house with the city's sewer system. The plumbing company could fix the problem, and indeed had done so for other houses on my block over the years. But the bad news was that the repair would cost me a fortune, somewhere around $12,000.

"See how your house sits up on a rise?" he waved a hand from the street to my house. "The sewer line runs right under the street, but by the time it gets to your house, it's pretty deep. If you lived level with the street, it wouldn't cost as much to dig down and replace it."

Gram, what did you do to me? Of course I needed a working toilet, but I didn't have that kind of money sitting around. I realized I should have started building up a savings account instead of paying extra toward my student loan and splurging on new furniture. I wanted to cry.

The plumber assured me I wouldn't have to pay it all at once, installments (with interest) could be arranged. So much for having a house free and clear. Lacking options, I agreed to the company's installment plan and signed the form so the work could begin. The plumber estimated the repair would be done in a couple of days.

I had to use the bathroom just thinking about it. I looked around, panic welling up. I noticed Mr. Jackson's front door was open, so I walked over and rang the bell.

"Denise! Come on in, what can I do for you?" he said as he ushered me inside.

I briefly explained what had happened. "Can I borrow your bathroom for a sec?"

"Of course."

When I emerged, he handed me a key. "This is a spare I keep around, just in case. Take it, and please use my bathroom whenever you need to until that gets fixed." He waved in the direction of my house, where a backhoe was pulling up. I shuddered at the sight.

"Thank you, I'll try not be much of a bother."

"Oh, you'll be no bother. I'm about to drive down to Santa Barbara for a few days to see the grandkids." Why hadn't I noticed the suitcase parked near the front door? "It's a good thing I hadn't left yet."

It was, indeed. I thanked him, wished him a good trip, and walked back to my house. Now I had three problems facing me—or four, maybe five. First, I had no idea how I was going to come up with $12,000 to fix the sewer, but I had signed an agreement with the plumbing company, so I was going to have to do it somehow. Second, I had to finish my project for Ian by Friday and here it was Tuesday already. Third, I still hadn't figured out how to tell my parents what I had learned about the origins of the money Gram had used to buy her—now my—house. At least I no longer needed to figure out how to tell them Angela and I weren't on speaking terms. And fourth, I still had no idea what it might mean to stop acting like a colonizer. The reading I had begun doing would probably eventually help, but at the moment, I felt overwhelmed by how much I didn't know.

Should I call Sean? Would unloading my problems on him help?

No, I knew Sean too well. Rather than listening he'd offer up his own solutions. He could be very well-meaning, but not necessarily helpful. I'd fill him in later.

As it turned out, I filled him in the next morning when he called to ask how my project was coming along. Returning home from Mr. Jackson's bathroom, I found a missed call and message: "It's me; call me when you get this". When I returned his call, I mentioned not having my phone while I was at Mr. Jackson's, which led to why I was there in the first place. That led right into the drama surrounding my sewer backup, and the problem of how I would pay the bill. I glanced out my front window, where a freshly dug trench seared down the middle of the front yard. The mini-mountain of dirt in what had been a garden felt like a rebuke to Mr. Jackson for helping me replace weeds with native plants.

"Ouch," Sean commented. "You seem to have one thing after the next going wrong these days."

"Angela came home," I countered, "and she's coming over in a little bit to help me with my project."

"Right," he acknowledged. "The project's what I was calling about. You're making good progress?"

I sighed. "I was until I got sidetracked yesterday. But I'm determined to have something respectable to turn in Friday. I hate the idea of an incomplete."

He laughed. "That's my girl. Since you'll be done Friday, I think we should do something fun this weekend to celebrate, before we go see your parents on Sunday. Sound good?"

"Yeah, definitely," I said, perking up. I had promised my parents I'd drop in as soon as summer school finished. Not a trip I was looking forward to, though. I hadn't yet told them about what I had learned about Gram's family. I knew at some point I would need to do so, and the longer I waited, the harder it would be. "Maybe we can go to the beach if it isn't foggy. Or drive up to Point Reyes." Point Reyes National Seashore north of San Francisco is one of the foggiest spots in the U.S., but one of my favorite excursion destinations despite the weather.

"You're on," he said. Then his voice turned toward serious. "Denise, I'd like to toss out an idea. I don't want you to say yes or no right now, just think about it and we can talk this weekend."

"Okay." I became wary. I hoped it wasn't a marriage proposal! As much as I cared for Sean and enjoyed his company, I couldn't see myself married to him. Whenever I tried to picture us together long-term, I drew a blank. I hoped that might change with time, but I wasn't sure it would. I didn't think he pictured us getting married either, although he seemed so drawn to the idea of family—mine in particular—that he could, well, who knew what?

"Tomorrow's Curriculum is expanding. Over the next year or so, there will be a bunch of new hires, and I'd like you to consider being one of them."

My jaw dropped. I had not seen this coming.

He seemed to read my silence correctly as he continued. "I know this is probably coming at you out of the blue, but here's how I'm thinking about it. First, you love science, and you love weaving science through your curriculum. That's what we do, Denise. We create online curriculum that works across subjects, and science linked with literacy is big with us. You'd be great at that, and I think you'd have a lot of fun with it. Right now you've done a U-turn away from science with your new fixation on how to include more Indians in your social studies curriculum, but social studies isn't your forte and it never has been."

I wasn't sure how to respond. True, I did love science. But I was also beginning to reevaluate not just social studies, but my whole curriculum, from a point of view I hadn't considered before. I was bothered by what I was seeing and determined to do something about it. Sean's characterization of this work as a "new fixation" irked me. He made it seem illogical and temporary.

Into the well of silence, I dropped an "uhhhhh."

"Let me continue," he said. "Second, you hate having to teach to tests. You've been having to do that a lot, and it'll continue when school starts up again in August. You're a creator working in an environment that keeps clipping your wings. You know I'm right."

"Yeah, that's true," I said.

"And third, teaching doesn't pay all that much, and now here you are with this repair bill staring you in the face. And who knows what else might go wrong with your house."

My voice began to return. "Sean, this repair job is a one-time thing. It isn't like the house is falling apart around me."

"How do you know?" he asked. "Denise, you need to get a home inspector to come in and give it a thorough going-over. That usually happens when someone buys a house so they know what they're getting."

Since I'd inherited the house I'd skipped that step, but it wasn't something I wanted to deal with at this moment. I said, "Sean, I appreciate you giving me this option to think about, and I'll consider it. But I'm not sure what to make of it. I hadn't planned on moving. I assume the job would require relocating into the city, and I'm not sure that's what I want to do. But I— "

"Relax. You might be able to work from where you are right now, and only come into the city once a week or so, once you get oriented to the work," he interrupted.

"But I wouldn't even know what I was doing," I objected. "It's online, and although I use online stuff in the classroom, I have no clue how to develop it." I felt as though someone had stuck me in an aviary. Suddenly wildly different kinds of birds were whizzing around my head, and when I'd try to look closely at one, two others would get in the way. The way this conversation was moving, I couldn't focus on one—bird or idea—at a time.

"You don't have to know all that," Sean was saying. "We have a tech team that takes care of it. You come up with the material, they figure out how to package it on the platform. And back to the pay scale, within a year, you'd probably be making double your current salary. Oh, and there's international travel now and then, all interesting and usually fun. And, we'd probably get assigned some of the same trips." I pictured him wiggling his eyebrows. "Just think about it. We'll talk more this weekend. I've gotta run, but I wanted to start this ball rolling."

With that, he rang off. I stared at my phone. How was I going to sort this out? Angela was my usual confidant, but I wasn't sure I wanted to mention this conversation to her, at least not yet. For one thing, talking about it would completely derail our work on my project. For another, she'd feel like I was considering abandoning her, and would this job possibility ever underscore her perception of me as privileged!

Although Sean might say I could work from home, if my prospective job were anything like his, it would entail long hours in the San Francisco headquarters. The better salary, tempting as it was, would come with a price.

At least I could find out more about Tomorrow's Curriculum. I threw breakfast together and set it down among the jumble of books by my laptop on the kitchen table. Over toast and coffee, I opened the laptop and searched for Tomorrow's Curriculum. I briefly scanned through their website, but realized it wouldn't tell me what I wanted to know. What kind of reputation did the company have? Why was it expanding? Maybe news articles would help.

I quickly found some articles from the previous month announcing that publishing giant Robinson-Woodrich was in the process of acquiring Tomorrow's Curriculum. Then a couple of shorter articles from about two weeks ago announced that the deal was being finalized.

Hmm. Why hadn't Sean mentioned this to me? Surely he knew that I, like any other teacher, was quite familiar with Robinson-Woodrich, since its name was on maybe half of the materials in my classroom. And, they published the main standardized tests used in about half the states, although not in California. But because they were elbow-deep in making a fortune from the curriculum standards and regulations that defined what teachers do these days, my knee-jerk reaction to Robinson-Woodrich was negative. Which was probably why Sean had been mum.

He worked for Tomorrow's Curriculum's global division. I remembered Jessica mentioning Robinson-Woodrich creating and selling curriculum in Third World countries that prepared call center workers. Was that a good thing for young people there, or a contemporary way of turning non-white people into cheap labor? I shivered with the thought as I wondered how large the worldwide Robinson-Woodrich footprint was, and how any of this might affect the work of Tomorrow's Curriculum. I was pondering what search terms to use when the doorbell rang.

I jumped up from the computer and opened the door. Angela stood on the step, scanning the trench in front of my house. I was glad she had agreed to come to the house rather than proposing a different place to meet. We were working at bridge-building.

"Just walk in, you don't have to ring," I said as I motioned her inside.

"I tried to but the door was locked." She looked around. "They sure made a mess. When are they coming back?"

"Any minute. Want a cup of coffee?"

She declined as she sat at the kitchen table, surveying books and papers that ringed my laptop like hotels around Union Square. "So if I'm going to help you, you're gonna need to show me where you are with your project."

I reached for a printout of what I had written yesterday while I closed the news website and reopened websites related to my project. Angela read the drafted rationale, overall unit plan, and sketches of a couple of lessons, nodding her head as she went.

She put the pages down. "I like how you're focusing on the Ohlone during the California Gold Rush."

"Thanks," I said. "When I put the idea of the Gold Rush and California Indians together, one of the things that popped out at me was something the California legislature passed authorizing white people to take Indian kids away from their families to be indentured servants, just by going to the Justice of the Peace."

"Holy shit!" she said.

"Yeah, that's what I thought. I should maybe add this stuff into the rationale. In 1848, the U.S. had just taken half of Mexico, and six days before the treaty was signed, someone discovered gold near Sacramento. Boom, the Gold Rush was on! Two years later, while California was in the process of becoming a state—and who wouldn't want to admit it as a state, with all that gold—the state legislature got busy passing laws enabling white people to turn Indian people into servants, or selling Indian people they thought were vagrants to the highest bidder for work. Indian people had no legal rights at all."

"This is so important to teach." Angela slammed her hand down on the table so hard that I jumped. She looked at me. "Sorry. But this stuff hurts, you know?"

"Yeah, I know," I agreed.

She continued, "You point out here that the mid-1800s were a crucial time for California Indians, but schools usually teach the Gold Rush as something totally disconnected. I like your idea of teaching the unit through perspectives of Ohlone people, the U.S. government, miners, and Californios. So many people clawing over each other's backs to try to make a fortune while legalizing racism. Geez, I didn't realize Congress authorized bounty money for killing Indians, or that a lot of whites who captured them sold them as slaves." She ran a hand through her hair as she gazed out the window, as though visualizing the brutality.

"No wonder the Indian population of California plummeted when the U.S. invaders took over." Her body clenched. Then she exhaled and returned her gaze to mine as she said, "You need to teach this. But I don't exactly see your plan. You're overly short on detail."

"That's because I got lost tracking down information about the different bands of Ohlone," I said. "I don't exactly have a plan yet. I had been thinking they were this one tribe, you know? But that's not how it is. Back before the Spaniards came along, they lived in villages scattered all over this part of California." I pointed to a map of villages. "They didn't see themselves as Ohlone, that designation was placed on them later on. The missionaries gave them Spanish names and forced a lot of them to work inside the missions, so after a couple of generations, they became known by mission, like the Dolores Mission Indians in San Francisco, or the San Carlos Mission Indians in Monterey. And then when Mexico took over, the Indian people were moved to ranchos to work, so they started being referred to by those locations. It's confusing, at least to me."

I pointed to the laptop screen and continued. "So I've been looking at all these different Ohlone websites. Not only isn't there one Ohlone nation, the Feds don't recognize them at all, even though various Ohlone tribes have been working for years to get federal recognition. You should read this page about the legal fight the Muwekma Ohlone have been waging against the BIA, even though the BIA admits their tribal status was never legally terminated. The Muwekma have presented all the required paperwork for tribal recognition, but the Feds still won't recognize them."

Angela squeezed in next to me and began to flip back and forth among various open websites. In the background, I heard machinery. The workers had returned for round two. And in class, Ian had gone back to pointedly ignoring me, even when I raised my hand to participate in a discussion the previous day. I didn't want to think about how he would grade this Gold Rush unit. If it weren't something I could actually use, I'd dump it and return to a much more manageable project.

Angela interrupted my musing, her eyes glued to the screen. "It looks like four, no five, no wait, seven, yeah, seven Ohlone bands are petitioning for federal recognition. I'm gonna have to find out more about how that works. You should include something about tribal recognition in your curriculum."

"I was thinking about that, but not in this Gold Rush unit," I said. "This one guy, Dorrington, he wrote up a report in 1927 naming which bands of Indians he thought were landless. Hello, why were Indian people landless? Anyway, in the process, he de-recognized over a hundred bands that had been recognized previously. And now they're having to fight to regain federal recognition they never actually lost. Sad, huh?"

Angela was studying something on the screen and not paying attention to me. Her eyes widened.

"What is it?" I asked.

"Can you believe it?" She turned to me, while pointing to a picture. "That's my dental hygienist, Martina Soto, standing next to her brother at a powwow in Pomona. Apparently she's a member of the Costanoan Rumsen Carmel tribe based in southern California. I had no idea."

She was pointing to a picture of several roughly middle-aged people, some wearing tribal regalia and others wearing jeans and T-shirts.

I said, "You're part Indian and you didn't know she was, too?"

"What do you talk to your dental hygienist about?" she asked. "I talk to mine about my gums, not my identity. Besides, you didn't even know I had Indian ancestry until a couple months ago."

"But she looks kind of Indian," I said looking at the picture again.

"So do most Mexican people," Angela replied. "But I don't go around asking them about their Indian ancestry. I wonder why Pomona? Ohlone weren't down in the southern part of the state."

"That's weird," I said. Then I had an idea. "I wonder what she would like fourth-grade kids to know about Ohlone people. I wonder what she'd think of what I'm trying to do with this unit. Can you ask her? When is your next cleaning?"

"I usually get it done sometime after Halloween. Pig out on candy and then go get the teeth cleaned. I suppose I could ask her opinion, though. I mean, you're getting me thinking about my own curriculum, too. Of course, she's just one person."

"Right, but maybe she could suggest other people we should talk to."

"But maybe not before Friday," Angela pointed out. "Anyway, while you're in class this afternoon, I'll call my dentist's office and see if I can set up a time to talk with her. In the meantime, let's try to lay out what was happening in the middle of the 1800s."

That night, I was about to get in bed when something made me check my email. After scrolling quickly through the usual junk mail, I was about to set the phone on the nightstand when I did a double take: an email from Ian, sent a half hour ago, subject line empty.

Curious, I opened it and read:

Denise, I've been rude to you and feel an apology is in order. Can you chat with me a few minutes before or after class tomorrow? Ian

He had been rude to me, true, but I figured his brusqueness was just part of his personality. Some people run hot and cold, and it's best not to obsess over why. When I was a kid, our neighbor Mr. Hagan was like that. Some days he was all, Denise, sweetheart, how are you? And other days he didn't seem to see anyone in his path as though he were in a different world entirely. Once I asked Mom what I did to make him mad at me. She said I didn't do anything, that was just how he was, and poor Mrs. Hagan had to put up it.

So I tried not to take Ian's curt behavior toward me personally. Well, emphasis on "tried." Something about him fascinated me since that coffee conversation, but after that, he didn't give me more teasers. Well, only a couple more class days left and he would be history, anyway.

What might he want to say to me? I sent him a reply:

How about after class?

Chapter Eight

Collision

I TOSSED AND turned, wondering what Ian had in mind. All night opposing images battled in my head. The warm Ian who invited me into his own uncertainty of learning to grapple with being a colonizer's descendant morphed into the cool university professor who kept all his students, me included, at a careful distance. Which was the real Ian and what did he want with me?

As my alarm went off, the light in my head came on—teaching evaluations students always fill out the last day of class! That had to be it: Ian didn't want a bad evaluation to tank his chances of being hired to teach another course. He was manipulating me! The funny thing was, I hadn't planned to trash him. He was a very good instructor. He had stretched my thinking. His questions about literacy pushed me in directions I hadn't known existed, giving me a new set of keys that might unlock more success in my classroom.

So he really didn't have to bribe me with an apology, if that was his intention.

When I arrived for class, a knot of students was gathered outside the door. I joined them to see what was going on. It turned out that Cheryl was displaying photos of her newly purchased wedding dress on her phone. I glanced at a couple of them, then continued on in.

"Good for her," said Patricia, who was right behind me.

"I suppose," I replied. "But I think romance is overrated, myself. I'd rather stay single."

A few minutes later, Ian had organized us to discuss questions we were struggling with as we finished our projects. Mine was: While teaching literacy, how can you teach respectfully how one nation colonized another?

"Why while teaching literacy?" Patricia asked.

"Because this is a literacy class," I replied. "That's what our projects are supposed to be about. I'm actually working on my social studies curriculum, but I can develop kids' literacy skills at the same time."

"So, do you want us to help you with the literacy part, or the respect part of the question?" asked Sheila, another fourth grade teacher I hadn't met until this summer. "You're talking about California history, so maybe you're asking how to teach the missions? Or U.S. annexation of the Southwest?"

"Annexation" is the euphemism textbooks use to characterize the aggressive U.S. conquest of the northern half of Mexico. I hadn't even started thinking yet about that part of my curriculum.

I replied, "I was thinking about the Spanish conquering California Indians, but you can apply the question to any other conquest. Did you know that right after Columbus stumbled on the Americas, the Pope, apparently speaking for God in his opinion, granted all land west of the Azores to Spain, by virtue of them discovering it?" I put "discovering" in air quotes. "But since people were already living there, the Spanish went on to clarify that Europeans had to actually occupy the land by building a fort or something. None of this was worked out with the Indians, of course."

Until two days earlier, I hadn't known about the papal bulls—edicts by the Pope—that eventually became the Doctrine of Discovery, and accepted as international law. After the Crusades, in a series of papal bulls over about forty years, the Pope sanctified enslaving non-Christians and taking their lands. It wasn't just a matter of Columbus not recognizing the Taino Indians as human, which was huge in itself; backed by the Catholic Church, Spain created a whole legal system imposing its power over most of the Americas. I continued, "I have no idea how to broach that history with fourth graders, especially considering how many of them have some Spanish ancestry."

Suzanne, a middle school teacher who rarely opened her mouth, spoke up. "Just because a lot of us Latinos have Spanish heritage doesn't mean we can't criticize what our Spanish ancestors did. I guess I don't see the problem, unless you have some kids from Spain who might get tweaked. But that still doesn't mean you don't teach it."

Suzanne was Latina? Walters must have been her married surname.

"I think Denise has a point," Sheila said. "People have a lot of nostalgia about the missions, even though they were a direct result of that Doctrine."

Suzanne replied, "Well, you don't have to teach just one point of view. Like, you could divide the kids into a couple of groups, Spanish priests and Indians, and have them debate their perspective after doing some investigating. I do things like that in my class. One of my best units unpacks the history of the King Ranch in Texas. Students research and play roles like Richard King and his business partners, small landowners, the Texas Rangers, northern Mexico ranchers, and Mexican *bandidos*. It's a lot of fun."

"We teach fourth grade," Sheila started to object.

"I like that idea," I said, ignoring Sheila. Fourth graders can handle opposing viewpoints. "I can see how to tie it with literacy, too, because the kids have to read something before they debate. Thanks, Suzanne." I had no idea how I was going to plan and write up all this by Friday, but at least now I had a direction.

Patricia turned to Sheila, who looked as though she was still trying to formulate an objection to Suzanne's idea. "So what's your project about? What can we give you input on?"

Two hours later, after Ian dismissed class, a line materialized in front of him as though he were selling tickets for the latest Leo DiCaprio movie. I overheard Cheryl, who got there first, describe her re-worked project in far more detail than necessary, apparently seeking his blessing. It looked like I would have some time to kill, so I turned to Suzanne, who was zipping up her backpack. "Thanks for that idea. Tell me again which school you teach at."

"No problem. I teach at Vazquez. You're at Milford, right?"

I nodded, embarrassed that she remembered where I worked while I remembered virtually nothing about her.

"You must know Jessica Westerfield," she continued.

I nodded. "I do. Not terribly well, although I like her."

"She's been a good ally to us on a new Raza Studies curriculum. Not many white teachers have stepped up to support us. She's special. Well, I gotta run." With that, she turned and left.

I felt as though a wasp stung me. Obviously, I wasn't one of the white teachers supporting them—whoever "they" were. Come to think of it, I had heard about a group of Mexican-American teachers working on a

Mexican-American studies curriculum. That must be what she was referring to. If I asked Suzanne more about it, would she tell me?

I felt conspicuous just sitting there as the room emptied, so I headed for the ladies' room. When I returned, Ian was wrapping up with Erin, the last remaining student. I gathered up my bag as Erin left. Ian caught my eye and pantomimed drinking coffee.

As we descended the stairs, he commented, "I'm always surprised how many students need to be reassured they're on the right track."

Not always on the right track myself, I just nodded.

"I'll look forward to seeing how your project has come along." He looked at me with a grin. "Not now, of course, unless you have a burning question?"

"No," I said. "I'll look forward to seeing how it comes along, too. It won't be all polished or anything, but I aim to give you something respectable. My friend Angela's helping me out a little."

"Good," he said. "And I'm glad to know your friendship survived."

We crossed the street and entered the coffee shop. "Same as last time?" he asked.

The shop was empty. I took a table away from the door, then studied Ian's back as he stood at the counter ordering two lattes. His brown canvas book bag, now draped over one shoulder, had holes where the stitching had ripped. Lightly bleached rings around a couple of dirty streaks suggested ineffective attempts at cleaning. In contrast, his blue plaid shirt looked freshly washed and pressed.

He set down the coffees, then took a chair. "Denise, I just wanted to apologize for being a bit of an ass with you." His brow creased.

"Thanks, but you don't need to apologize," I said. *Of course he does*, said a voice inside my head. *He's been rude, and rudeness demands an apology.* But another inner voice warned me about this attempt to buy a good teaching evaluation.

"The thing is," he continued, "I rather like you. Y'see, you remind me a wee bit too much of my soon-to-be ex-wife Rachel, although in many ways you aren't like her at all."

I would have dropped my latte, were it not already securely placed on the table. I stared at him, my jaw hovering down to my boobs.

"She's tall, athletically built, like you. Blond hair, although yours is shorter," he continued. "That first day I saw you in class, you wouldn't remember this, you had your back to me for just a second before you turned around, and I thought, my god, what's Rachel doing here?"

He took a sip of coffee. I simply didn't know what to say, and was confused about the direction this conversation might be taking. He shifted his weight in his chair as though a different body position would make him—or me—more comfortable. He continued, "But once I got over that initial shock, I realized I was attracted to you on your own merits. Especially last time we were in here." He waved his hand to indicate the space. "Although I realize that for you, romance is, what did I hear you say, overrated?"

I felt heat rising from my neck to my hairline. He had obviously heard me grousing about Cheryl. And he was attracted to me? My god, this wasn't about teaching evaluations at all! I must have looked stupefied because he asked, "You're single, right? Just checking."

I nodded.

He plowed ahead. "Y'see, your values, at least what I'm aware of, are a lot like mine. You ask many of the same questions I ask. That's very different from Rachel, which is why we're in the midst of a divorce."

My voice finally returned. "Ian, back up. This conversation is moving in an entirely different direction than I thought it would. Yeah, my love life is kind of stagnant at the moment. And this is the first you've mentioned your married life, although of course that isn't something that would just come up in class. But right now I feel like I've been dropped right into the middle of, oh, I don't know what. Okay, you're right, my feelings were hurt when you pretty much ignored me after being so open with me earlier. But—" Where to begin?—"Tell me about Rachel."

As he leaned back in his chair, his shoulders relaxed. I seem to have moved the conversation to slightly less sensitive ground. "I was completely smitten when I first saw her on a beach in Tauranga, where my sister and her family live. She was there on holiday with a couple of friends, and we managed to hit it off. Then she returned to California where she lives, and, well, I came over here a couple of times to visit her. This all moved very quickly, you understand, and during my third visit, we decided to run off and get married."

I tried to picture an impulsive Ian eloping with a bikini-clad woman he fell for on the beach. The image just didn't fit this smart, methodical, organized teacher.

"Not something you'd expect of me, eh?" he asked as though reading my mind. "It wasn't until we were married that I realized she's far more materialistic than I am. When I met her, she was working in a pre-school center, so I thought she liked little kids. Good potential mum, you know? Turns out she was also working on her real estate license, and once she got that, she was off into the million-dollar house stratosphere, leaving kids in the rear-view mirror. She kept visualizing us in one of these mansions she was selling, overlooking some magnificent vista." He shook his head. "The part about working with kids? Just a short-term way station which she said totally cured her of any thoughts about motherhood."

"Then here I come along questioning turning homelands into real estate," I said, avoiding alluding to my teaching career, which he might interpret as me volunteering to be the mother of his children. My stomach fluttered at that thought. I hoped I wasn't blushing.

"Yes, finally a beautiful lady who makes sense to me. Rachel and I separated in March. Our lawyers in Los Angeles are battling out the terms of a divorce. She's trying to get as much as she can out of me, which is funny, really, when you think of it—it's a bit like trying to squeeze water out of that rock over there." He pointed out the window. "She seems to think my PhD is worth something, but so far all it's gotten me is this part-time job that barely pays rent."

"And you're having to fork over for a lawyer?"

His face squeezed up like a prune. "But it'll be over soon. Anyway, so here I am trying to figure out if you might have any place in my life, while my head keeps pointing out that I tried a tall blond Californian once and it almost ruined me. Not to mention that you're a student in my class, and I don't want to get bounced for sexual harassment."

My muddled head couldn't string two words together to make a sentence.

Ian said, "I can tell by your face that I'm tossing you a curve ball. I should have waited at least till the end of the course, but I couldn't. I was afraid that after tomorrow, you'd disappear. I know it's presumptuous to even think you might have any interest in a used Kiwi who doesn't have much to offer except a weird sense of humor and a decent moral compass."

I knew I should tell him I already had someone in my life. He would be embarrassed, but that would save him from digging an even deeper hole. Yet, I didn't want to mention Sean. Sean was—well, he was safe emotionally. No great bells and whistles, but security and comfort. Ian, on the other hand, had turned my insides into pudding.

Trying to compose myself, I replied, "Ahh, yeah, you have surprised me. Not in a bad way, just in a, well, a surprising way. Umm, well, maybe after you've graded my project, we could have coffee again?"

"I was thinking of something a bit more stout." He grinned. "Let's leave it at that, and I'll contact you in a few days."

We stood and gathered up our things. I was amazed my jelly knees held me up. Ian deposited the coffee cups in the garbage, and we left.

I had walked two blocks past my car before I came back down to earth. What was it about him that felt like magic? I couldn't put my finger on it, but I knew it had been years since I had experienced a similar feeling.

I thought about Angela's comment that I already had a boyfriend— Sean—whom I didn't appreciate. But even with an effort to appreciate him more, I knew we didn't make magic together. Sweet and handsome as he was, he never blew me off into the clouds like this.

But falling from the clouds was excruciatingly painful. Not an experience I wished to repeat. I wasn't sure what to do.

When I entered class on Friday, I dropped my project, nicely printed, onto a pile that had begun to form on the table in front of the room. He winked at me. I hoped I wasn't blushing as I took my seat. I flipped open my laptop, checking email as a time filler before class started. A message from Angela:

We're on with Martina Soto Monday morning at 10. She's jazzed about your project. I'll meet you there. We'll talk before then of course! ☺

Then a message from Sean:

Sitting here in boring meeting, day-dreaming of the weekend with beautiful you. Pack your overnight case, I'll be by to get you as soon as I can get out of here this afternoon.

১৯১৯১৯

TWO A.M. SUNDAY morning. I flipped over again, careful not to disturb the snoring lump in bed next to me. Sleep eluded me. Whenever I started to drift off, I slid into Ian's arms—but it was Sean who was curled up beside me. I shouldn't have let Ian say as much as he did. I should have stopped him, told him I already had someone. Someone who wouldn't hurt me.

On the other hand, maybe I should have simply run off with him, abandoning everything else in my life. Forget reality and take a chance.

Sean had picked me up late Friday afternoon as he said he would. Off we went to Point Reyes, where he had reserved a room in a romantic lodge. Over seafood and wine, he toasted my completion of the summer course. I was surprised. Finishing a course mid-way through a degree program doesn't merit a fancy celebration, and besides, our relationship was built mainly around casual activities—long walks, movies, visits to my parents. It seemed Sean had an agenda, but none emerged. Maybe he felt me slipping away and was trying to reel me back in.

Saturday morning as we walked on a trail, I broached the subject of Robinson-Woodrich buying Tomorrow's Curriculum.

"Sean, I'm just not comfortable with them," I said. "My impression is that they're predatory. They're out to make big money, that's their main agenda, and even if Tomorrow's Curriculum has a more humanitarian mission, they'll mold you into theirs. Why didn't you tell me they bought your company out?"

"Because I knew you'd react just like that," he said. "I have no love for Robinson-Woodrich either, but I figured you'd have this knee-jerk reaction, just like what I'm seeing right now."

I didn't like his tone of voice. It felt demeaning. I said, "So you were going to keep me in the dark, is that right?"

He exhaled loudly. "Look, Denise. First off, I wouldn't call Robinson-Woodrich predatory. They're very good at playing the game of capitalism, and capitalism is a fact of life. If you don't like it, well, what can I say? As far as Tomorrow's Curriculum goes, we still chart our own mission. Robinson-Woodrich may own us now, but they don't control us."

"And how long will you remain independent from them?" I asked.

"We're not independent, we're getting resources from them, for heaven's sake. We'll be able to expand our operation, do things we hadn't been able to do before. They have a much broader global reach than we did, and they have money to do things we couldn't." He looked at me as though I were a recalcitrant child.

I barreled on. "So I hear the curriculum they peddle in Third World countries trains young people for low-wage jobs American corporations export, is that right?"

Sean looked exasperated. He started walking on ahead of me. I followed. After a minute, he stopped and turned back to me. "Denise, I don't know exactly where you're getting this stuff. Robinson-Woodrich *does* help prepare young people for jobs so they can become economically independent. But whether you like that or not, that isn't what *we* do. Our academic curriculum links local knowledge with English literacy and our domestic standards-based curriculum. Period. That's what we do and that's what we'll continue to do. You can join us or not. I'm not trying to talk you into something you don't want, and I'm sorry if I gave that impression."

I couldn't think what to say. Maybe he was right. Maybe my reaction had been too automatic, too overblown, too much a product of complaints I'd heard over the years about the expanding Robinson-Woodrich empire and its growing control over what teachers can and cannot teach. And it was true that Sean hadn't been twisting my arm. All he had done was offer me an opportunity, and here I was, snapping at him.

I apologized, and Sean apparently accepted my apology. One of his virtues was that he rarely stayed angry for long. Me, on the other hand, I couldn't shake my unsettled feeling about the direction in which Tomorrow's Curriculum seemed to be headed.

When we arrived at my parents', they surprised me by revealing they had taken up golf.

"Golf?" I asked, almost choking as I pictured them in plaid shorts and visors, grass flying from their divots.

"You'd be surprised how many people our age play," Dad said. The age part didn't surprise me, since most of the people I noticed on the local golf course had white hair.

Mom continued, "We signed up for lessons at the country club. Do you remember Jeff and Susan Miller? They're in the class as well. We go out as a foursome now and then when it isn't too hot."

Susan Miller, pink and fluffy like cotton candy, had been a kindergarten teacher for as long as I could remember. She must have retired.

Dad announced, "We're taking you two to dinner at the country club tonight."

Mom was looking at me. "Don't look so shocked, honey. People our age do take up new interests. That isn't entirely the province of the young."

"I'm glad. I just didn't know you had an interest in golf."

"We didn't either until we tried it out," Dad said. "Walking around the course is good exercise, and the game's a challenge."

"We figured out how we can spend a little more on ourselves," Mom added. "With retirement approaching, we were afraid we'd have to tighten our belts. But we got a financial advisor who showed us what we can actually afford while continuing without overspending."

"In January, we're going on a cruise through the Panama Canal." Dad sounded like a little kid about to visit the state fair.

Mom put her hand on mine. "Your Gram left you in good shape, Denise, so since we don't need to worry about you, we can finally do a few things for ourselves."

Dad proffered a brochure and a trip booklet. Spreading the documents across the table, he shared the fun he and Mom had deciding on a cruise, the first in their lives. He had always wondered how the Panama Canal's locks worked, so that became the deciding factor. He was considering buying a new camera for the trip. Any thoughts I had about asking them for help with my sewer bill had evaporated.

"Adult ed through the school district offers a photography class on Thursday evenings this fall. I'll probably sign up," he added.

Over dinner at the Country Club, I mentioned the course I had finished and the Gold Rush unit I had redesigned, with Angela's help. I was about to convey Angela's greetings when Dad exclaimed, "The Gold Rush! As a kid, I loved studying it. I remember my teacher arranging a field trip so we could pan for gold. I forget where we went, but I loved sluicing and anticipating a bright lump of gold in my pan. Never happened, but the possibility gave me quite a thrill."

"That's not what we're doing," I said. "A lot of the mining took place on the homelands of the Nisenan and Miwok people. The miners just came in and started digging on someone else's land. The Indians worked with them for a while, but before long the miners started murdering them, and the murdering just escalated. For California's Indian people, the Gold Rush was the beginning of outright genocide. Mexicans treated the Indians as laborers, but then the white miners treated them as scum to get rid of."

After a moment of silence, Mom said, "*That's* what you plan to teach your kids? Why in the world would you do that?"

"Because it's true," I said. "I was taught a sugar-coated history and you probably were, too. I want to get at the truth of what really happened."

"Honey," Dad said, "What you just said may be the truth, I don't know where you got it, but it may be. But it was also a long time ago. I don't quite see the point of upsetting little kids by telling them about—"

"Genocide?" Mom's voice sounded aghast. "Isn't that a little harsh?"

"Yeah, Mom, genocide was very harsh. That's why I can't dance around it," I replied.

My parents glanced at Sean, who shrugged his shoulders as if to say, "Don't blame me."

"Well, at least check with your principal before you mention genocide. There may have been some shootings, but genocide?" Mom was having a hard time wrapping her head around that idea.

"One thing I agree with, honey," said Dad, obviously trying to turn down the heat. "Some of the teaching of California history has become too commercialized, so I appreciate you doing your own research to create something new to use in your classroom. Have any of you seen those kits they sell these days for making models of missions?"

Mom was still frowning, but Sean jumped in. "They sell those things at Walmart. I happened to notice a pile of them on display the other day when I ran in there for something." Sean's remark reminded me of my classmate Nancy as she gushed over the mission unit.

I said, "I'm just trying to put Indian people back into the history I teach. After the first couple of chapters in our California history textbook, they pretty much disappear. What kids don't learn is that Indian people are still here, despite white people's attempts to kill them off." I probably had a "last word on the subject" look on my face because my parents and Sean just stared at me.

Finally Mom said, "Well, I hope you don't come across in your class as opinionated as you sound right now."

A waiter appeared to clear the salad plates, which moderated the mood of the table. When he left, Sean said, "I assume Denise has told you all about her problem with the aging sewer?" Conversation picked back up again, with everyone weighing in about my aging pipes, the repair job, and the bill I now had. Dad reiterated Sean's advice that I hire a home inspector.

By the time we got back to the house, everyone except me seemed to have forgotten the tense exchange earlier. I had to give Sean some credit for calming the waters by steering the conversation toward things we could all laugh about together, like a news story about Amazon surpassing Walmart as the largest retailer by selling sex toys, and another one about a convention of people dressed as animals being herded outside because of a gas leak in the convention hotel.

"Can you imagine all these people dressed up like lions and bears hanging out on Chicago's sidewalks?" said Sean as laughter rolled through him.

Later, Mom pulled me aside. "I wouldn't worry too much about the house," she said. "I imagine you'll be moving in with Sean before too long, married, I hope."

I stumbled trying to figure out how to respond. I finally whispered, "Mom, I don't exactly feel in love with Sean, and I don't think he's in love with me. He's a great friend and I totally enjoy being with him, but . . ."

She cocked her head as she looked at me. "Denise, what more could you want? He's stable, fun, employed, handsome—and besides, your dad and I are hoping for grandkids one of these days."

So there I was, sleeping with Sean in my parents' house. They were hoping our relationship would eventually produce grandkids, while neither he nor I was thinking in those terms. Worse, I was trying to rein in wild fantasies about another man. I tried burying my head in my pillow. Why did I have to be an only child? If only my parents had someone else to pin their hopes for grandchildren on!

And I still hadn't told them how my research linked Gram's house with the theft of Ute people's land. How could I possibly approach such a touchy subject after the way they reacted to my Gold Rush unit?

The next morning, I tried to sound upbeat, but Dad could always read me. "What's wrong?" he asked. "I can tell something's bothering you."

What aspect of my current predicament did I want to share? I chose at random: "I might stop teaching and take a different job."

"What? I thought you love teaching." Dad sounded surprised, and Mom's mouth dropped open. It was clear that even Sean hadn't expected that from me.

"I have to figure out what to do." Words tumbled out. "Sean suggested I apply for a job in Tomorrow's Curriculum. I love teaching, but the work there could be interesting, and the salary will be a lot more than I'm earning right now. At least I'd be able to afford to keep up the house. Right now it's a stretch to pay off the sewer repair while I'm still paying off my student loan." Tears began to well. "I'm sorry, but maybe I never should have agreed to take Gram's house."

Mom placed a hand on my arm while giving me a sympathetic look that was probably meant to remind me of the previous evening's thought that I might not need the house much longer anyway. Which was not the direction I wanted the conversation to take. I blurted out, "And anyway, Gram wouldn't even have had the house if her grandparents hadn't helped steal land from the Utes."

That was a show-stopper. All three of them gaped at me. Dad gasped, "What are you talking about?"

I took a deep breath. "Dad, do you remember the story about Gram's mother being the first white child born in Colorado?"

"I've heard it, but what does that have to do with anything?" he replied.

"When Angela and I went to Colorado in June, one of the things I did was track down more information about that story, and about the whole process of white people taking land from the Utes around Steamboat Springs. I found out that Gram's grandfather got a homestead within a year after the Utes were run out of the state."

When no one reacted, I continued. "It cost hardly anything for a white person to get acreage back then, just mainly the cost of surveying. But he seems to have sold that land a few years later to buy property in Steamboat Springs that he transferred into Gram's mother's name."

Dad said, "He abandoned her and their kids."

I said, "He did, and eventually ended up in jail. That's in a census record. But before that, he turned the property over to Gram's mother. Maybe he wasn't quite the scumbag you thought. Anyway, she sold it and bought land in California right before the Great Depression. Gram inherited money from that sale, which she used to buy the house I now live in. Don't you see? The house that's now mine came into the family because Gram's grandparents got a chunk of land taken from the Utes."

Dad's eyes blazed. "That is the flimsiest reasoning I've ever heard. Where are you getting this stuff?"

"I have the documents, Dad," I said.

"And you're letting your anger about your own money problems addle your brain. You seem to forget all the work your grandparents and great grandparents did so you can afford to have a good job and a nice place to live. And now here you come with the gall to insinuate your family were thieves?" I had never seen Dad so angry. It was as though I had snuck up behind him with a kitchen knife.

Sean caught my eye. "Denise," he said, motioning zipping the lips. That angered me.

"Well, Angela's grandmother gave me a Ute perspective on how that all went down. And Angela didn't even speak to me for about two weeks after that out of anger for what our ancestors did."

"That's enough," Mom barked. "Denise, I don't know where all this is coming from, but if you can't show some respect, I think it's time for you to leave."

My hands were shaking. I felt like I should try to take back something I had said, but as I quickly thought over my words, I couldn't identify what.

"Look, Mom and Dad," I said. "This stuff was all really hard for me to grapple with when I was first confronted by the documents in Steamboat Springs. So I can understand— "

"No, you can't," Mom declared. "I thought you had more backbone, Denise. Here you are, a homeowner with no mortgage to pay, and the first thing that goes wrong, you blame everyone else. Even the very people who are responsible for you having your house. And this thing about the Utes that you seem to be dragging in for no reason I can see . . ."

"Angela's grandmother is Ute. I talked with her. Her people lost their homeland in Colorado so our people could set up housekeeping there."

Dad gaped, as though trying to figure out what part of my statement to respond to, then said, "Angela doesn't look Indian."

"What do you think an Indian looks like?" I asked, momentarily forgetting my similar reaction only weeks earlier.

Dad sputtered, apparently unsure how to respond. In that moment realized my parents, lacking any personal relationship with an Indian, or at least with someone they knew as Indian, had only media images to work with. I tried to think what to say next that wouldn't shut the conversation down entirely.

"Well, I don't care if she's Chief Joseph," Mom declared. "If Denise can't show respect for her dad's family, she isn't welcome in this house."

"Mary—" Dad touched her arm. Mom looked like she was biting her tongue.

Dad looked at me. "I don't know where all this is coming from, Denise. But I think you need to go back home and think carefully about what you're saying. Maybe this course you took planted some crazy ideas in your head. Or Angela, I've always liked her, but maybe she's trying to manipulate you for some odd reason. When you've calmed down, I expect you'll feel silly for the wild accusations you've made. When you're ready to apologize, let us know."

I hated to leave them in anger like this, but could think of no response they would listen to. And they knew Angela. How could they suddenly cast suspicions on her? Had I brought this impasse on, myself? Had Gram brought it on without knowing it? As a teenager, I had numerous arguments with my parents, but none like this. I felt as though a precious object had just shattered, but I couldn't figure out if it was because I hit it, or because a deeper fissure in the earth had produced a sharp quake. Either way, though, I wasn't sure it could be put back together, and that realization brought on a profound sadness.

Chapter Nine

Seeing for the First Time

MONDAY MORNING I arrived at Coffee and Such to meet Martina Soto, my head still reeling from the blow-up with my parents. Sean had not been much help processing it, since he more or less shared their point of view. We barely talked during the ride home. I wanted to stand my ground, but our deeply conflicting interpretations of the ancestors and Gram's house shook me.

Was it even a good idea to meet with Martina, or should I just drop the whole thing? Maybe I was heading into something that on both professional and personal levels would drown me. The thought of jumping over to Tomorrow's Curriculum felt almost soothing.

But the meeting was already set up, so there I was. On a rushed phone call the previous night, Angela mentioned learning that Martina had grown up in the Bay Area. Her mother, who was Rumsen Ohlone, was born in Pomona but moved north as a teenager. About ten years ago, Martina began going to southern California regularly as she realized how much the tribe there was doing.

"And I found out why they're in southern California," Angela had said.

"Why?" I asked.

"Because, when the Americans took over California right around the time of the Gold Rush, they started murdering Indians right and left. The Rumsen people were recruited to work on a vineyard near Pomona, so off they went. Interesting, huh? Something to put in your unit."

I found Angela seated at a table with a woman who looked to be in her forties, short black hair and long silver earrings framing a broad face.

"We just got here," Angela announced as I approached. "Martina, this is Denise. Denise, Martina."

I took a seat across from them. "Pleasure to meet you," I said to Martina. "This is my treat, what would you like?"

"We already ordered," said Angela. As if to verify, a voice announced her order was ready.

"Let me get it," I said as I moved toward the counter to place my order.

A couple minutes later, cappuccino in one hand, Martina said, "Angela told me a bit about your project. I think it's great that you're trying to give more attention to California Indians, although I'm not sure how I can help you since I'm not a teacher."

I pushed aside the fight with my parents and dove in. "Let me give you some background, and then we can figure out where to go from there," I said, encouraged that her face showed interest. I told her about inheriting my house from my grandmother, becoming intrigued by the two white child stories, then tracing the links between the Utes' dispossession, my ancestors' homesteading, and the money trail leading to my house. I explained that while pondering what to do about benefiting from theft of Ute land (a voice in the back of my head wondered whether my broken sewer pipe might have resulted from a curse on my house), I confronted my ignorance about California Indians, which became increasingly obvious as I juxtaposed my social studies curriculum against what I was reading. I mentioned my professor from New Zealand who had shared with me how he came to grips with descending from the colonizers.

Martina listened as I talked, nodding now and then.

Angela jumped in. "This is personal for me, too, Martina. You know my grandmother is Ute, but my other grandparents are white, and at least one of them descended from a homesteader, too. We got to thinking we should start with our relationship with the peoples who are indigenous to where we live, except I think you're the only one we know."

"Chances are I'm not, but a lot of us are still working out our identities, which are pretty mixed anyway. I certainly can't speak for all Ohlone, and I can't speak for my tribe either," Martina said, brow wrinkling.

"We understand that," I said. "But you can point us in some direction. Maybe."

She asked what I had been reading. I described various websites and articles, which had seemed comprehensive at the time but now felt scattergun. But she said, "You have a decent start. Now, what was your question again?"

"One question has to do with what I should teach fourth-graders," I replied. "That's when kids study California history."

"Well, I suppose the first thing you can do is give a different perspective about the missions," she said, eyes darkening. "My own kids had to build a model of a mission, complete with Indian workers. When I asked why they thought Indians were working there, my son said it must pay pretty well. After I told him the Indians didn't get paid, couldn't leave, got whipped, and a lot of them died, he ripped up his project and refused to turn it in. The teacher gave him an F on it."

Stunned, all I could do was mumble, "Oh my god." I rapidly replayed my own sketchy teaching of the missions to recall whether I had done anything like that. I probably hadn't, but had there been Indian kids in my class? Maybe. I didn't know.

Martina continued, "Imagine using the same process to teach about Southern slave plantations or Nazi concentration camps. A book you should get if you don't already have it is *Bad Indians*. The author makes that comparison."

I jotted the title on my iPhone notepad. Angela explained, "She's not only reworking perspectives about the missions, she's trying to weave Ohlone history into the whole California history curriculum, right up to the present. We both are, actually."

I blinked. This was the first time Angela actually said out loud her intention to rework her curriculum.

"But that's where we got stuck," she continued. "We wondered what the tribes would like California kids to learn."

Martina considered. "Well, certainly the fact that we still exist. So many kids think we're not around anymore. Even adults think so. By the way, Esselen, Yokut, and Miwok were in this general area, too. I'm not Esselen, but the incorrect belief that Esselen are extinct is still around. So exposing students to living people would be big."

"I believe the East Bay Regional Park District has just finished an Ohlone Curriculum for teachers," Martina added after a sip of coffee. "Try looking on the Internet to see if it's available."

I wrote it down.

"When I was growing up," Martina continued, "for a long time I thought we were Mexican. We lived in a predominantly Mexican neighborhood, and with a name like Sanchez, well. My dad is part Mexican, part Salinan, and a few other things. My mom is mostly Rumsen

Ohlone. When I was small, sometimes I asked her what we were. She'd say, 'What do you think we are?' I'd say, 'Mexican?' She'd just hug me and say, 'You're so smart,' or 'You're so beautiful.'"

Angela said, "I knew I was part Ute, but didn't know what that meant. Not many Utes in California."

"No, but there are a lot of Indians in California," Martina said. "However, in my parents' generation, that wasn't seen as a good thing. My mom would have tried to pass as white if she could, but she's too dark, so she just let people think she was Mexican. But a lot of the stories she used to tell me were different from stories my Mexican friends heard at home, so that's why I'd ask her who we were."

"Stories like what?" I asked, while silently registering the parallel with Carol Walker's effort to pass as white.

"Oh, like, she'd tell me about an old gravesite near Pomona where her ancestors are buried. When her people die, their spirits go west across the sea. When she was a child, her mother sang to help the spirits of departed people on their way. Growing up, my family didn't do Day of the Dead celebrations like my Mexican friends' families." She thought a moment. "I remember a song Mom sometimes sang in a language that wasn't English or Spanish. It was in our language, of course, but I didn't know that at the time. She said she learned it from her grandmother." She hummed a few notes. "I've forgotten most of it. Mother didn't know what the words meant, but liked to sing it because it reminded her of her grandmother."

Martina smiled into her coffee. "Mom told me her grandmother had her eat poison oak when she was a child. Just one leaf at a time. She never developed a rash in her life, so she figured her grandmother knew how to build up tolerance to it."

"Did you eat poison oak?" Angela sounded dumbfounded.

"No, I never had the guts to try it," Martina replied. "It might work like a vaccine that gives you just enough antigens to stimulate your body to produce its own natural immunity, but I'm not sure."

The scientist in me, intrigued, made a mental note to look into the chemistry of this practice later on. I asked, "How did you decide to become a dental hygienist?"

Martina laughed lightly. "When I was in high school, that's what my best friend's aunt did. Tia Rosa, that's what we called her. She asked me one day what I planned to do when I graduated from high school."

"Where was this?" Angela asked.

"Over in Martinez, that's where we lived at the time," Martina replied. "I wasn't even sure I'd stick around to graduate. I think I was in eleventh grade then. She told me I had the markings of a healer, whatever that meant, and she thought I'd be good doing the kind of healing work she did. I didn't think too much about it, but she kept giving me nudges and bits of information here and there. She even took me to work with her one day."

"She must have been determined," I commented.

"Oh, that she was. At first I couldn't see why I'd want to put my hands in other people's mouths, but when she showed me what she actually did, it seemed interesting. She just kept after me. She got me to enroll in the community college, then Hayward, that's what they called East Bay back then. Then she steered me into the professional training program she had completed. Tia Rosa was smart. She saw a lot of girls dropping out of school and having babies without any plans for a future, so she made sure that didn't happen to me or Carmen."

In response to our puzzled looks she added, "Carmen was her niece, my best friend."

I asked, "Did Carmen become a dental hygienist, too?"

"No, she's a school principal in Martinez. Tia Rosa steered her, too, but not in the same direction as me."

"Are they Ohlone?" I asked.

"No, they're Mexican. Tia Rosa passed on a few years ago," she replied. "As I said, I grew up in a mostly Mexican neighborhood and thought I was Mexican for many years. Tia Rosa figured out I was Indian before I did. When I finally told her, she just said it was obvious to her after meeting my mother."

Martina studied her coffee, then looked directly at me. "Where are your people indigenous to, do you know?"

I had no idea what to say. I hadn't been asked that question before. I asked, "You mean, where did they come from?"

"Where were they before they were colonizers? What is the homeland of your ancestors? I usually don't ask white people this question; most think it's offensive. But you seem open to it."

"I hadn't thought about it like that before," I replied. "I guess England, Sweden, France, maybe Ireland, I'm not sure."

She just nodded thoughtfully but didn't say anything. She seemed to want to give me space to think.

"Martina," Angela was saying. "To go back to the question about what kids should grow up learning, or even what non-Indian adults today might do, given the history of conquest, what would you say?"

"Oh, my. I'm not sure," she replied.

I added, "Like, if I wanted to make restitution or something, given that I benefited from the theft of Ute land, what should I think about doing?"

Martina shifted in her chair as she thought. Finally, she said, "It isn't like you can just do something and make hundreds of years disappear."

"No, I didn't mean—" I began, then stopped. Maybe that's what I did mean. Maybe deep down I was hoping she could give me the steps to take, the good deeds I could do. If I knew what to do and did it, then maybe I wouldn't feel guilty. I would have done my bit to address colonization. Check it off and move on to something else.

But what had Ian said? He had to learn to stop acting like a colonizer, and that was a whole lot harder than finding one or two things to do.

"One of the things you need to understand," Martina said as she watched my face recalibrating, "is that we're in the process of trying to reconstruct our own nations. The tribes aren't all in the same place with that. But try to imagine a calamity striking your society, and 95 percent of the population gets wiped out. With that goes a tremendous amount of knowledge. The survivors are left traumatized. Their descendants, still dealing with trauma, are trying to reconstruct as much of the nation and its knowledge as they can with what's left."

I nodded.

"That's work we're engaged in. It probably isn't something you can help us do. In fact, one of the most unhelpful things is when outsiders try to tell us what we should do or who we are."

Angela nodded. "I've heard my grandmother say the same thing. She once told me that when Indian people in Colorado Springs stopped trying to be white and started being Indian again, it wasn't clear what that meant."

"Some of us are trying to gather the old stories," Martina said.

"And then tell them to the young people," Angela added. "That's what my grandmother does, she tells stories and helps the kids figure out what they mean for their lives today. She's told me a lot about different ceremonies, like the Bear Dance."

"I'm not familiar with that one," Martina said.

"The Utes do it every May. It's a big celebration of spring, honoring bears as they come out of hibernation. Then there's the Sun Dance in summer, when men dance around a cottonwood pole out in the sun for three or four days. Some of them commune with spirits of their ancestors while dancing—that's what Grandma told me."

"Do you know if your grandmother's people ever participated in the Ghost Dance?" Martina asked.

"She said some of them did for a while." Angela looked at me. "The Ghost Dance was a ceremony that called on the ancestors to return and make the white people go away. White people tried to outlaw it, but Grandma said no one paid much attention to them. But after a while, they just quit doing it because the ancestors didn't actually return, and the white people were still there."

Angela turned back to Martina. "Grandma also told me a story about her grandfather who joined a large group that went into Wyoming to find a place where there weren't so many white people. They thought they might join up with Sioux, but the Sioux had enough of their own problems and didn't want ours as well. After a year or so, they ran out of food and finally came back to Utah."

As I watched Martina and Angela go back and forth with stories, I realized uncomfortably that I had little to contribute to the conversation. Being white, I also felt a bit like the subject of their conversation, and not in a good way, although I don't think they noticed. Maybe I should just forget about working on my curriculum. This could get too complicated, and didn't Martina say that outsiders like me got in the way? Especially outsiders who descend from the white people that created the Indians' problems in the first place. Maybe I should stick with science, since that was what I knew best. That was what Sean said. Maybe he was right.

"Denise?" I realized Martina was looking at me. "I think we lost you there for a minute."

"Oh, well, yeah, I was just thinking how little I know, and maybe I shouldn't try to mess with my curriculum because I'd probably get things wrong."

Martina's eyebrows knitted into a frown. "Goodness, that isn't what I intended. Personally, I'm thrilled to meet a teacher who's actually interested in us. Not the fictitious Pocahontas version, but the tribal people who are here now. If you have Indian kids in your class, you can always invite them and their families to help you. You don't have to be the expert all the time, you know."

I studied my empty coffee cup, not wanting to admit that I wasn't sure whether any of my past students were Indian or not. I looked up. "Yeah, but I just don't know that much. You know? Even after reading websites and books and stuff, there's still so much I don't know." I let my frustration hang in the air like cigarette smoke.

"As I mentioned earlier, I'm not a teacher," Martina said. "I can't give you advice on teaching any better than you can give me advice on cleaning teeth."

A chuckle broke through my frustration.

"There's a teacher you should talk to, Oscar Ortiz. He's Ohlone, and he teaches high school literature. Let me see if I can find his contact information." Martina retrieved her phone from her bag. After locating his contact information, she forwarded it to Angela. "Just tell him I sent you, and tell him what you're working on."

"I think I've heard of him," Angela said. "He coaches baseball, doesn't he?"

"Yep. He was a minor league player for a while. His kids play baseball, too. But he knows as much about Native literature as he does about baseball. More, actually. And he has a great sense of humor," Martina said. Then she turned back to me. "Hang in there with us. It sounds like you've gone from not seeing us, to seeing us. Believe me, that's an important step. We are visible, once you start to see us and pay attention."

Angela coughed. "Like you peering into my mouth the last few years, and me only now realizing you're Indian."

Martina laughed. "Yeah, like that. Anytime you want to talk or bounce something off me, Denise, you know where to find me. But do contact Oscar; I think you'll enjoy meeting him."

"We will, thank you. And thank you for taking the time to meet with us," I said as we gathered our cups and napkins for disposal.

"By the way," Martina said. "If you're not already planning to attend the Bay Area Indian Heritage Festival on Saturday, you should. You're familiar with it, aren't you Angela?"

"No," Angela said. "I guess I should be, huh?"

"It's worth going to. Maybe I'll see you there."

As we walked out, Angela's expression seemed to ask if I was okay. I nodded, then said, "I need advice."

"As in more coffee?"

Within ten minutes, I had unloaded the dilemmas that were literally keeping me awake at night, minus Sean's suggestion that I work for Tomorrow's Curriculum. I wasn't yet ready to talk to her about that.

Angela's reaction to Ian's revelation, my weekend with Sean, and the blow-up with my parents was, "Holy shit." She stirred her coffee. "Well, for one thing, you need to talk directly with Sean. And your parents . . . that's a hard one because usually they're sweet."

"Usually they are," I agreed. "I probably knew there was this other side to how they think, but now that I've actually seen it, I don't know what to do about it. Sean's head may well be in much the same place as theirs, but he mostly kept his mouth shut. What's hard is that I care about all of them and don't want to hurt anyone. My parents think I've flipped out. I really want to figure out how to get them to see my point of view. And I'm clueless how to tell Sean I don't want to marry him when he's never even mentioned marriage."

She placed her palms on the table. "Well, maybe you don't need to say anything to Sean just now. It doesn't sound like he's thinking marriage, anyway. And, it could be that you never hear from Ian again, right?"

"I suppose." Although I was pretty sure I would, and I knew I wouldn't turn him down.

"The immediate question is what to do about your parents. Shit." Angela thought, then said. "Maybe I should go visit them with you, kind of like, back you up?"

"I don't think that would help. No offense," I said, recalling Dad's speculation that Angela may be at least partially to blame. "They'd probably feel even more defensive. I mentioned meeting your grandmother; they might think you had a bad influence on me or something. Maybe I'll take them my data and see what they make of it."

"Data? Your parents are wondering if you lost all respect for the family and you're going to bring data?"

"Good point. Geez, I have no idea what to do," I said glumly.

"So just sit on it. Meanwhile, I'm up for going to the Bay Area Indian Heritage Festival. I'll find out the details. Bring Sean along if you like. Or Ian. Or both of them and we could make it a double."

I glared at her, although I knew she was just joking. "Yeah, right. But yes to the festival. That sounds like a great idea. And Angela? Thank you for setting up this meeting."

"No need to thank me, I got as much out of it as you. I'm excited to have learned more about Martina."

I put my head into my hands. "And now I've gotta find a home inspector."

"A home inspector? For what?" she asked.

"Well, when I got Gram's house, I never thought to wonder what was about to fall apart. Obviously, the sewer line was in trouble. Both Sean and Dad have told me I need to get the home inspected so I know what's about to go next. Although what I'd do about it . . ."

"I know someone. A guy I went on a date with." She retrieved her phone from her bag and began scrolling through contacts. "He was boring as a date, but he has his own home inspection business. Okay, here it is, Josh Fenstermacher. I can't believe I actually kept his number."

She hit his mobile number then waited. "Josh? It's Angela Walker, I bet you thought you wouldn't hear from me again," she said. "No," she replied to something on the other end, then, "Yeah, me too. Hey, I have a friend who needs her home inspected." Something on the other end, then, "Yeah, she's right here, let me give her to you. Her name's Denise."

A minute later, we had set an appointment for late afternoon of the first day teachers in my district return to school. Not great timing, but his earliest opening.

I got home to find Mr. Jackson pulling something from the dirt burying my new sewer pipes. Apparently, he had just returned from Santa Barbara.

"Hey there," I called to him. "I thought you'd be away longer, but I'm glad to see you back. How was the family?"

As a shadow passed over his face, I recalled him telling me once that losing his wife was like falling into a dark hole he could never escape. He replied, "Everyone was fine. The girls are busy with summer soccer teams and swimming lessons. They're growing too fast, pretty soon they won't be kids anymore." He paused as though reflecting, then continued, "I always imagined Glendora and I would watch our grandchildren grow up together, then leave this earth at the same time. Now here I am, an old man by myself."

"What happened?" I asked, not knowing what to say.

"Nothing happened. Autumn and Jimmy couldn't have been happier to see me. The two girls—well, they adore their grandpa, but they're as busy with their own lives as Autumn was at their age. Autumn, every year she looks more and more like my Glennie."

When Mrs. Jackson had died of stomach cancer, I was angry that such a warm human being had to experience a long, painful decline. I cried at her visitation, and then again at her funeral. But busy as I was with my own life, I had not considered the cavernous hole her death left. As far as I could tell, Mr. Jackson had picked himself up and carried on, becoming increasingly active with the NAACP. I had never considered the private hell he lugged around with him.

He said, "I didn't stay as long as I had thought I might. I felt a little too much like excess baggage, so I decided to come on back. Now, I see you have some work to do." He held up some dirty, stringy stuff.

"What is it?" I asked.

"An iceplant root. Damn, I thought we had it all. This stuff is hard to extricate once it's insinuated into a patch of ground. It just keeps coming back."

"You have a keen eye," I commented.

"I've been looking at it for years. They used to plant it liberally to control erosion. But the more conscious people are about native plants, the more they recognize the problem with invasive species."

A penny dropped. I had admired Mr. Jackson's yard for years without thinking about its abundance of native plants—the blue ceanothus every spring, the California fuchsia and honeysuckle in summer, and blue-eyed grass with periwinkle blossoms nestled in amongst the rocks. I only now realized he planned it that way.

"Your yard— " I began.

He chuckled. "Your Gram and I used to have long debates about which kinds of plants to grow. She figured, as long as they thrive it doesn't matter whether they're native or not. Now take those hydrangeas over there." He pointed to the colorful shrubs in front of the house. "Your grandmother and I had some deep discussions about them when she put them in. Since the hydrangea originates in Asia, it's a foreigner here if you think historically. It isn't invasive in that it doesn't crowd out its neighbors, but it drinks more than its fair share of water, which is a problem in this semi-arid climate. Your grandmother actually knew a lot about native plants, although she wouldn't admit it because she liked growing a lot of stuff that isn't native to here. But she was always good about keeping out the aggressive invaders."

Invaders like Orville and Sally?

Where did that thought come from?

I shoved it aside as I remembered the painful row with my parents. My expression must have changed because he asked, "What's wrong?"

Although I had just unloaded to Angela, Mr. Jackson's mention of Gram reminded me how deeply I loved my family, warts and all. So I told him what had happened the previous day.

When I finished, he put a hand on my shoulder. "And it hurts because you care about them, am I right?

"Yes, exactly," I sobbed. "I don't know what to do. The more I learn, the more I realize that I can't just turn around and go back to how I was thinking before I looked into the history of my family and the Colorado land."

I thought about Angela's reaction to researching her Norwegian ancestors in Nebraska. She found a homestead record issued by the O'Neill/Ponca Indian Reservation land office, but was puzzled because there is no Ponca Indian Reservation. Digging around, she learned that in the 1870s, the state legislature tried to remove all Indians from Nebraska so white people could have the land. Several tribes, including the Ponca, were driven on foot to "Indian Territory" in Oklahoma. When the chief and some others tried to return, they were arrested and jailed, and the chief was put on trial. He won. But while the Ponca could return home, they had no home to go to, so a small reservation was created. After World War II, the federal government terminated all tribes. The Nebraska Ponca were removed from tribal rolls, and lost their land as well as federal recognition. After vigorously lobbying the state legislature, they eventually were restored recognition in exchange for agreeing never to petition for a reservation.

Angela was angry, but she focused her anger on the Nebraska legislature rather than her ancestors. Could I be clearer about directing my own anger toward colonial policies rather than Dad's ancestors?

I said to Mr. Jackson, "All the almost twenty years I spent as a student in school, and I never learned the histories of the people of the land we now occupy. Just a sugar-coated version of a little bit, way back then, but that's all. What a terrible commentary on our education system, huh? Now at age thirty, I'm finally starting to learn what I should have been learning all along. I can't just unlearn what I now know in order to make my family comfortable. We're like that invasive ice plant you're holding. We don't want to admit we are, but we need to if we're going to do anything."

"Well, you'll figure out a way to build a bridge to them. This very minute, they're probably having much the same conversation, trying to figure out how to build a bridge back to you."

I nodded, not the least bit sure what I might come up with.

"Now," he said, "I don't know what you were planning on doing with this fresh mound of dirt in your yard, but if you want some help, you know where to find it."

Wiping one eye with the back of my hand, I said, "Well, I'm not doing anything else today. What ideas do you have?"

Before he could reply, my ringtone blasted from inside my bag. I retrieved my phone, but didn't recognize the number.

"Hello?" I said, hoping it wasn't a telemarketer.

"Kia ora, Denise," came a familiar male voice with a New Zealand accent. "Did I catch you at a good time?" "Ian!" My heart stopped.

"First things first," he said. "Your project turned out very well, considering the limited time you had to work on it."

"That's great," I said.

"Second, having just turned in grades, I'm now at liberty to ask you if you'd like to have dinner with me on Friday."

❧ ❧ ❧

FRIDAY EVENING, I was still trying to decide which jacket best complemented my denim skirt and tangerine T-shirt when the doorbell rang. *Ian must be here!* I grabbed my navy-blue shoulder bag and white denim jacket, hoping the color combination didn't look too Fourth of July, and ran to the door, heart pounding.

"You look ravishing," he said by way of greeting.

"Thank you. Want to come in? Where are we going?" Questions tumbled out like popcorn. I felt silly.

"I made a reservation at the Wooden Bucket. Does that sound okay?"

I nodded. The Wooden Bucket was new; I hadn't been there yet. As we walked to his Honda Civic, he pointed to the swath of fresh dirt connecting my house with the street, still visible under newly planted flat ceanothus. "New pipes?" he asked.

I sighed. As we drove off, I told him about my backed-up sewer system and the plumbers' repair job. But since I didn't want to get into its cost and my resulting financial problems, I concluded, "I and a neighbor spent much of Tuesday on hands and knees in the dirt landscaping."

"Almost makes me glad I don't own a house," he commented. "Here we are."

The Wooden Bucket, occupying a renovated warehouse, had been opened the previous year. Normally I think of warehouses as shabby structures with bad lighting and an ambience for murder. I've watched too many cop shows. This one, however, boasted thinly-shaded floor-to-ceiling windows and potted plants scattered among tables. The hostess seated us next to a window.

I had fretted over what we might talk about. What if he wanted to plunge into a serious relationship, starting now? What would I say, and what would I do with Sean? Or, what if the conversations we already had used up what we had to say to each other? What if he, like some people, talked at length about himself, reducing me to passive listener? Or what if we both stumbled along, trying to fill airspace by leaping from topic to topic without landing on anything either of us cared about?

Ian must have had the same worries. After putting in our drink orders, he said, "So I'm not sure where any of this goes. As I said the other day, you intrigue me but I'm skittish about rushing into anything."

Whew! I must have looked relieved because he added, "That's okay?"

"Yeah, totally," I replied. "I'm not great at relationships. And while I feel like I know you as a teacher—a really good one, by the way—I don't know you as a person. You know, your life, like what made you decide to become a teacher, what you like to do when you aren't working, what your family is like . . ." I trailed off. I was starting to ramble.

But his face relaxed as his eyes crinkled into a smile.

By the time our dinners came, we had shared numerous stories about our lives and how we became teachers. We described embarrassing moments (on his first day of student teaching, the head of school mistook him for a parent who happened to have the same surname), odd coincidences (my former fifth-grade teacher turned out to be principal of the school where I student taught), and funny moments (Ian's students taped tacks to his chair as a joke, but the tacks barely penetrated his bulky wool trousers, so he couldn't figure out why the kids were snickering). He said he missed teaching primary, but found university teaching more interesting than he had anticipated. What we didn't talk about was any concurrent love interest in either of our lives. I knew I should at least mention Sean, but I didn't.

"Obviously with adults, it's more about playing with ideas than managing behavior. But the homework I have to grade is much more massive." He grinned. "By the way, don't forget to pick up your project in the department office. I know most professors email your work back, but I think better when I write on a hard copy."

I hadn't forgotten, but I hadn't picked it up yet so that nothing he had written might mar this evening. "I'll get it Monday," I said.

"In any case," he continued, "I like what you're on to very much. The research projects and role-playing you designed do a brilliant job connecting literacy with social studies, as well as opening up questions about what the United States takeover of California meant for the Indigenous people."

I felt my face flush. A brilliant job? "Thank you. It still needs work before I can use it, but I have a couple months before we get to that period in California history."

"How are you thinking about starting the year in a way that sets the stage for amplifying the visibility of Indigenous Californians?" he asked.

A less eloquent version of that question had paralyzed my brain as I worked in the garden. I had plenty of first-week plans ready to go, but none for how to introduce Indigenous Californians. I studied my water glass, then finally said, "Ian, I have no idea. I'm afraid I'm trying to take on something too big. You can't believe how much I read just for that one short unit I gave you. It's so confusing because I hadn't realized how many different tribes and subtribes are in California. Where do I start? Angela's dental hygienist said I should start with living people, but she also said I should take on the missions. And I don't even know who in my class is Indian."

I felt like a volcano. Magma, having built up for weeks, finally erupted. This wasn't just about a unit plan, or even about a strategy for getting to know local Ohlone peoples. Rather, I was beginning to glimpse the enormity of what it might mean to stop teaching like a colonizer. It was much easier to rip out patches of wooly thyme and stray iceplant roots than it was to invert the entire point of view that guided my work, my life, my family, myself.

"Ow!" he exclaimed. "You've been sitting on a lot here. Let's back up. Why are you taking teaching advice from a dental hygienist, may I ask, although it sounds to me like reasonable advice."

"Angela knows her. She's Ohlone. And she gave us the name of a high school literature teacher to talk to who's also Ohlone. We haven't contacted him yet. But I'm just in over my head. Sometimes I think, you know, about when I majored in geology at the university, all those classes I had to take developed my science knowledge in some depth. And now here I am, working on something that's not only completely out of my field, but also matters to people—it's about peoples' lives. I'm going to get a lot of things wrong. After all, I'm not Indian, I didn't grow up learning any of this stuff, and my whole way of looking at the world is white. Maybe I should stick to teaching science instead." I felt tears begin to well in my eyes.

Ian took my hand in both of his, saying, "You'll be okay. At times I still feel like that."

I couldn't imagine what he meant. Maybe he was just trying to make me feel better.

"You might think that course you just finished was bicultural," he said. "It had a lot more readings by Indigenous scholars than most university courses do; I used some Māori cultural protocols like starting off with a *karakia* every day. That's more than I'd have known to do, say, ten years ago. But how many of your classmates will be better teachers of American Indian students because of that course?"

I was stumped. "I don't know how many even *have* Indian students. Whenever you asked, it was like most of us didn't know or hadn't thought about it." His nod indicated he had noticed. I continued, "But at least, I'd hope we'd be better teachers of whoever we have in class."

"Yes, of course, I do too. But if what I'm doing isn't helping to repair, even in a wee way, generations of damage done by colonization, then, well, I still have a long way to go."

I studied my hand, still firmly in his. It felt good there. And I hadn't expected this kind of reply from him. I thought he would give me encouragement, even pointers. Now here he was saying he felt as unsure as I did.

142

"Ian," I said, "if you aren't even sure what you're doing— "

He held up a hand. "That's not exactly what I said. I'm on a journey, Denise, and so are you. Sometimes I wish it wasn't a journey but rather a destination that I'd already arrived at. But decolonization is a journey that ultimately involves power-sharing and repatriating what had been taken, whether it's land, labor, or both."

"Did you repatriate land?" I asked.

"Not me personally, no. In my family, my generation doesn't have much to repatriate. But repatriation in New Zealand is worked on at the governmental level, primarily through two ways. One way is through direct negotiations with the government by large tribal groups such as Ngai Tahu and Tainui. In the other way, following the Waitangi Tribunal's recommendations, the government passed specific legislation to return funds or land to particular tribes. Myself, I've been a strong supporter of Māori land rights. I don't always know what I'm doing, but I do have a sense of direction. I also stay in contact with a few Māori mates in New Zealand, and a handful of Indian people here. Those relationships developed over time, by the way."

"A journey, yeah, okay," I said, knowing I'd need to think about this. "Maybe I shouldn't have taken Gram's house at all. Maybe Ute spirits disrupted the sewer line. Maybe they pushed Gram off the front porch when she broke her hip. And maybe they're about to disrupt something else in the house in order to push me out."

Listening to myself, I thought I sounded whacked out, but I continued. "It wouldn't just be the house they're striking out at, either. It's my relationship with Gram, who was the dearest person to me, but who inherited the money made from stealing their land. If they can break up my love for Gram, then maybe the spirits think that would be justice." I paused, then added, "I know that sounds pretty crazy."

Ian's steady grey eyes looked into mine as they crinkled at the corners. "We have spirits in Aotearoa, too, but I don't recall hearing about them breaking sewer lines."

Tension drained from my body. I laughed.

Our server, who had taken our plates, returned with dessert menus. Ian flipped his open. "What do you fancy?"

"I don't think I could fit another bite into my stomach," I replied, surprised I had managed to clean my plate despite the intensity of the conversation.

He studied the menu, then beckoned our server. "One piece of key lime pie, two forks. And a long black, ah no, I mean coffee Americano for me."

"I'll have decaf, black," I said.

When the server left, I raised my eyebrows. "Long black what?"

"It's what we call espresso with hot water. Americano is similar, you can usually get that here. I could live here the rest of my life and without thinking still ask for a long black. So tell me about your family. You mentioned visiting them a week ago."

My head slumped into my hands. Tears weren't far behind. Since my mother threw me out of the house, although I had stewed, obsessed, and complained, I hadn't actually cried yet. Since I've always been able to patch things up with them eventually, I figured I could do the same with this. But I didn't anticipate them accusing me of disrespecting the family and telling me to leave. Mr. Jackson thought I would figure out how to build a bridge back to them, but I felt stuck and it hurt.

Ian leaned over the table and put his hands on my shoulders. "Hey, there," he said. "I'm sorry if I opened a sensitive subject, but do you want to talk about it?"

I tried to force back tears as I mumbled, "I didn't mean to start weeping."

"No apologies, please," he said. "You don't have to talk about it if you don't want to."

"It's just—well," and the story poured out. "They accused me of disrespecting them and the work Dad's grandparents and great-grandparents did, and they basically threw me out until I change my story. Ian, I have no idea what to do now. I've considered going back to show them some of the documents I have copies of and ask what they think. But, I don't know. Damage has been done and I don't know what to do."

He thought a moment. "I went through something similar with my parents, but they were already a bit prepared by the visibility of Māori land claims settlements, especially the Ngai Tahu settlement in the South Island. They were able to say, ah well, maybe our own kin did steal land, and maybe a lot of Pākehā today don't want to give it back, but there are some wheels in motion. Here in this country, you hardly see anything close to that, so most white people here don't seem to think about it at all."

"So what do I do?"

144

"It sounds like their biggest concern is that you might not respect them, is that right?"

I considered his question. "That's probably right. Them personally, and the rest of the family in general."

"So, are they right?"

"What is hard for me to respect," I said slowly, "are the ancestors who knowingly took other people's land. The only way they could justify doing that was to regard them as less-than-human. I know that's how white people saw things at the time, but I can't respect people who overtly dehumanized other people like that. With later generations, it's fuzzier because I don't know how much of this history they actually knew. White people learn not to see Indian people at all except as historical artifacts. But if you know you're still occupying stolen land, it's like you're standing on someone's foot and you finally hear the person say, 'That hurts, get off.' Then if you don't move your own foot, well—"

He nodded. "So you're trying to figure out where to move your own foot to."

"Yeah. And I suppose I don't know what my parents should do till I figure out what I should do. I'm not sorry about what I said to them, but I do still love them."

"Do they know that?" he asked.

"Maybe not," I replied. "You're giving me an idea for how to deal with them. Thanks. When it comes to what I should do, I can't help but wonder what the Utes would want me to do. Not just me, but all of us who have inherited benefits from our ancestors' theft."

"I supposed you could ask," he said.

"Ask who?"

"Well, you'd need to look on the tribal website. What issues is the tribal council working on? What are the current land issues? You could talk with people, although you shouldn't just jump in cold without gathering information that's publicly available." When I didn't say anything, he added, "I'll help you if you'd like."

"Okay, thanks," I said as I realized our server had quietly deposited the dessert and coffees.

Ian picked up one fork and nodded toward the other one as he said, "I can't eat all this; you need to help me."

❧❧❧

I AWOKE SATURDAY morning still dreaming of Ian's arms around me. Although his long, lingering kiss on my doorstep communicated desire, he had turned and left before I could invite him in. I wasn't sure when I would see him next, but figured it wouldn't be long.

I couldn't dwell on Ian, though, since Sean and Angela would be arriving in a few hours. When Sean had called to work out getting together this weekend, I talked him into attending the Bay Area Indian Heritage Festival with me and Angela, and he agreed. I wasn't sure why, since this wasn't an event he would have chosen. And I wasn't sure why I invited him.

At any rate, he showed up ahead of Angela, greeting me with, "Since you're on vacation right now, you shouldn't be working."

"Huh? What do you mean? I'm not working," I said as I poured him a glass of lemonade.

"Isn't that what this festival thing is? More work on your curriculum?" he asked.

"No. Well, yes. But no, it isn't. I'm genuinely interested. I haven't been to something like this before. I'm starting to pay attention to the people whose land we occupy," I replied. "I'm learning how our government policies tried to exterminate them. But they're still here and much more interesting than most schoolbooks portray. Like, you know, in my classroom I have a few children's books about Indians a long time ago, and my social studies textbook has a little bit about what people ate and how they built their houses centuries ago. But that isn't how the books treat white people."

Sean blinked, then said "Yes, ma'am" just as Angela walked in. He said to her, "She's giving me a history lesson."

"Good," Angela replied. "Ready? Let's go."

A half hour later, we arrived at the county park to find the parking lot full, but street parking still available. A few jeans-clad teens were milling around the gate. A family hauling three small children was walking in the direction of their car. Smoke with a mouth-watering smell rose from a grill somewhere inside the grounds. We found a spot for the car and parked.

Admission was free. I had anticipated the grounds being packed, but while I saw perhaps a couple hundred people, the park was not jammed. Lining the central field on both sides were booths of various kinds. A jewelry vendor immediately drew Angela's and my attention. I grabbed Sean's hand and pulled him over to the booth so I could look. Fine silverwork encased stones of varied colors in earrings, pendants, and bracelets, one of which already adorned Angela's wrist.

"What do you think?" she asked, displaying the silver and coral bracelet.

"Very nice. Don't you want to look around first?" I asked as I fingered a pair of fine drop earrings made out of what looked like malachite and silver. The sweater-clad woman sitting inside, hands busy with embroidery, looked up.

"Those were made by a local artisan," she said. "The ones on this rack are $35, and the ones on this next rack are $50. You can only buy his work at events like this; he doesn't sell to the stores."

I glanced up at her, then back at the earrings. "Really beautiful. We just got here, I can't start buying things until I've looked around."

"I can," Angela announced. "How much is this?"

While Angela paid for the bracelet, I strolled to the next booth, pulling Sean along with me. He was looking around as though trying to take in what the festival had to offer. Following his gaze toward the central field, I saw a large man holding a pole decorated with feathers on one end, surrounded by children and adults who were probably their parents. He looked like he was talking to the children, perhaps telling a story, although I couldn't hear him well enough to make out.

The next booth's table banner announced "Indian People Organizing for Change." Two young women chatted behind the table. Noticing me, one of them handed me a brochure as she said, "If you haven't heard of us, we represent an organization that's working on reclaiming Ohlone sacred spaces."

The other added, "We're trying to bring back the kind of spaces our ancestors had for gatherings, where our ancestors actually were."

A couple of posters drew my eyes to information handouts about projects. One read "Sogorea Te' Land Trust" above a photo of what could be the Oakland skyline. The other read "West Berkeley Shellmound."

"What's a shellmound?" I felt dumb as I asked the question. I had heard the term, but hadn't paid much attention to it.

"Our ancestors made huge mounds of shells and other things near shorelines," one of the women said. "The mounds got flattened and buried as cities were built over them. We're trying to create a park in West Berkeley where one of the oldest shellmounds used to be, to honor and teach about our people. The city is proposing an urban project right on top of it. They offered us an old parking lot to use, but it isn't in the right place. We're trying to get support."

I picked up a flier that displayed a beautiful proposed park. Angela, pointing to the Sogorea Te' Land Trust poster, said, "I've heard about this. What a great project!"

The first young woman smiled. "It is. We also want to build a community garden there to teach how our ancestors took care of the land. It was hard to get traction at first with the Feds not even recognizing us, but we've made progress. You can read about our work, and if you want to make a contribution, you can." She flipped over the brochure I held and pointed. "We have a suggested tax here on the back for people who live on our lands and want to help us out. This is the website."

"Thanks," I said. I stuffed the brochure into my bag as Angela asked one of the women how the Sogorea Te' Land Trust project had started. My brain was spinning. Who knew that the minute I entered this festival, someone would offer me specific information about a local land reclamation project and how people can help?

Sean had drifted to the next booth, which featured books and CDs. As I caught up with him, I heard a familiar voice behind me yelling "Angela! Denise!" Turning around, I saw a hand waving, then Martina Soto appeared. "I'm so glad to see the two of you here. When did you arrive?"

"A half hour or so ago," Angela said. "How long have you been here?"

"Since about noon. Say, your timing is good. See that man over there?" She pointed to the large man who had been talking to children. He was now walking to the perimeter of the field as a group of young male dancers assembled for the next event. "That's Oscar Ortiz, the literature teacher I told you about. He just finished telling traditional stories to the children."

I tried to get a better look. He appeared to be a sturdy six feet tall, wearing jeans, a plaid shirt, and a grey cowboy hat. I couldn't see much of his face behind his sunglasses. He was talking with another man who had elementary-aged children hanging onto each hand.

"C'mon, I'll introduce you," Martina said, turning in his direction. As we followed, I told Sean that Oscar was an Ohlone high school teacher Martina thought might be able to help us with our curriculum.

"And who is Martina?" he whispered. "Another teacher?"

"She's Angela's dental hygienist," I explained. "But she knows enough about what the schools don't teach about Ohlone people that she's actually helpful to us."

"See? I said you came here to work on your curriculum," he said, poking me playfully.

We passed the dancers—young men painted with diagonal black and white stripes on their chests and arms, and under their lower lips. Bands of dark fur held large feathers to their foreheads. An older man wearing a T-shirt and hat appeared to be giving them final directions. Oscar caught sight of Martina and waved as the man he was talking to pulled the two children toward the Porta Potties.

"Hey, lady," he said with a large grin as we approached. He gave Martina a quick bear hug, then looked at us and asked, "You brought friends?"

"You never know who I might show up with," Martina said. "Let me introduce a couple of local teachers. Angela here teaches sixth grade and is one of my patients. Denise is Angela's friend. And this is—I'm sorry, I forgot your name?" Martina apologized to Sean.

"Sean Grayson." Sean extended his hand. "I'm not a teacher anymore, but I work with a small curriculum company."

The two men shook hands as Martina continued, "Oscar, a few days ago I was telling Angela and Denise about you. They're working on weaving local Indians into their curriculum, and I thought you might be able to give them some ideas."

Oscar smiled broadly. "Sure, besides baseball, teaching about our people is my favorite thing to do."

"He coaches little league, and used to be with the minors," Martina explained to Sean.

"Who'd you play with?" Sean asked. Our afternoon had finally hit on something Sean could relate to.

"San Jose Giants. I dreamed of playing major league, but wasn't good enough," Oscar replied. "My kids play baseball, so now I coach."

Drums indicated the start of dances, and the cluster of young men began to move rhythmically.

"These guys are good," Oscar said, indicating the dancers. He turned back to me and Angela. "Why don't you give me a call and we can set up a time to meet. I have a ton of stuff in my classroom I'd be happy to share with you." Fumbling in a back pocket, he pulled out and proffered a business card.

I took it and slid it into my bag. "Thank you so much. We'll contact you soon."

A sudden burst from the drums drowned out his reply. The dancers picked up the rhythm as they shuffled into the central area. I scooted forward to get a better view.

I was impressed by their athleticism. As they danced, the young men leaped and swooped as gracefully as herons without losing the beat. They were followed by a smaller group of young women dancers, equally graceful, clad in white leather dresses and shell jewelry, holding fans made of feathers. I was so intrigued watching them that I forgot about Sean until I felt his hands on my waist.

Turning, I caught his eye and whispered, "Thanks for coming."

"It's fun watching you and Angela enjoy yourselves," he replied.

When the dancers had finished, Angela announced she was famished and was heading for the booth that sold fry bread and Indian tacos. "I haven't eaten since breakfast."

Sean looked skeptical. "I was thinking we could go out somewhere for dinner after we leave here."

"We can. That will be dinner. This is lunch," Angela said.

"While she's eating, Denise, you two should check out the basket display." Martina pointed to one of the booths. "You missed the demo, it was going on earlier this afternoon. Baskets are such complicated works of art. I hate hearing the phrase 'basket weaving' being used to refer to simple, mindless activities. It isn't that way at all."

As we approached the booth, Martina continued, "The woman leading the demo explained where the grasses come from, and how they're harvested and prepared for weaving. Then she invited someone from the audience to try to follow her as she wove a simple piece. I didn't volunteer, although I had tried it before and couldn't believe how hard it is to make the piece look like anything."

When we reached the booth, I was awed. There were baskets of varying sizes with complex geometric designs, baskets with shells woven into them, and baskets with two colors of feathers. A triptych displayed pictures of grass harvesting, then various stages in the weaving process. Behind the table, two middle-aged women chatted with an elderly woman in a wheelchair.

Angela reappeared with a half-eaten Indian taco. As she and I oohed and aahed over the baskets, I noticed Sean behind us, looking around but not really giving the basket display much attention.

For the next half hour, while Angela and I continued to find things of interest—a booth selling children's books, two more jewelry and beadwork booths, a short performance by a children's dance group—Sean seemed to withdraw. Coming here was not how he had pictured us spending time together. Yet for me, this was exactly the right activity. I felt like I was seeing so much for the first time. I had met Oscar Ortiz and was excited to visit his classroom and talk with him. I had gotten to know Martina a little better. I was blown away by the intricacy of the artwork I had viewed. And I couldn't wait to find out more about the Sogorea Te' Land Trust. While Sean was punching away on his cell phone, I was feeling energized by what was around me, absorbing everything like a plant taking in water.

Sean perked back up after we left. "I got us tickets for *Mission: Impossible 5*," he said. "We have just enough time to get to the theater."

"It opened yesterday, didn't it?" Angela commented.

"Yep, and we'll be able to get in without standing in a long line." He unlocked the car, piled us in, and set off for the theater.

So that's what he was doing with his cell phone. Sean loved movies. We had seen *Mission: Impossible 4* together. He had also seen earlier movie and TV episodes, some of them multiple times. Angela hadn't, so as he drove, Sean gave her probably far more background than she wanted, recalling his favorite scenes in considerable detail. Having spent the afternoon leading Sean around through an event he didn't quite relate to, it was now my turn to follow him.

I was thankful later that night that he fell asleep before trying to initiate sex. Ian wasn't far from my thoughts; sex with Sean didn't hold its usual appeal. I wasn't sure how to manage two men in my life. The only reason I was comfortable managing one was that Sean was so easygoing and undemanding. While Ian had managed to peel back layers of my defenses as if they weren't there, Sean and I seemed to have a tacit agreement to leave each other's defenses alone. Which kind of relationship did I actually want? I wasn't sure.

Sean would be leaving Monday for a ten-day business trip to Mexico. His absence would give me some time to think about what I wanted relationship-wise and work-wise

Before falling asleep, he said, "I know you aren't thinking about work for a few days, but I still want you to consider applying for a job with Tomorrow's Curriculum. I don't think you'd regret it. Just think about it. Okay?"

"Okay," I said.

Chapter Ten

Ride the Uncertainty

WITH A FEW free days remaining before returning to work, I chased from my mind Tomorrow's Curriculum, as well as my parents, my sewer repair bill, and my relationship quandary. When Angela called about our date with Oscar Ortiz, I was excited. His school was on a different schedule from ours. Teachers were back, and he was looking forward to seeing us Wednesday afternoon.

Entering his classroom felt like entering a contemporary art museum. Posters of artists, writers, and political issues filled the walls. Two bookshelves were crammed full. Sculptures and baskets graced every available surface. My eyes were drawn to a basket about eight inches high woven with reeds, some curled in a way that made it appear layered.

"Beautiful, isn't it?" said Oscar. "That one was made by a Penobscot artist. You can pick it up, if you'd like."

I had a fear of breaking things, probably a vestige of my parents taking me to museums as a child. I left my hands at my side. Angela was saying, "Thank you so much for taking the time to share with us."

"Yes, thank you," I echoed as I tried to remember where the Penobscot Nation was located.

A warm smile lapped across his broad face. "Very happy to do so. As I said the other day, sharing knowledge of our people is one of my favorite things to do."

He offered us a couple of chairs at a circular table in the corner. A pile of books and papers sat on the table next to a large cardboard box.

"I put most of my children's literature in this box for you two to borrow," he said. "These are things your library should get if it doesn't have them already."

I opened the top flap, seeing titles such as *Kunu's Basket: A Story from Indian Island* and *The Christmas Coat: Memories of My Sioux Childhood*. "This author's local," he said as he held up Yamane's *Weaving a California Tradition: A Native American Basket Maker*.

"Look at this, a book about a jingle dancer, and another about a powwow," exclaimed Angela. "I need to get copies of these for my classroom."

I sifted through a few more books, then commented, "My school has a handful of children's books about Indians, but I don't think we have any of these. At least, I haven't noticed them."

"Most non-Indian people can't tell the difference between what's good and what's stereotypic," Oscar said as he turned toward his computer. "Take a look at this webpage." He opened *American Indians in Children's Literature* as he explained, "This blog is by a Nambe Owinghe woman with a PhD. The general rule, especially when you're just getting started, is to look for books by Indian authors, rather than non-Indian people's books about us."

Angela and I both jotted down the URL.

"Now," he continued, "you need to know what to do with books like these. You can't just hand them to kids and assume that's it."

"That's why we wanted to talk with you," Angela said. "We're both trying to make the people who were originally here more central to what we teach."

I added, "If Cynthia Jorgenson leaves us alone. I was going to say 'drops dead,' but that wouldn't be cool."

"Your principal?" Oscar asked.

Angela replied, "No, both of us have okay principals. She's is the testing honcho in our district, or at least the person who worries most about aligning our curriculum to what's in the tests."

"Glad I teach high school literature," Oscar said as he raised an eyebrow. "In any case, here's what you need to think about. Kids generally like the stories in this box. But most kids think they're just cute stories by simple people who aren't around anymore. Not so much with the jingle dancer and powwow stories; it's easier to locate those in the present. But some of the animal stories that teach values, history and even science, those stories need to be read in a context that develops students' understanding. Does that make sense?"

"At a general level, yes, but I need more detail," I said.

"Of course," Oscar said, pointing. "You see that map over there? Go look at it."

We stood and walked to a poster entitled *Native American Nations: Our Own Names and Locations.* I felt disoriented. The map depicted North

America with lines designating U.S. states and Canadian provinces, but the place names were in languages I didn't recognize. As I studied it, I realized it located Indigenous nations before colonization, using nations' own names for themselves. Nunt'zi appeared to be what Ute people called themselves. Ex'celen was the name for people I had learned as Esselen. Nations covered the continent.

Angela, who had been absorbed paging through the children's books, now placed her hand on the word Nunt'zi straddling Colorado and Utah. I wondered what she was feeling, probably seeing her grandmother's tribe's own name for itself for the first time. Oscar simply sat quietly until we returned to our chairs.

"Thank you," she finally said. "I feel like I've just seen a part of me I didn't realize existed."

He nodded. "What kids today need to learn is that Indian people aren't just a cultural group, or even a bunch of cultural groups. We aren't a minority group, either. Indians are sovereign nations working to re-establish nation-to-nation political relationships with the United States, as well as with each other. That map helps to show what I'm saying. We're dealing with a lot of other issues, of course, not the least of which is that many of us have been pushed out of our homelands and are trying to rebuild in a place that isn't home. These kinds of issues show up in our literature."

"Yeah, I've read a couple of Louise Erdrich's novels," Angela commented.

"Good," he said.

I had been pawing through the box of children's books. I commented, "It doesn't look like most of these were written by Ohlone writers. I was thinking of starting with Ohlone, but you're showing us material by people from many different tribes."

"Well, yes," Oscar replied. "Your California history would focus on the people who are indigenous to California, of course, especially in the area where you live. But Ohlone people aren't the only ones writing, and you shouldn't limit yourself. Besides, Indian people from various nations dialog with each other constantly. You need to work with the big picture as well as the local picture."

He was silent for a moment, then picked up some Xeroxed pages. "Another thing to think about is that Native literature is more than novels and stories. I encourage people to think broadly. Take this piece, for instance, and by the way, this is something you can use in your fourth-grade social studies curriculum." I read the title of the copy he handed me: *The Narratives of Lorenzo Asisara.*

"This is a first-person account by an Indian who lived in one of the missions, taken in the form of three oral histories at different points in time. Almost everything written about the missions is from perspectives that aren't Indian. This is the most extensive piece I'm aware of that's in an Indian voice, and the story it tells isn't what's usually taught in the schools. Take it, I have the book I copied it from."

I could definitely use this. I wouldn't even need to create a new unit, I could just put this right into our study of the missions, and in doing so, change the whole point of view.

Angela was asking, "Do you have anything for kids about the Doctrine of Discovery? That's what was used to justify not letting Indian people own land."

Oscar's eyes narrowed. "That's not exactly right. It was used to justify taking non-occupied land, and it gave exclusive right of buying Indian lands to the conquerors. A lot of our ancestors were forced into selling. But as individuals, we can own land."

She looked puzzled. Oscar continued, "It's complicated. You're right that the Doctrine has been a tool to take our land. If a tribe sold land, they had to offer it to the U.S. government first."

"So can you buy a house? Or sell it to a regular homebuyer?" I was confused.

"Yes, of course. Individual Indians can own land just like you can. But tribes do not. That's an important part of tribal relations with the Feds. The U.S. government holds tribal lands in trust for tribes to use, but has final jurisdiction over the land. There are limits on your own land ownership, by the way. Just because you hold a title to a plot of land doesn't mean you've seceded from the U.S."

As he continued to talk, I began to feel overwhelmed. He knew so much, and I had only begun to scratch the surface. At the same time, he was someone I could bring my questions to. If you hand me a book, I will read it, and he certainly had enough to keep me busy. I didn't have to know California Indian history all at once. I could learn in small pieces, like I had done while developing my Gold Rush Unit. Maybe the greatest gift Oscar was giving us was his conviction that we were able to learn, that our quest to rethink our curriculum was worthwhile. After all, he didn't have to spend this August afternoon with us.

"Thank you," I said as we stood to leave. "You have no idea how helpful you've been. I've been feeling like I was taking on way too much, like I don't have the background, don't know where to start, and as a white person, I shouldn't be trying anyway. Now, for the first time in over a month, I feel like maybe I can do this, one step at a time." I couldn't wait to show these books to Ian, and to tell him about Oscar.

"Me too," Angela said. "Even I have some Ute ancestry, I was raised as white. I've been kind of helping Denise, and sometimes fighting her—"

"And sometimes not speaking to me."

"Right, sometimes being angry at you for being white. And wanting to rip the white out of me."

"Those feelings won't just go away," Oscar said. "But you can lean into them, work with them, ride them while you're learning. Believe it or not, you'll become stronger."

I wasn't sure how leaning into and riding pain and uncertainty would make me stronger. But then again, maybe what he was talking about was a little like the painful moments during a massage, when the therapist pushes into a knot in your muscles. Rather than tensing up or telling the therapist to stop, I had learned to open myself to the pressure, to lean into it, to take in pain as a part of letting tension go.

Oscar had one more thing to give us. "I almost forgot. This is a flier for a public presentation Friday night that you might find interesting. The speaker, Dr. James Oatman, is a Miwok scientist on the staff of the California Department of Forestry and Fire Protection. His research is on California Indian traditional forest management, and he'll be talking about how knowledge of Indigenous management practices can improve what we are doing."

"We should go to this," Angela said.

"Definitely," I agreed. My science major in college had not included anything about Indigenous science, a field I was dimly aware existed but knew nothing about.

Gathering up the box of books and handouts, we thanked Oscar again and left. For the first time since I began rethinking my curriculum in relationship to American Indian knowledge, I felt energized.

❧❧❧

FRIDAY EVENING, IAN, Angela and I settled into our fourth-row seats in Miller Auditorium where Dr. Oatman would be speaking, after rushing through a quick dinner of hamburgers and fries. Angela's first opportunity to meet Ian had occurred over food we were stuffing into our mouths. She seemed to like him. At least that's how I interpreted her surreptitious thumbs-up signal partway through dinner.

Only about a third of the auditorium seats were occupied. Given all the concern about wildfires in California, we had expected a larger crowd. But maybe most citizens didn't see the relevance of Indian people's knowledge to addressing a contemporary problem like wildfires.

A wave of voices rolled in from behind us. I turned to see what appeared to be an undergraduate class filtering into the auditorium.

Ian took my hand and squeezed it as he whispered, "Thanks for letting me tag along."

My stomach did a little flip. I leaned over and kissed his cheek.

At that moment, a white-haired man wearing glasses walked across the stage to the podium. "I'd like to welcome you to this evening's lecture. We have a real treat in store for us. I'm Professor Michael Bowen, chair of the biology department just down the road. I'll be introducing Mark Wolff of the California Department of Forestry and Fire Protection, who will introduce Dr. Oatman. But first, please take a moment to turn off the ringer on your cell phones."

As I reached for mine, Ian whispered into my ear, "I love these layers of introducers. This bloke will introduce that bloke, who will introduce another bloke before we get to the guest of honor."

A jeans-clad, bearded young man hopped up onto the stage from the first row. Mark Wolff thanked Professor Bowen as he gave a plug for the university's biology department. Placing a hand above his eyes as though to shield them from the glare of lights, he playfully scanned the crowd. "I see at least three classes of university students out there. Wup, here come some more." The back door rattled open, and about ten people filed in, taking seats near the back.

"Come on up to the front, there's room," Mr. Wolff said. He then adopted a more formal posture as he shifted into a short introduction to the work of the Department of Forestry and Fire Protection. He explained that the severity of several wildfires over the past few years had led the Department to seek new perspectives about forest management.

158

"Ironically, our search for a new way of looking at the problem led us to ancient practices we are now learning from. Here to tell us about his research on those practices this evening is Dr. James Oatman." Mr. Wolff shuffled papers, apparently searching for Dr. Oatman's bio.

He continued. "Dr. James Oatman, who is from this region, can trace his ancestry back through many generations of Miwok people. He recently completed his PhD in Ecology at the University of California, Davis. He'll tell you about the research his dissertation was based on, so I won't do that. I will say, however, since he came to work with us a couple of years ago, I've found Jim to be not only a brilliant scientist, but also a warm human being who has been a delight to have as a colleague. Please join me in welcoming Dr. James Oatman."

Clapping, Mr. Wolff stepped back from the podium as a tall man, long dark hair in a ponytail, walked onto the stage. He wore jeans, boots, a white shirt and a leather vest. Out of the corner of my eye, I saw Angela freeze.

"What is it?" I whispered. "Have you met him?"

"No. Maybe. I don't think so. But he's gorgeous," she whispered back.

I jabbed my elbow into her ribs as I whispered, "Get serious." But I had to admit she was right.

Dr. Oatman projected onto the screen a map of California's recent wildfires. He spoke briefly about the size and destructiveness of some of them, and the evolution of policies prohibiting burning. Then he changed the image to a grainy photograph of an elderly Indian man with a child, explaining that this was a photo of himself with his grandfather. It was from this grandfather that he had first heard stories of how his ancestors had managed the land and its resources, and the role rotating controlled fires had played in that management system.

"For a long time, I just thought he was telling stories. I'd go to school and see pictures of Smokey Bear telling us to prevent forest fires, and then I'd hear my grandfather tell about his grandfather's grandfather using fires to manage and diversify the kinds of plants that grew. I couldn't reconcile in my mind these two different paradigms about land management, especially since none of my teachers seemed to think Indian people knew anything worthwhile." He went on to describe a course he took as a freshman in college from a science professor who had become interested in Indigenous science. "Folks, this was the first time I became aware that there is such a thing as Indigenous science, and it completely changed the trajectory of my life. Up to that point, I wasn't sure why I was continuing to go to school, other from the fact that my parents insisted on it. But now I could see a purpose for myself. Any of you out there who are teachers, your work can completely transform your students' lives."

Did he know Sean was trying to lure me out of the classroom? I felt as though Dr. Oatman was looking directly at me when he said that, but of course he wasn't, he was talking to the audience in general.

Dr. Oatman described reading everything he could get his hands on related to Indigenous science, and thinking about what he was learning in relationship to his now-deceased grandfather's stories. "I learned that the old people weren't just telling stories, they were keeping knowledge alive, hoping their words would plant seeds of knowledge within the young people. Too often those seeds wither and die. But they can be nurtured to grow, and I have several mentors to thank for that."

The slide on the screen now showed a group of young adults outdoors, perhaps college students, sifting through sand. Dr. Oatman described his research into the controlled burning practices of his ancestors, and how the research team documented burning in the past by analyzing layers of earth. I dug out my iPhone and typed notes furiously as he talked. I wondered where I could find some of his work to read, since he was talking faster than I could keyboard.

By the end of his lecture, my brain felt wired and my thumbs cramped. He took several questions from the audience, then it was over. The lights flashed back on.

"You seem to have written a book there," said Ian with a grin, indicating my phone.

"I've heard of Indigenous science, but this was the first time I learned enough that it made sense to me," I replied. "I kept thinking back to avenues my science courses could have taken in the university, but never did."

"I wonder if he's spent any time in Aotearoa New Zealand," Ian said. "Quite a bit of traditional knowledge work is being done there. Say, Angela, you're awfully quiet."

"I'm just blown away," she exhaled. "Sometimes it felt like he was channeling my grandmother. But then he'd jump into all this research I'm sure she has no clue about. I can't wait to tell her about it." Pause. "And he's gorgeous."

By the time we ambled out of the auditorium, it had almost emptied. As we passed a small knot of people in the entrance hall, Angela, struggling to get into her jacket while holding her large shoulder bag, planted an elbow in the back of one of the undergraduate students. "Oops, 'scuse me," she said.

At that moment, her shoulder bag slid off her arm, falling onto the floor. As she stooped to retrieve it, another hand picked it up for her. The student stepped back, and I realized the hand belonged to James Oatman.

"Let me help you with that," he said as he held her jacket so she could slide her arm into the sleeve, then handed her the bag.

"Thank you," she said. "And thank you for doing this work. I wish my grandmother were here."

He cocked his head. "You have a grandmother who's interested in Indigenous land management?"

"Yes, although I don't think she knows it's called that. She lives in Colorado. She's Ute, and her stories remind me of some of the stories you told," Angela replied.

He smiled. "And you are?"

"Angela Walker, and these are my friends Denise Fisher and Ian—I'm sorry, I forgot your last name."

"Ian McAlister." Ian offered his hand and the two men shook.

"Sounds like you might be from New Zealand," Dr. Oatman guessed.

"Right-o. Ye've been there?"

"A couple of times. Mainly to visit the Institute for Indigenous Science at—how do you say the name of the *wananga* in Whakatane?"

"Te Whare Wānanga o Awanuiārangi," Ian replied. "The University of Canterbury has a pretty interesting program, too."

"I've met some people from there. Are you connected with one of those programs?" The students had drifted off, and we were now walking out the door and toward the parking lot.

"No, not at all," Ian said. "I taught reading in a primary school near Hamilton for a few years, then studied for my PhD in Literacy at Waikato University. I'm here temporarily, teaching university courses for teachers."

My stomach lurched at the word *temporarily*. I had to remind myself that of course, Ian would probably return to New Zealand. I wondered if he imagined taking me with him. Goodness, that would complicate my life planning.

We reached the car. Angela, sounding shy for the first time in her life, turned to Dr. Oatman and asked, "How can we get copies of some of your work? Denise tried to write down everything you said, but I think she missed some things."

He laughed as he pulled a wad of business cards from one of his pockets. "Just send me an email, and I'd be happy to send you PDFs. Including a piece I wrote about my grandfather that your grandmother might find interesting."

We thanked him, then proceeded to get into the car. As Ian pulled out of the lot and into the street, he chatted about the Indigenous science programs in New Zealand. He didn't seem to notice that Angela and I were each preoccupied, me with the possibility he would move back to New Zealand, and Angela, I guessed, with Dr. James Oatman.

The next evening, by the time Ian picked me up for dinner, I could scarcely hold back the question that had plagued me all day. As he started the car, it spilled out: "Ian, I need to know something. You told Dr. Oatman you're here in the U.S. temporarily. Does that mean you plan to return to New Zealand?"

He switched off the ignition and looked at me. "No. At least not immediately, anyway. I'm here because I married Rachel, and now that we're getting divorced, I assume I'll return at some point."

I stared straight ahead so he wouldn't be able to read my eyes. Of course I had no right to assume he would stay here for me. Especially considering Sean was still part of my life, although at the moment I wasn't sure why.

"Denise, look at me," Ian said.

I swiveled around to face him. His eyes studied mine. He asked, "Do you think we may have a future together?"

"Maybe," I said, nodding. But I couldn't promise him a future I wasn't sure about myself. Was I ready for a long-term commitment? Until a few days ago I had assumed Sean to be the most likely candidate. Perhaps what I really wanted was reassurance that Ian would be here for me, even if I couldn't yet promise him anything. He seemed to sense my uncertainty.

"Then let's live with some ambiguity for a while, okay?" he asked, cupping my face in his hands. "If it turns out that we do have a future together, then we'll have to decide where that future will be located. I'm open to options. But I think for now, we're both exploring. Right?"

Exhilaration (Ian might actually want to stay with me!) danced with relief (no need to decide anything right now). He was neither planning on leaving right away, nor on spiriting me to New Zealand. I could live with ambiguity for now. I nodded.

"Right, then," he said as he started the car again. He turned and gave me a thoroughly inviting kiss, then unset the parking brake and pulled out into the street. "More later where that came from," he said with a wink.

๕ ๕ ๕

SUNDAY I SLID into my usual seat at the café where Angela and I often had lunch after volunteering at the Red Handle.

"You were missed," she said. "People asked about you. I said you weren't feeling well."

"Thanks." When I woke up next to Ian, I realized I could either send him home to keep my volunteer obligation, or text Angela that I wouldn't make it but would see her afterward. A picture of a lump under rumpled sheets was all she needed.

"Ian seems right for you," she commented. "You had this glow Friday night that you don't usually have. Where does that leave Sean?"

"I don't know," I replied. "Thankfully he's in Mexico right now. I think Tomorrow's Curriculum is starting a project there. But him being away gives me some time to think. Not that he's around all the time when he's here in California."

This was true. Sean showed up on most weekends when he wasn't traveling. But he lived and worked in San Francisco. And for reasons I hadn't quite figured out, we spent most of our time together at my place in Cypress View (or sometimes at my parents' house), not at his apartment. He seemed to like having his own space. Not for the first time, I wondered if he might also be seeing someone else. At any rate, there were sides to him I didn't know very well. That had suited me. Until now.

"Ian and I are figuring out where we're going," I continued. "He gets me in ways people usually don't. Present company excluded of course. By the way, how's Internet dating going these days?" Angela hadn't mentioned it since early summer, and while I didn't want to rub in her face the fact that I now had two men in my life while she was still searching, I was curious.

"Boring," she replied. "Occasionally I troll to see what's out there, but I've realized I'm tired of the tacky dates I was coming up with. Working in an elementary school, it's hard to meet guys who are older than ten."

"Well, you could try volunteering in an old folks' home," I said as I flipped open the menu.

"I thought those places were populated mainly by women," she commented.

"They are, but some of the male seniors seem pretty spry."

"Your usual?" Janice, our usual server, was hovering. It's funny, I felt like I knew Janice since we chatted almost every time I ate there, but I actually knew nothing about her life. Was she married? Did she have kids? Did she work there only on Sundays?

"Yes, thank you," said Angela.

"Me too," I added, returning the menus. "Your good memory keeps us coming back, you know, Janice."

She rolled her eyes with a grin as she turned and left.

I said, "I'm stoked after our meeting with Oscar and then hearing Friday's lecture. The lecture gave me this brainstorm for linking science and literature, and maybe social studies. I'd start with the current problem of forest fires and drought, which I'd connect with the weather and erosion topics in the science curriculum. There's also a topic on relationships between engineering, technology, and the natural world—I might bring that in, too. Anyway, drawing on Dr. Oatman's talk, we'd then move to Indigenous science and his research on traditional California Indian land management practices. What do you think?" Before she could respond, I asked, "By the way, has Dr. Oatman sent you anything yet?"

"Not yet," she replied. "I just emailed him yesterday."

"Okay. Well, what do you think of that idea? I might be able to use some of the children's literature Oscar recommended, if any of it actually fits."

"It's an idea," she said slowly, as though I were a sixth grader beginning a project she knew would never work out. She was used to hearing me brainstorm. Sometimes she helped me shape ideas, other times she gently laid them to rest. This time seemed to be the latter.

Our sandwiches arrived. After plowing into the first few bites in silence, Angela said, "Rather than trying to come up with this stuff all by yourself, why don't you look at some of the curricula that are already available? For instance, I've been looking at a wonderful curriculum website about land stewardship, created by the Indian Land Tenure Foundation. You can access it online. It's got background stuff for teachers to read, blow-by-blow lesson plans, links to teaching resources you can use, connections with standards, everything. And it's really good."

Duh. Why hadn't it occurred to me I wasn't the first teacher to become interested in Indigenous science? I took out my phone to make a note.

"Thanks. I feel stupid for not having thought to see what's already available."

"You aren't stupid, believe me," she said. "I was hunting around online yesterday for what I might be able to use, and discovered more than I anticipated."

"Like what else?"

"There's an Ohlone Curriculum produced by the East Bay Regional Parks. It's for third grade, so we probably wouldn't be able to use it in our classes, but it's loaded with information. Actually there seem to be several pieces of curriculum and other resources about California Indians— including a coalition of people working on a whole California Indian curriculum. Sacramento State University's College of Ed has a bunch of great resources vetted by California Indians on the web. They sponsor summits where educators like us can learn about how to use those resources."

Using my phone, I googled what she said, and there it was. Easy to find, and free.

Angela continued, "Montana has Indian education lesson plans on their website for all of the main subject areas."

"Montana?"

"Yeah, it's cool," Angela replied. "It's set up by grade level, so all you have to do is click on a subject area and grade level, and voila. Science is even there; so's math. Last night, looking through the language arts plans, I found a bunch I could use, complete with readings and PowerPoints. I also found a tribal sovereignty curriculum for Washington State. It's Washington focused, but there's quite a bit you or I could use."

Maybe there was more to work with than I had realized. "So what are you starting the school year with?" I asked as I finished jotting down the websites she mentioned. After faculty workdays next week, kids would be arriving on Thursday.

"Well, I'm not starting out with anything. I mean, not anything new. I'm just doing what we did last year. What I want to do is hunt around and find things that seem best for sixth grade, preferably plans someone who knows more than I do has put together and tried out. I admire all your work developing that unit from scratch for Ian this summer, but I don't see doing that for my whole curriculum. Not if I can find things that are ready to go. I also want to work with the other sixth-grade teachers in my building rather than just striking out on my own. We are a team, after all."

Good point. I'd need to at least fill in my principal Sarah about what I was working on. I finished my sandwich, then said, "Sean has this crazy idea that I should apply for a job working where he works."

Angela regarded me. "What? In San Francisco? No way, I hope."

"He brings it up every now and then, and I just blow him off," I said. "The only reason I'm even mentioning it is that this talk about what we might do in our classrooms clashes with what the administration says we can do. That gets frustrating. There are days when I really do think about doing something else."

"Well, yeah," she said. "All teachers feel like that on one occasion or the next. But, you're not really thinking about just taking off, are you?"

Why was I even bringing this up? Surely I wasn't actually considering going to work with Sean in San Francisco, even if he had tried to tell me I wouldn't need to relocate there. I could do much of the work from home. So it wouldn't necessarily disrupt my life, and it would make good use of my creativity.

I replied, "No, it isn't something I'm actually considering. I just get this cold lump in my stomach when I think about going back into the classroom with all these ideas of what I could be doing with my students, and then hit smack into the reality of what is allowable."

"Well, so do I," she replied. "That's why we eat out so often. We keep each other sane. Heaven knows we'll need to do something to hang onto our sanity starting next week!"

Chapter Eleven

Fraud Unmasked

I DUCKED OUT of school a few minutes early Monday afternoon to meet Home Inspector Josh Fenstermacher at my house. The first day back after summer vacation had given me a major headache.

During the morning staff meeting, our principal had tried to establish an upbeat mood as she welcomed everyone and introduced two new teachers. A new sixth-grade teacher had relocated to California from Iowa, and a new first-grade teacher, who looked like she was still in high school, had just completed her teaching credential locally.

Sarah then moved to this year's initiatives for raising students' reading and math achievement, although the results of the spring tests were not yet available. Eye contact among several teachers said, Here we go again. That's probably when my headache started. We would phase in a new math curriculum, starting with kindergarten and first. I sensed Cynthia Jorgenson's hand at work behind the scene. As Sarah talked, I noticed a stranger who looked about twenty-five. Sarah hadn't introduced him yet. Was he a new administrator? A visitor? He looked like a salesman.

". . . Bill Mayer, a representative from Robinson-Woodrich, who will give us an overview of the new math curriculum," Sarah was saying.

Yep, he was a salesman, there to plow more Robinson-Woodrich products into our classrooms. Bill Mayer leaped to his feet and proceeded to dole out brochures and instruction booklets like sheet music for a choir. For the next hour, he whipped us through a PowerPoint presentation of the new the math curriculum, involving us now and then in solving problems or trying out online math games. The curriculum wasn't bad—there were features I could see myself using—although I didn't regard it as the magic bullet he made it out to be.

The afternoon left us free to prepare our classrooms for students. Although I was as prepared now as I had been the previous year, I still didn't have a plan for making California Indians more visible in my curriculum, beyond the unit I wrote for Ian's class and things I had begun to collect. I had an idea for starting out, though. I could begin with the concepts *indigenous* and *indigeneity*, developing them in relationship to the concepts *migrate* and *invade*. I found a couple of lesson plans using these in curriculum guides Angela had suggested, but not tailored for fourth graders. But I wanted to use them to get my students to begin to explore their own families' indigenous roots, picking up on the question Martina had asked me. I could also apply them to science, differentiating between indigenous and non-indigenous plants and animals. I wanted students to know that people, plants, and animals have always migrated, and to begin to think critically about when migration becomes invasion.

I had been mulling this idea when Sarah stopped into my classroom to welcome me back. When she asked what I was working on, I told her briefly about the unit on California Indians during the Gold Rush I had written for Ian's class.

"Interesting. Have you shared it with the other fourth-grade teachers?" she asked.

I shook my head. "Not yet."

"You should. You know you don't all have to do the exact same thing, but this sounds intriguing. They might think so, too."

"I'll do that," I told her. I suspected my two counterparts would want to continue with the same Gold Rush unit they had taught in the past, but it wouldn't hurt to give them a copy of mine.

"Do you know Donna Reyes?" Sarah continued. When I gave her a blank look, she said, "Donna's a fourth-grade teacher at Libertad Elementary. I met her in a workshop this summer. She's Indian, but I don't know which tribe. She seems very knowledgeable. She presented some of her work on her own curriculum at the workshop, and I thought she was very impressive. You could try to get together with her. She might have some ideas to share with you."

I thanked Sarah and asked if she could send me Donna's contact information.

Later, as I pulled into my driveway, I noticed a white van trailing me. It parked, and a man as thin as a fencepost emerged carrying a clipboard. His crisp white shirt and black slacks contrasted with grey curly locks loosely pulled into a ponytail.

"Denise Fisher?" he asked as he approached.

"That's me," I said, fumbling with my keys. "Thanks for coming."

"Hi, I'm Josh," he said. "I'll start with the exterior, but before you go inside, mind looking at this checklist?" I caught a whiny undercurrent to his reedy voice. No wonder he didn't make it past the first date with Angela.

We went over the list of things he would inspect, and I signed the form. As Josh began traversing the perimeter of the house, I ran inside.

About fifteen minutes later, the doorbell rang. "Mind if I come check out the interior?" Josh asked. Amazing how the timbre of a person's voice can make a simple statement sound like a snivel. He waved one hand at me as he said, "Go ahead and do whatever you'd normally do. When I'm done, I'll go over everything with you."

I was dicing carrots to put in a salad when Josh approached. "Can I pull you away for a few minutes?"

"Sure," I replied as I rinsed and dried my hands. "Let's sit here." I indicated the kitchen table.

"I'll email you a copy of this," he said as he took a chair. "But let's review what I saw, starting with the exterior." He flipped to a page entitled *Roofing*. "The biggest problem is that your roof needs attention. I found evidence of leakage in three places inside, and from the outside, it doesn't look like the roof has been replaced for a long time."

"Replaced?" I asked. "As in, I need a new roof?"

"Possibly. If I were you, I'd get a roofing company to look at it before the rainy season starts."

"How much—" I gulped.

"To reroof the house? Depends. Anywhere between six and ten thousand, I imagine. But maybe they'll decide you don't need a whole new roof just yet."

I pictured winged dollar bills flying away. I wasn't sure where they would come from.

He continued. "There's the beginning of a wasps' nest under the eaves of the garage. You should get that removed."

I had noticed what I thought were bees, but hadn't paid attention to where they were coming from. "What else?" I asked, dreading what might be coming next.

"Those are the most immediate things needing attention outside," he said. "The external façade is in reasonable shape, considering the age of the house. The gutters and drain system are functional although when you get the wasps' nest removed, you should also have the gutters cleaned out."

"Can you recommend someone?" I asked, realizing I had no clue who to hire for this work.

"Sure, I'll give you some names before I leave. Let's see." He flipped the page. "Your electrical system is fine. Your windows are in decent shape, although you should consider getting double-paned windows to save on indoor heating costs."

Josh continued running through the list. When he finished, I had three things needing immediate attention (a toilet to replace, the roof inspection, and the wasps' nest removal), things that would need attention in the next year or two (replacing the badly rusted garage door, installing fans in the bathrooms, and repairing a crack in the driveway), and a list of optional upgrades, like double-paned windows. He also pointed out that the aging water heater and furnace would need replacement at some point.

"You're lucky you still have that older model of washer and drier, the kind they used to make before they put computers into everything. Those old appliances might keep working for another decade or two," he commented. "The newer electronic appliances, like your fridge, don't last nearly as long." That revelation surprised me. Gram had replaced her old fridge and stove just before she died. I assumed the washer and drier would go next, but maybe not.

Josh let me know his bill would arrive via email along with his report. As I walked him to the door, I thanked him, even though I felt as though he had just dumped a pile of shit on me.

I returned to the kitchen and picked up his written recommendation for a roofing company and a handyman. How was I going to pay for all of this? Gram, what did you get me into?

There was, however, one somewhat bright light in Josh's report. He had given me a reason to approach my parents. Ian was right: they probably wondered whether I still loved and respected them. Now I had a conversation opener: I had followed their advice about hiring a home inspector.

I picked up my phone and speed-dialed their number, fingers crossed that Dad would be the one to answer since he would be more likely than Mom to listen to me.

"What's up, Denise?" Dad greeted me.

"Hi, Dad. I followed your and Mom's advice about getting a home inspector to look over the house. He just left. That was a good idea, although I learned there are leaks in the roof and a few other things needing fixing. Soon."

"Well, good," he said slowly. "Not the leaks, but good that you had someone come and look things over. What else did he find?"

"A wasps' nest, a hairline crack in the toilet, a crack in the driveway. Some appliances that won't last as long as I'd hoped. Maybe next time you're here, you can help me prioritize getting them fixed," I said. When he didn't respond, I added, "Dad, I'm sorry about upsetting you and Mom when I was there. I can't simply forget what happened in history, but that doesn't affect how I feel about you and Mom. Or Gram, for that matter."

Finally he said, "Well, I wish you would forget the whole thing. You can't go back and change what happened in the past. Even if the information you have is correct, which it may not be."

I wanted to defend my information. But over the phone probably wasn't the best venue for what would surely become another argument, so I said, "Maybe I can show you what I found and see what you make of it."

"That isn't the point," he said. "It feels to us like this whole business has made you disrespect your own family. Maybe not your mother and me, but certainly the people I descend from. You're portraying them like a bunch of thieves, and for no purpose that's clear to me."

I decided to drop it for now. "Well, Dad, I just want you and Mom to know I love you, and I took your good advice."

"We love you, too, and I'll pass on your message to your mother when she gets home," Dad said.

"I was thinking about driving up to see you both on Sunday," I said. Actually, I hadn't been thinking of it until that minute, but doing some repair work on my relationship with them, and doing it soon, seemed like a good idea.

"You're always welcome here, you know," Dad said. "Sunday isn't the best day for us, though, since we've already planned a round of golf, but if Saturday works, we'd love to see you."

I agreed on Saturday.

"And bring Sean along if you can," Dad added.

"He's in Mexico," I replied.

"Well, no matter. We'll see you Saturday. Oh, and if you don't already do this, project your budget out six months or so. That'll help you get on top of these unexpected bills."

"I'll do that, Dad. Bye for now."

I felt relieved to have a line of communication reestablished with my parents. I wasn't going to back away from what I believed was the impact of my ancestors' homesteading, and I had no idea how I would approach my parents on Saturday. Maybe I should just avoid the whole subject and talk about other things.

I called Angela. "What's up?" she greeted me.

"Josh Fenstermacher just left. He is hands down is the most dismal person I've ever met," I replied.

"You mean his voice? A complete turnoff," she agreed.

"That and his depressing information. He thinks I need roof repairs sooner rather than later, and I need a new toilet because a hairline crack is starting to run up my water bill. I'm beginning to wish houses didn't need toilets. And I need to get a wasps' nest removed. Oh, and my property tax bill just arrived." I sighed deeply.

"Ouch! Sorry to hear that," she replied. "Maybe you can get an outhouse installed in the backyard. Just kidding!"

"Yeah, right. Well, I figure I can pay for this stuff if I don't use any electricity, don't drive anywhere, eat one meal a day, don't buy anything for my classroom—"

"You could take out a loan," she ventured.

"I already did, to get through school, to buy my car, and now to get the sewer line fixed."

"Ugh. I'm really sorry you have to deal with all this," she said. But I caught an undertone in her voice saying, *Welcome back to the world of teachers who have housing bills to pay.*

I slumped down on the kitchen table and buried my head in my hands. How did it happen that the previous week I had felt buoyed with possibilities and now I felt defeated? Our faculty meeting all morning brought me right back into what I hated most about my job: the expectation that I conform to someone else's expectations of exactly what I should be doing in my classroom rather than making my own professional judgments. Social studies was the only subject area now where I had some leeway, at least until the powers that be decide we should skip it to expand the time for drilling kids in reading and math.

And now I had bills piling up.

I had told Sean I'd think about considering a job at Tomorrow's Curriculum. What would be the harm in looking? Like window shopping?

I opened the company's website and looked under "Employment Opportunities." Based on the number of job listings, it appeared that the company was indeed in the process of expanding. About half the listings were for software engineers, computer scientists, or educational technologists. But I found a couple for science curriculum specialists.

I clicked on one of them. "Are you ready to shape the future of science for the elementary grades?" the website asked.

"Sure," I answered.

I learned that the person hired for this job would be using her "highly trained brain" to create "fun, engaging, and interactive science learning activities that are aligned with specific learning outcomes." My B.A. degree would qualify me, but an advanced degree was preferred. Good reason to finish up the M.A. program. My teaching experience, as well as my creative thinking and attention to detail would also be "highly desirable."

This job description was more intriguing than I had anticipated. I couldn't imagine Cynthia Jorgensen, or even our superintendent, expecting teachers to use their highly trained brains to create fun classroom activities, at least not in schools like the one I worked in. I wondered if Tomorrow's Curriculum actually treated its employees as well as its website suggested. I could always ask Sean. I hunted around for a pay scale, but all I found was the statement, "Salary and benefits negotiable."

I could apply online. Sending in an application wouldn't obligate me to anything, but might get me in the door so I could try negotiating a salary that would allow me to pay off my loans and whip the house into shape. Maybe they'd even let me work from home rather than requiring me to move to San Francisco.

But as my fingers approached the keyboard, I recalled Bill Mayer earlier in the day pitching Robinson-Woodrich's version of what we teachers should be doing in our classrooms. Would this job transmogrify me into a science version of him? I pictured myself in a black suit and crisp white blouse, chirpily taking teachers through my plans for their work. I almost gagged.

On the other hand, a job like this would not only solve my money problems, it might also smooth things over with my parents. Although they seemed satisfied having a daughter who was a teacher, they would surely be proud of me moving up from there. And the focus on science would allow me to stop trying to reimagine social studies with local American Indian tribes at the center, which despite Oscar Ortiz's encouragement and the websites Angela unearthed, I was finding challenging. I just didn't have enough background knowledge, and meeting Oscar made that painfully obvious. I also had to admit that a science job might diminish my guilty obsession over having a house obtained by stealing Indian peoples' land, since I wouldn't be thinking about Indian history every day.

What would Ian think of all this? He would probably be disappointed in me. He would think I was running away from a challenge rather than facing it. I could call him and vent, but I didn't want to come across as whiney. Besides, he was on his way to Los Angeles for the rest of the week to wrap up divorce details with his attorney. He wouldn't need my problems added to his own.

I bookmarked the job at Tomorrow's Curriculum, then did a quick email check. There was Sarah's message with Donna Reyes's contact information. What the heck, I thought, I'll give her a try. I typed:

Dear Donna, I'm a fourth-grade teacher working on including California Indians in my curriculum. I'm eager to meet you after my principal Sarah Peel spoke highly of you. She met you in a workshop this summer, and thought we might be able to share some curriculum ideas. Any chance of grabbing a coffee sometime after school next week? From deep in the trenches, Denise Fisher, Milford Elementary

I put my laptop away, then slouched into a chair in front of the TV to watch the latest episode of *iZombie* before turning in.

❧❧❧

WEDNESDAY EVENING I was putting the finishing touches on a new welcome activity to do with my new class the next day, when my phone rang. It was Sean, back from Mexico.

When he asked how I was, I started on Josh Fenstermacher's report, but didn't get very far.

"A new roof, huh?" Sean said. "Those older houses can be a pain. At least yours is in way better shape than a lot of the houses I saw in Mexico

City. I had the best meeting with these English language school directors there. After I showed them the kinds of things we had been working on, they were hooked, and I think we're gonna have a great contract within the month."

How had we gone so quickly from my problems to Mexico's English language schools? "That's wonderful," I said. "Sean, I, uh . . ."

"Now I've got a boatload of paperwork staring me in the face," he continued. "Stuff that piled up while I was gone, plus some plans I need to sketch out for the Mexico project. Your classes started this week, didn't they? How'd things go?"

"Kids show up tomorrow," I said. "The first part of the week was, well . . . Say, do you know a Bill Mayer? Salesman for Robinson-Woodrich?"

"No, I don't think so," he replied. "Why?"

"Oh, nothing. I just get tired of these sales reps coming in and telling us what we should be doing. This one reminded me of a shoe salesman."

There was a pause on the other end. Sean and I seemed to have conflicting agendas for this conversation, and I pictured him trying to figure out what to say next.

"Denise, I hope you weren't expecting me this weekend," he said finally.

Ah, so that's what he was dancing around. "No, not necessarily. I'm visiting my folks on Saturday." I didn't add that I was seeing Ian on Sunday.

"Good. Maybe we can connect next weekend, or if that doesn't work, the one after that," he said.

"Sean, we don't have to get together, you know," I said. "This isn't like some kind of obligation."

"I didn't mean to suggest that it was," he replied.

I took a deep breath. "I guess I should tell you that I've met someone else recently."

Silence. Then, "That's not a problem, Denise. You're free to see whoever you want. This was never an exclusive relationship anyway."

"What?" Our relationship wasn't exclusive? It had been for me.

"Back when we started seeing each other, we agreed that we could see other people if we wanted. You remember that, don't you?" he said.

"That was eons ago," I said. Then the light bulb went on. "Are you seeing someone else?"

"Only now and then, no one regularly. I figured you were doing the same thing."

"I wasn't," I replied. "You were it."

"But you seemed okay with the casualness of our relationship." He truly sounded puzzled.

"I suppose I was. I just wasn't interested in dating around, and I imagined you felt the same. Well, I never asked you, I just assumed. Now I think I might be ready for something more."

"So, you're telling me goodbye?" he asked.

Was that what I wanted? Sean had become such a good friend that I couldn't imagine kicking him out of my life entirely.

"Sean, for me, relationships are exclusive. I need to try this new one out and see where it goes. But I still regard you as a friend." The tears forming in my eyes caught me by surprise. After all, hadn't I been planning to have this conversation at some point? I continued, "At first, I thought our relationship would go somewhere, then realized probably not, but I wasn't ready for an intense relationship anyway. But through the time we've spent together, I've come to care about you a lot, and I enjoy your company."

Suddenly my phone rang. I looked to see who it was. Ian! Should I take the call or let it go to voice mail?

"Hang on a sec, Sean," I said. "I've got a call here I need to take. Don't go away."

I put Sean on hold. "Ian!" I greeted him.

"I hope I didn't catch you at a bad time," he said. "Looking forward to the new crop of kids tomorrow?"

I tried to sound cheerful as I replied that I was, very much. "How are things in LA?" I asked.

As he began to tell me his about his lawyerly experiences over the past couple of days, I realized this could go on for a while and I still had Sean on hold. So I said, "Ian, can I call you right back? I'm on another call."

"This can wait until I see you," he said. "Are you okay? Your voice sounds a tense."

"Oh, I'm fine," I lied.

"Well, get a good night's sleep and we'll talk when I get back." He hung up and I returned to Sean.

"Sorry about that," I said.

"Your new guy?"

"Yeah. He's in LA right now."

"Okay. Well, I won't take you off my speed dial. But I hope this new relationship gives you what you need. You'll let me know?"

"Yeah, I will. Geez, my parents are gonna kill me. Mom was ready to go shopping for my wedding dress. She really wants grandkids sooner rather than later. And she and Dad like you a lot."

"Maybe they can just adopt me," he joked. "Seriously, Denise, I'm not sure I'm cut out for marriage. I think you are, but me, not so much. And kids—well, you'd be a good mom, but I don't see kids in my future at all."

We mumbled an awkward good-bye, we'll talk soon, then hung up.

I poured myself a glass of wine as a jumble of feelings welled up in me. I felt like I had just lost a good friend, even though we agreed to stay in touch. But on the other hand, Ian drew me like a magnet. I had known I'd need to choose between him and Sean, and now I had. But Ian could tell I was upset about something. I hoped he wouldn't worry.

I opened up email and scrolled through new messages. A reply from Donna Reyes had come in:

Denise. Yes, we can talk. How is Friday 4pm at Starbuck's on Main and Fourth? Donna

Hmmm, terse. I sent back an even shorter reply: *"Great, see you then."*

⋞⋞⋞

WHEN I ENTERED Starbucks on Friday, every seat seemed occupied. Was Donna here yet? And without knowing what she looked like, how would I know? I glanced around. Over in a corner, I saw a woman whose long black hair was gathered into a beaded barrette, hunched over a notebook, her pen moving across a page. I threaded my way to her table.

"Donna?" I asked.

"Yes." She looked up at me. "You must be Denise. Have a seat."

"Let me get a latte first," I said. "Can I bring you anything?"

"No." She returned to the notebook in which she was writing, an almost-empty coffee cup perched on the corner of the table. "Maybe you can toss this." She handed it to me without looking up.

A couple minutes later, latte in hand, I slid into the chair across from her. I wasn't sure what to say. "Thanks for agreeing to meet with me."

She flipped shut her notebook and looked at me. "Sure. So you said you're trying to include more Indian people in your curriculum?"

"Well, yeah. As I've realized it's written from the perspective of the colonizers, I've been trying to rework it more from American Indian perspectives. But I'm a novice. My principal thought you might be a good person to talk with." My palms sweated as I tried to read the mask of Donna's face.

"And why do you want to do this?" she asked, placing her forearms on the table and crossing her slim hands on her notebook.

I thought a moment. "I grew up not thinking about the impact of my ancestors on the people whose land they took. As I've become more cognizant of the ongoing impact of colonization, I've started looking more closely at what is, and what isn't, in our curriculum. I don't want my students to grow up as ignorant as I did. For a masters course this summer, I created a unit about the Gold Rush that focused on how U.S. policies brutalized California Indians. I had to read a ton of stuff to write the unit."

"And so you'd like to borrow some of what I've created, is that right?" she asked.

"Well, I was interested in sharing ideas and resources," I replied.

"Doesn't sound like you have much to share yet. Are you doing all this work by yourself, or are you collaborating with any Indian people?"

"I'm working with my best friend Angela Walker. She teaches sixth. She's part Ute."

Donna stared at me without blinking. "Never heard of her. Is she a member of the Ute Nation?"

"No, I don't think so. Her grandmother is, though, I think," I said.

"Look," Donna said, "I've been working on my curriculum for about four years. I've put a lot of work into it. I don't just give it away. I especially don't just give it away to a white person who wants to short-circuit doing her own work."

I felt as though she had thrown fire into my face. I must have blanched because she said, "That probably didn't come out sounding nice. But I meant what I said. We're done giving you people what's ours. If you want to share with us, you have to earn that right."

Did she want a copy of my Gold Rush unit? I asked her.

"I've already completely rewritten how I teach that period in history. Quite frankly, I'm not sure you would have anything to offer that I could use. Have you ever taken coursework in Indian history or literature?"

I hadn't. I shook my head.

"I supposed if you want to do some serious work, you could start there. Otherwise, what you're doing strikes me as trying to assuage your own guilt, but without the knowledge to do it well, and without the tribal connections that would give your work, and you, some integrity."

My face went up in flames and my lungs forgot how to draw breath. She stared at me a few seconds more, then picked up her notebook and pushed back her chair.

"I'm sorry I bothered you," I managed to mumble.

"I can see I've hurt your feelings," she said as she stood. "That wasn't my intention. I just become impatient when I see Anglo teachers dive into our business without a clue what they're doing, and assume they can speak for us. I'm sorry if I'm interpreting you wrongly."

With that, she stood, pivoted and walked away.

I sat immobile for what felt like a year, oblivious to the chatter around me. A young man came over and asked if I was using the chair opposite me. I told him he could have the whole table, I was just leaving. And I did.

I slumped over the steering wheel in my car for quite a while. At first I wanted to defend myself. I was trying to do the right thing, after all. Unlike so many teachers, at least I recognized that our curriculum ignored California Indian perspectives, and I was trying to do something about it. Shouldn't Donna have given me some credit?

But deep down, I had continually questioned my own ability to decolonize my curriculum well, and Donna had confirmed those doubts. Of course Angela didn't recognize what a fraud I was—she had only begun to tune into her own Ute ancestry. Oscar Ortiz, well, he was probably generous with everyone. But Donna had touched a chord that, deep inside me, I knew to be true—I was so thoroughly socialized as a colonizer's descendant that even my attempt to act in a relationship of reciprocity turned out to position me as trying to take knowledge and then take credit.

Chapter Twelve

Another Door

I WALKED THROUGH my front door and threw myself on the couch. I couldn't face anyone, not even Angela or Mr. Jackson.

I should never have tried to pursue the first white child story in the first place. Why didn't I just let it go? Why did I have to track down that information in Steamboat Springs, and then have the gall to think it revealed an injustice I could do something about? I was completely over my head, terribly unsuited to tackling what had happened in the past. I couldn't even rework the basic story in my own lousy curriculum without stepping on Indian toes.

Sean had said I should stick with what I knew. He was right. Forget rewriting social studies and literature—I could snuggle up to my old friend science, my college major. If I were a fake in attempting to challenge colonialism, at least I could explain geological systems and plant phyla with integrity.

I sat up, retrieved my laptop from my bag, and opened the Tomorrow's Curriculum website. Quickly I located the science curriculum development job. The opening was still there.

Within an hour, I had filled out the online application, complete with cover letter and updated curriculum vitae. I hit send. Then I grabbed a spoon and pulled a half-eaten quart of chocolate ice cream from the freezer.

I should have felt relieved, but instead I felt forlorn.

Suddenly my ringtone sounded. Ian! Back from LA, most likely. I answered.

He greeted me, voice chipper. "I'm a few thousand dollars poorer now, but got everything sorted. You survived the first week?"

I tried to match his mood, but my effort felt forced. "Looks like I have a lively class this year. More boys than girls. They'll keep me on my toes."

"I give a mean back massage," he offered.

"That sounds perfect. How's Sunday?" I replied, knowing very well he was thinking of sooner rather than later.

When he didn't reply immediately, I added, "I promised my parents I'd go see them tomorrow to try to mend fences. Sunday didn't work for them. And right now—well, I'm just beat. I wouldn't be good company."

The tone of Ian's voice told me he was disappointed, but we agreed on Sunday afternoon. After he hung up, I berated myself for screwing up this relationship already, before it had even launched itself very far off the ground. Maybe I should call him back and tell him to come right over. But I really was in a terrible mood, and I didn't want to offer him my worst side.

The next morning, as I drove to my parents' house, I reflected on my relationship with Mom. Sean had drawn my attention to how she must have experienced the clash between her own sense of order and the chaos of a newborn. Although she wouldn't have meant to take frustrations out on me, surely that's exactly what happened. But as a baby, I had no way to understand her impatience when I took longer to eat than she wanted or cried for no discernable reason, or her exhaustion when I demanded midnight attention. As I grew up, I feared I didn't quite measure up to what Mom wanted, so I became cautious around her. I worked hard to please her, but didn't relax with her like I did with Dad.

The roadmap we had worked out for dealing with each other wasn't the roadmap we needed now, I realized. I needed to be able to disagree with Mom, to make choices she wouldn't make, within a relationship we both trusted. But that wasn't what we had. How could I reorient our relationship from one of me trying to please her, to one of me being myself without her interpreting that as rejection?

I had no idea how I was going to navigate the next few hours.

When I arrived, I offered to take my parents to lunch, but Mom had already picked up assorted salads and cold cuts from a deli.

"I've got good news and bad news," I said, trying to appear chipper and upbeat. "The bad news, more or less, is that Sean and I split up. We're both good with it, though, and we'll still be friends."

Of course they were surprised. I went on to explain that neither of us had seen our relationship as permanent, and recently I had met someone who might become more central to my life than Sean had been.

"Mom, I know you want grandkids, but as long I stayed with Sean, they weren't going to happen. This doesn't mean Sean is splitting with you, though," I added in an attempt at light-heartedness. "He'll still probably show up at your door now and then. He thinks of you as his substitute parents."

"Is that the good part of your news?" Mom asked cautiously.

"No. The good news is that I've applied for an exciting new job at Sean's company. No guarantees I'll get it, of course, but it suits me well and I have an 'in' on the staff."

Surprise registered on both their faces. "Honey, I thought you liked your current teaching position," Dad finally said.

"I do, but this one offers some amazing opportunities." I summarized the job description, and the contrast between it and my first days back at work. "The thing is, I'd actually get to use my brain," I concluded. "And you know how much I love science. That's what I'd be focusing on. Plus, the pay is better."

Although their facial expressions had warmed as I talked, I had imagined they would be more excited. They appeared to be searching for how to respond. Then Dad put an arm around my shoulder. "If this makes you happy, it makes us happy. But you said you and Sean split up, so how would that work?"

"We're still friends," I said. "He's been trying to get me to apply."

Mom said, "If we don't seem bowled over with enthusiasm, it's because this just seems rather sudden, to us at least. You always sounded so happy working with the children."

"It isn't all that sudden," I said. "Maybe I haven't complained to you about all the testing we have to do, and the directives we get not to stray from the textbooks, but that's been a reality for some time now. Sean mentioned a good month ago that I should look into their new positions. I did that, but had to think about it."

"Well, then maybe this will be a good opportunity," said Dad. "You seemed to get such a kick out of working with kids despite everything else, though. Will you have a chance to do that with this new job?"

"No, at least not like now. I'll probably be able to try out my ideas on kids, but not in the same way of really knowing a class. I mean, if I stopped having contact with kids altogether, whatever I create would lose touch," I said. Which was a good point: Sean never mentioned working directly with kids. This was something I would need to ask about when or if I was invited for an interview.

"I don't have the job yet," I continued. "Who knows, I might not even get a call."

"Does this mean you'll be moving to San Francisco?" Mom asked as though she hadn't heard me.

"I don't know," I said.

"I bet Angela isn't too happy about that prospect," Dad commented.

"I haven't really talked with her about it yet," I said as I recalled her reaction when I mentioned it a few days earlier. She had blanched at the idea of me not only moving away, but also, I suspected, being handed an opportunity other teachers, including her, might want.

"So if you move into San Francisco, what will you do with the house?" Mom asked in a barbed tone. "After all, if it comes from stolen property, as you seem to think, that could be why you'd want to take a job somewhere that would give you reason to unload it."

I was dumbfounded. I had not expected this reaction and wasn't sure what to think. "Mom," I said finally, "Mr. Jackson and I did a lot of work fixing the yard back up after the sewer line repair. I haven't considered getting rid of the house. Look. I never meant to upset you. Maybe I shouldn't have tracked down all that information, but I did, and the story it pointed to has been rough to deal with. But now I'd like to put it behind me and turn over a new leaf. If I get this job, maybe I can do that."

Having briefly considered inviting Ian to accompany me today, I was glad I hadn't. For one thing, how would I have told Mom and Dad I broke up with Sean when Ian didn't know Sean existed? For another, what would he think of me essentially saying that while I was fully aware of descending from the colonizers, I had no intention of learning what decolonization might mean because I didn't want to upset my parents any more than I already had? Or, that because another fourth-grade teacher I didn't even know had told me in so many words that this was work I had no business doing, I had jumped at a way out that an ex-boyfriend suggested?

Come to think of it, what was I going to say to him tomorrow?

The rest of the afternoon, my parents and I seemed to playact our old selves. We tacitly agreed to back off any further mention of land theft. Nor did we discuss the job at Tomorrow's Curriculum any further—particularly since at this point all I had done was submit an application.

Instead, we shared trivialities of our everyday lives and stories from the past, which I realized was one of the main dances we had used over the past few years to weave us together, particularly me and Mom. But I had changed, and maybe they had as well. Now our relationship needed to change. Having no clue what an evolved parent-daughter relationship would look like, however, we doubled down on the routines and conversation topics that had seemed to serve us in the past.

As I drove home, I pondered what I might do to nudge my relationship with them away from its childhood underpinnings and toward something more adult. How could we keep, and even strengthen, our love, but on different terms?

On Sunday morning my alarm blasted me awake. I was surprised I had set it. I should have been sleeping in. As I ascended into a semi-alert fog, I realized the noise was my ringtone, not my alarm.

"Hello?" I mumbled into the phone.

"I'm waking you. I'm sorry, but we need to talk. Can I come over?"

Ian! I bolted upright. "Of course! Give me a few, okay?"

I scrambled into the shower. I thought we had plans for later. Why was he coming over now? As I was pulling on jeans and a sweatshirt, the doorbell rang. Opening the door, I saw Ian holding two cups of Starbucks. He entered, handing me a cup.

"I know I shouldn't be presenting myself this early, Denise, but I hardly slept last night." He sank into a chair. His hair was scruffy as though it hadn't seen a comb since yesterday. Just like mine.

He looked directly at me. "There's something you aren't telling me."

When I started to object, he said, "Just hear me out. The night I spent here with you, while hunting for tissues to wipe my nose, I happened to notice a box of toiletries in the cabinet under the sink. Men's toiletries. I don't expect that you've been living like a nun, so I put it out of my mind. But you've been odd on the phone the past week. That time I called when you had someone on hold, it felt as though you couldn't wait to get me off. You didn't want to see me Friday after I returned from LA and although I have no specific reason to doubt that you spent yesterday with your parents, frankly, I'm not sure if you're telling me the truth.

"That's where I was," I said, sounding lame since everything else he said was true. Why had I not thought to hide Sean's stuff when Ian was in the house?

"I respect your privacy, but I do not tolerate deceit. If you have someone else in your life, just tell me. But don't pretend I'm one thing to you when I'm actually something else."

I set the coffee down. "You're right, I was keeping something from you. I've been wrestling with a huge dilemma, and was afraid if I told you about it, I'd show a side of myself you wouldn't like."

"Try me," he said.

I fortified myself with a gulp of coffee, burning my upper lip in the process. Then I told him all that led up to applying for the job with Tomorrow's Curriculum—my growing frustration with what teaching had become, my alternating between enthusiasm and deep doubt about my ability to decolonize my curriculum, then Donna Reyes's confirmation that I should just stick with science. "Several times I almost picked up the phone to call you, but I was afraid you'd tell me to persist in something I didn't think I could do. Stiff upper lip and all that. But then my financial problems led me to realize I had another option: applying for this other job. I knew you wouldn't think it was a good idea, but I figured it could help me pay my bills and might even help me calm the waters with my parents."

He was leaning back, arms folded across his chest, brow furrowed. "So how did you identify this job in the first place?" he asked. "I had no idea you were even looking."

"An ex-boyfriend told me about it. He works there," I replied.

Ian's eyebrows rose. "An ex-boyfriend? Not the owner of said toiletries, I hope?"

"We're just friends now. I had been seeing him when I met you, but realized the relationship wasn't going anywhere. So we mutually agreed to break it off," I said as my palms sweated.

"You had been seeing this bloke when we met, but this is the first I'm hearing about it? Denise, I know you had a life before me, I wouldn't expect that you didn't. But it would seem relevant that you'd at least mention you were seeing someone. You certainly had the opportunity. You broke up when?"

"Ah, about four days ago." I felt horrible admitting it. "Ian, he's history. That relationship didn't have legs, it wasn't going anywhere. He's a friend, and he helped me with some of my problems, but when you and I started seeing each other, everything missing from that relationship became obvious to me."

"But it isn't exactly over, not if you're planning to work with this chap." Ian's voice chilled.

"Not work *with* him," I said defensively. "He had told me his company was expanding, and when I decided to see what he was talking about, what kinds of job openings they had, well, I found one that sounded so much like me that I decided to give it a try."

"And this company is located where?"

I rubbed my neck. How did he have such an uncanny ability to zoom right in on things I didn't want to tell him? "It's headquartered in San Francisco. But so much of the work is online that I could probably do it from here. I'd be creating on-line curriculum modules that connect science with literacy, and that could be used in different countries around the world." I knew I sounded defensive.

"That sounds like the kind of global colonizing curriculum Robinson-Woodrich is into," he muttered.

I looked down. My face must have gone crimson because he stared at me. Then he stood and pulled his keys from his pocket.

"You're going to work for bloody Robinson-Woodrich, aren't you? That's what this is about."

"I'm just looking into it as an option. I haven't even had an interview. Besides, I'd be creating science curricula, not—not call center prep crap." I knew my reply missed his point, but I had to clarify that my bags weren't packed. Yet. And that subsuming local knowledge under U.S. knowledge isn't a form of colonization. Or maybe it is, but I'd rather not think of it that way right now.

"Denise, I thought we might have a future together, but it seems I'm wrong," he said. "What I'm having trouble with is reconciling the passionate and socially-conscious woman I had come to know with this—this secretive, or dishonest, I'm not sure which—this coward."

I shot back, "Well, that's what I thought about you for a while this summer, when at first you were really open to me, and then you shut the door on me."

He looked surprised. "Yes, alright, but I've told you what was going on with me. You know the story. It's different."

"Maybe. Maybe not; I'd need to think about that. But now you know my story. Ian, you need to understand that Sean and I are a thing of the past, whatever does or doesn't happen between you and me. And I wish you could appreciate how scared I've been about not measuring up, about jumping into something that's way over my head, and then stepping on people without realizing it." The dam holding back my emotions broke, and I began to sob.

Ian finally said softly, "Denise, I can't help you figure out what you want. That's something you need to do for yourself. When you figure that out, then let's talk. Okay?"

I nodded, wiping my eyes.

Ian stood, walked to the door, and left. I felt as though I had just lost everything.

Chapter Thirteen

Like Daenerys Targaryen and Julian Bond

OVER THE FOLLOWING week I channeled my energy into teaching. God knows I needed something other than my own problems to preoccupy me. Having lost Ian hurt too much to think about. And I felt small for having compromised my values. I even avoided Angela, which was so unusual she knew something was wrong.

"I need to take a rain check on dinner Friday," I said when she called Thursday evening.

"Big weekend plans with Ian?" she asked. I could picture a knowing look on her face.

"No. I, uh, I just need some time to myself."

The line was silent for a moment. "You sound bad, girlfriend. What's up?"

"Everything went sideways, Angela." I felt tears forming. "I've disappointed Ian. I think I've disappointed my parents too. I'm not sure. Mostly, I've disappointed myself. I just need to sort things out."

"I'm a good listener, if that would help."

"I know you are," I said. "Right now, I mostly need to listen to myself. I know you're there for me. That means a lot. As soon as I'm ready to talk to someone, you'll be the first to know."

"Just holler, okay? By the way, don't forget that next weekend is Labor Day and I'll be in Colorado visiting my grandmother. I'll still have my phone though," she said.

"Okay. I love you, Angela," I said.

That conversation had been a week ago. Now, as I was packing up papers and books to take home for the long weekend, my phone rang. Not recognizing the number, I considered not answering, but then again, it could be important. If it was a telemarketer, I'd just end the call.

"Is this Denise Fisher?" asked a female voice I didn't recognize.

"Yes, it is," I replied.

"Ms. Fisher, this is Alexandra Mayo from Tomorrow's Curriculum. I'm calling because we are very impressed with your qualifications for the position you applied for, and would like to set up an interview with you here at our San Francisco headquarters," she said.

"Oh!" I exclaimed. I hadn't given the job much thought all week. I tried to gather my wits as I said, "Gee, that's wonderful. I, ah, I'm teaching Monday through Friday, except next Monday of course, which is a holiday—"

"Yes, of course," Alexandra said. "We were wondering if you might be available Saturday a week from tomorrow, say around 1:00 p.m."

"Yes," I said. "I can do that."

"Good. I'll follow up with an email confirming the exact time and location of your interview. This will give you an opportunity to tour our facility, if you haven't been here before," she said.

"Great. Thank you," I replied.

"You're welcome. We look forward to meeting you." With that, she hung up.

I stared at my phone. Suddenly the prospect of leaving teaching and taking a job with Tomorrow's Curriculum—and Robinson-Woodrich—was no longer hypothetical. As I pictured myself working there, I visualized a door. Was it opening or slamming shut?

As I drove home, my brain seemed to shut down as though it had fallen from my head into a swamp. I should be sorting out my problems, coming up with a plan, setting priorities. But everything in my life felt discombobulated. Thoughts refused to string themselves together. I could concentrate on how my kids had done on a math quiz, but could not sustain two seconds thinking of my parents, Ian, Angela, my house, or even what I wanted to be doing a week from now.

I took out a frozen pizza, popped it into the microwave, logged into Netflix, and started series one of *Game of Thrones*. I had watched about half the episodes since the series started four years earlier, but hadn't systematically experienced them in order. So I reasoned this would be a great way to spend Labor Day weekend.

For the next two days, I was not Denise Fisher. I imagined myself as the beautiful exile Daenerys Targaryen, who starts out timid as a little brown rabbit, but eventually leads an army into battle. I fantasized about my blond hair growing long enough to braid like hers. I imagined myself perched atop a horse or playing with baby dragons. I projected myself into her love affairs and her quest to be queen.

Sunday afternoon I ran into Mr. Jackson while I was going out to retrieve the previous day's mail. He was wearing a suit and seemed to be returning from something.

"Church," he replied to my query. "Then a short meeting to finalize preparations for an event memorializing Julian Bond." He peered at me. "You do know who he was, don't you?"

Although several news shows over the previous couple of weeks had dedicated stories to Bond's life and death, I had barely noticed them and couldn't say I knew much about him. I had heard of him, but that was it. "I know he was a long time civil rights activist," I replied. "He did something with the NAACP, didn't he?"

"Oh, yes. Julian Bond was national chair for about a dozen years." I felt silly. I should have known that. Mr. Jackson continued, "That's where I met him, at one of the national conferences. But even earlier, I can still clearly recall hearing him speak back when I was about twenty, still green behind the ears. I had been out in the streets with everyone else protesting housing discrimination, when we heard about this fiery young legislator from Georgia who had helped found the Student Nonviolent Coordinating Committee. He was coming to speak on one of the local college campuses. It was open to the public, so a bunch of us crowded into a VW bus and went. He's probably the main reason I didn't give up the struggle back then."

I didn't know Mr. Jackson had been active in protests, but then why would I think otherwise? I asked, "Like today's Black Lives Matter?"

He cocked his head and smiled. "Different times, but something like that, yes. Anyway, Bond was a giant among giants. He had a backbone of steel and was never afraid to fight for what he believed in. But he was also a gentleman. One-on-one, he was soft-spoken and seemed to actually listen to whomever he was talking with. He didn't act like he thought he was more important than anyone else. You ought to come to this event we're planning."

I realized Mr. Jackson could have been describing himself—kind and courteous, but also tough with a clear moral direction. A little bit like Daenerys Targaryen, whose character I had inhabited vicariously the past couple of days.

"Ummm, can I talk to you for a few minutes?" I asked.

"Yes, of course. Come on inside." He unlocked the door and ushered me in, then said, "You look a little peaked. Is something wrong?"

I slumped down into a chair. "Everything is wrong," I mumbled. "It all started when I realized where much of the money came from that Gram used to buy her—now my—house." To Mr. Jackson's puzzled expression, I added, "I've already told you about that, I know."

"And this has been weighing on you, hasn't it?" he asked.

Up until that very moment, I had not verbalized, even to myself, how difficult it was to reconcile living my life as I always had, with the knowledge that I was living it on stolen land, in a house purchased via stolen land. And how hard it was to reconcile my love for my family with their ongoing acceptance of that theft. I could think about other related things—the glorification of missions in my fourth-grade curriculum, Oscar Ortiz's wonderful collection of books, Mrs. Walker's work with youth at the Indian Center in Steamboat Springs—but I had been avoiding naming that central contradiction in my own life.

I replied. "What weighs on me is that I wouldn't have the house if the Utes' land hadn't been stolen. And the Ohlones' land, too, for that matter. If you don't know that what you have was stolen, well, you live in a kind of moral oblivion. But when you do know and you don't do anything about it, then yeah, it eats away at you. See, starting with the class I took this summer, I've been trying to make my social studies curriculum less from the colonizers' point of view and more from the California Indians' point of view, but I haven't done that with my own life. I mean, I'm trying to reframe how my students think while I continue to come home to stolen property every day. Does that make sense?"

"Yes, it does; it makes a lot of sense," he replied.

"And so rather than charging into battle to do what I know in my heart is right, I've been waffling and dodging, worrying about my parents' feelings, worrying about whether I'm suited for this work, worrying about my bills."

"Now you're losing me," he said as I paused. "Let's go back to charging into battle?"

"I've been watching *Game of Thrones*," I said with a tiny laugh. "I've been imagining I was one of the heroines, Daenerys, who goes from being this quiet little don't-rock-the-boat nobody, to a warrior, literally, for what is right."

"I see." He nodded as his face communicated that he had never watched *Game of Thrones* and could not visualize who I was talking about.

"Well, the thing is," I continued, "I know what's right, I know what I should do, but I've been afraid to face that."

"And what would that be?" he asked sounding unclear about where I was going.

"I should sell my house and give back what was stolen. I can't give the land my ancestors took back to the Utes—it was sold generations ago. But I can give back proceeds from that sale. The thing is—where would I live?" As I said this, I realized that the main reason I had never seriously considered returning stolen property was that I couldn't visualize "what then."

Mr. Jackson leaned back in his chair as he regarded me. "You have a lot of courage, Denise. I truly didn't anticipate this was where your thinking would lead you."

"Well, it did lead me there. It would be the right thing to do. But if I just give away the whole house, what do I do, pitch a tent in your yard?"

For some reason, that image struck me as funny and I laughed. Mr. Jackson joined in my laughter. Then he mused, "Between the sale of the land in Colorado and your grandmother buying this house, then giving it to you, I suspect other sources of funds have become comingled with those derived from the land. Now, it's true that if you study the roots of those other funds, you'll probably find more land stolen from other tribes, and maybe even some slave labor. But you probably won't be able to trace all that in enough detail to parse it out, and in any case, I suspect no one wants to leave you destitute."

I heard Ian quote his Māori friend saying, "No one's gonna chuck your mum out into the motorway." I thought about the money I was putting into fixing the sewer pipe. My grandparents had spent money over the years fixing one thing or another. And Gram had probably also inherited something from her father, even if it wasn't the amount she had inherited from her mother. There was no way I could completely untangle where everything that went into the house had come from.

"So—?" What was he getting at?

"What I'm suggesting is that if you sell the house—a very bold move, I must say—then keep enough for yourself to get a toehold in the housing market. And you'll want to get your loans paid off," he said. "You might decide to rent, or you might buy yourself a small condo, using a little bit of the sale of the house as a down payment."

I must have looked confused. He studied my face, then said, "Denise, you can give the entire proceeds from selling the house to the Ute Nation, but at least pay off your own repair bills first."

He had a good point. I would need to give some thought to the multiple sources of funds that had gone into the house over the years, without diminishing how Gram paid for it in the first place.

The thought of selling the house brought to mind my impending job interview. My stomach clenched. "So here's another problem," I said, telling him about the job at Tomorrow's Curriculum and why I had applied in the first place.

Mr. Jackson frowned. "Is this a job you want? Something you'd be running to, rather than using to run away from something else?"

As soon as he said that, I knew it would serve mainly as an escape from other problems. Ever since Alexandra Mayo's call on Friday, I had avoided thinking about the job. It felt more like a beam about to crash down on my head than a warm embrace.

"Denise," Mr. Jackson said, "if this job was right for you, you'd be excited about it. You'd be telling me all about it. The fact that you aren't doing that speaks volumes."

I nodded.

"One more thing," he continued. "I'm not a teacher, so I can't claim to know exactly how things are done in your profession. But you mentioned that your administrators won't let teachers be creative with their curriculum. Is that true? Even if you are meeting their expectations and your students are learning what's expected?"

"That's the message they keep giving us," I said.

"Let's go back to this—what was the name of that heroine of yours on TV?"

"You mean Daenerys?" I asked.

"Yes. How would she respond in your situation?"

I blinked. "I have no idea—" I began. I visualized her riding into my classroom on her horse, baby dragon in one arm. But she was not thoughtlessly defiant. She was simply strong and self-assured in pursuit of what she knew was right.

"I think she would honor the expectations of her that she saw as legitimate and wise, but refuse those she saw as unwise. And she'd try to explain herself as clearly as she could," I said. "But I don't have dragons to back me up."

Mr. Jackson laughed. "Neither did Julian Bond. But he had the strength of his convictions, and the ability to speak eloquently for what he believed in."

"I can't speak eloquently," I objected.

"You'll learn," he replied. "As for your parents, Denise, you may make choices they never understand. But make sure they know you love them, while also loving yourself well enough to stand on your values."

I didn't know what to say, so I walked over to him and threw my arms around him. "Thank you, Mr. Jackson," I said.

He hugged me back, then disengaged himself as he reached into his jacket pocket. He pulled out an envelope, and extricated two tickets from it.

"For our Julian Bond event," he said.

I was surprised. "How much?" I asked.

"My gift. I want you to come, and I want you to learn about this man. Knowing something about him may help you down your own road," he said.

As I took the tickets, I knew that the person I most wanted to bring with me was Ian. If Ian would even talk to me.

I ran home, opened my laptop, and started brainstorming:

Student loan: about $42,000 left to pay. Car: almost $6,000 left. Sewer repair bill: $10,000 left. Cost of fixing the roof and other things?

I hadn't tackled those yet, so I didn't know what the expenses would be.

Some condos nearby were listed at $330,000. Would a $50,000 down payment be enough? Houses like mine—probably with major repairs done—were selling for twice that. So if I sold this place and paid my creditors . . .

I was staring at my attempt to sketch out a financial plan when my phone rang. Angela.

"Are you back?" I greeted her.

"Yes, and I can't wait to tell you what my grandmother and I came up with. Okay if I come over?" Her words tumbled out like excited puppies.

A few minutes later, as she slid into the chair next to me, Angela's face danced.

"What's up?" I asked. "You look like you just got tickets to see Taylor Swift."

"Well, you know how we were trying to figure out who to collaborate with on our work to indigenize our curriculum."

Was *indigenize* a word? I supposed it must be. I put my hand up. "Angela, I'm out. I had the most discouraging—"

"Huh? Let me finish." She grabbed my hand. "I told Grandmother what we're working on. While I talked on and on, she just listened with this funny look on her face. When I paused to get my breath, she told me she had just returned from the rez in Utah. While she was there, she talked with a few teachers at this cool elementary school where her two great-grandchildren go—kids of cousins I haven't even met yet. Honestly, Denise, I can't wait to go there with her and meet my relatives! I've got an uncle, an aunt, and some cousins, and what would you call their kids? Anyway, that's what we're doing when I visit over Christmas. I hope—"

"Angela," I broke in. "Slow down, get to the point. So your grandmother told you about your relatives on the reservation, is that what you came to tell me about?"

"No. Sorry, I got carried away." She took a deep breath. "Okay . . . This elementary school has pretty much the same textbooks we use, but they're working with someone from the university and one or two community elders to develop more Indian curriculum. They have this old supplement about Utes called *Earth People* that was put together over twenty years ago, and it has a lot of good information teachers can use, but it's dated. And you can't just fold it into all the subject areas. None of the teachers are Indian, either, but they want to integrate more Ute knowledge into their classrooms. And they also want to bring in knowledge from other tribes."

I nodded, trying to figure out where she was going.

"Well, Grandmother's idea is that we collaborate with them, maybe adding a few teachers from here. You know, a California–Utah partnership. One of the older teachers at that school loves the idea. We could start off meeting by Skype or something, and then share plans by email or even work jointly on Google docs. As soon as we can afford airfare we can go visit, maybe around New Year before school starts up again." Angela's eyes sparkled. I hated to rub off the shine, but I had to.

"That sounds like a wonderful thing for you to get involved with." I measured my words. "But I don't think I'll be joining you."

"What? Why not?"

I sighed. "Well, mainly because I can't do this kind of work. I simply don't have the background. I've never even taken an American Indian studies course. I have no authenticity with Indian people. I'm a fake, Angela. I didn't tell you yet about my meeting with Donna Reyes who teaches fourth at Libertad. This was a week ago, a little more than. She's Indian, and in the space of less than ten minutes, she called me out. She could tell I haven't studied American Indian history and I know hardly any Indian people. When I naively suggested we share curriculum units, she scoffed. She said white people have already taken too much from Indian people, and I certainly don't have anything she might want. Deep down, I know she's right. I should never have tried to take this on in the first place."

"And you didn't say anything about this to me? I knew something was eating at you." Angela's face looked as though I had blindsided her. I suppose I had.

"I know you don't see me that way, and you'd try to out-argue everything she said. But I needed to let the truth sink in for a while. And so I realized I should just stick with what I know best, which is science."

"That's garbage," she said.

"So then I applied for a job at Tomorrow's Curriculum. It looked pretty interesting, actually. And it pays well. Well, then they called me for an interview. I'm supposed to go to their offices in San Francisco this next Saturday."

Angela's jaw dropped. "No! No, no, no! You can't be saying this."

I grabbed both of her hands. "Angela, you knew all along I wasn't sure what I was doing. It wasn't at all clear to me what to do about the fact that I descend from your grandmother's colonizers. I thought maybe I could tackle how we teach the next generations about White–Indian relationships, but how can I do that when I don't have the knowledge, and you're the only Indian person I know well, and you aren't . . . you're—"

"I'm not Indian enough?" She wrenched her hands free. "Who are you to say who is Indian and who isn't? And how can you think of just running away?"

"Hold on. I'm canceling the job interview. I realized working for Tomorrow's Curriculum would be running away from the teaching I love," I said.

"Then what?" Angela said, plainly angry. "You're staying but decided to keep teaching the colonial curriculum because of this Donna person? You're shitting me. I don't even know her. I can't believe you're taking her more seriously than you take me."

"It's like . . ." I tried to think of the right words. "She spoke to what I already feared was the truth."

"Well, she's wrong, and my grandmother thinks so, too." Angela pulled her cell phone from her bag and dialed a number. Suddenly her face brightened. "Hi, Grandma. I'm sitting here with Denise." She paused. "Yeah, truly. Well, we were talking about that, but Denise doesn't think she's capable of working with the school." She glared at me. "Yeah, that's right. Apparently, some Indian teacher here gave her an earful about how white people can't do this work, and it shook her up badly." Pause. "Okay."

Angela handed me her phone. "She wants to talk with you."

I hesitated, then took the phone. "Hello, Mrs. Walker."

"Denise, I understand you had an uncomfortable conversation with one of our young teachers," Mrs. Walker said. "Can you tell me about it?"

"Okay, although I don't know what good that will do. My principal suggested I talk with this fourth-grade teacher she had met who's Indian. So I contacted her and she agreed to meet me, but I'm not sure why. She really didn't seem to want to talk with me." The words just tumbled out as I explained what had happened. "But she was right that I don't know what I'm doing, and I probably don't have any right to presume to speak for Indian people at all."

When Angela handed me a tissue, I realized tears had begun to stream down my face.

Mrs. Walker said, "Let me give a different perspective, then you can decide for yourself what to do. I haven't met this Donna Reyes, of course, but I have met many young people your story reminds me of. Something you should remember is that our people are still dealing with generations of trauma. It affects us in widely differing ways. There used to be a young Arapahoe working here at the Indian Center. His name was Victor. He was brilliant, one of the smartest young people I ever met. He knew Arapahoe history in such detail that he could have written a book about it. Maybe by now he has. But he felt the wounds from that history as though each was freshly inflicted on him every day. And I supposed in a sense they were. As I say, different people deal with trauma in different ways. In his case, he could not trust white people at all. He didn't stay with the Indian Center very long because we have to interface with white institutions. I don't know where Victor is now. But I thought about him as you described your conversation with Donna."

"Okay," I said, "but that doesn't mean she isn't right."

"Let's take one of the things she said, your lack of background knowledge. That's true. But I also know you've been reading a lot because Angela has told me about this. Would taking a university course in Indian history benefit you?"

"Well, yes," I said.

"And are there such courses at one of the universities near you?" she asked.

"I suppose. I haven't looked yet," I replied.

"Well. You should look into it. Perhaps you and my granddaughter can sign up for one together. She needs to build her knowledge, too. With respect to who you are collaborating with, Angela has told you about my idea. Now to the matter of why you would be doing this kind of work. Denise, in the short time I spent in your company, I was impressed by your willingness to listen. When I was telling you some of my stories, you didn't argue with me like some people do, and you didn't try to coat them over with sugar. You let me speak and you listened with respect. In my mind, that ability is essential to reconstructing relationships between Indian people and non-Indian people. You are open to learning. Even the questions you are asking right now about whether you have any right to work with us tell me that you are someone I can work with, and someone the teachers in the school I have in mind can work with. Do you hear what I'm saying?"

I nodded, but was so overcome that I couldn't reply. Angela gently took the phone from my hand as she gave me a tissue.

"Thank you, Grandma," she said softly. "Denise will speak with you later, but right now she's digesting the impact of your generosity." They exchanged a few more words, then hung up.

Angela wrapped her arms around me and let me cry into her shoulder. "I'm getting you all wet," I finally said.

"That's what sisters are for," she replied.

I looked into her face. "That's the first time you've called me your sister."

"Yeah," she said. "I always blew it off when you'd refer to me that way partly 'cause you didn't seem to recognize privileges you have that I don't have, but also because I don't even get along with the sister I'm actually related to. So the whole idea didn't seem worth much. But over the past couple of months, I've watched you take on something that means a lot to me, and in a way I respect. I even respect your doubts about yourself, which tell me you recognize how your privilege gets in the way."

"Thank you," I said as I grabbed her hand. "Speaking of privileges, I need to tell you something else I'm thinking about," I said.

"Another bombshell?"

"Probably. You know how this house was bought from money derived from selling stolen land. I should return what was stolen, don't you think?"

"The land?" she blinked.

"No, I don't have the land. I mean the money that came from it. I can sell the house and give back some portion of what it sells for. I'm trying to figure out what portion makes sense."

"You'd do that?" Angela breathed. "I'm blown away."

"Well, I'm thinking in that direction. But I have no idea how that would work. The only person I know who's a member of the tribe is your grandmother. I assume she's a member," I added.

"She is. And you'd sell this place?"

"I'm considering it," I replied. "Look, Angela. This house is the most tangible benefit I have from my family's history of colonization, and look at what it's doing to me. It's eating up my finances, it's pushing me into making decisions I wouldn't make otherwise, and it's corroding me from the inside. If the land hadn't been stolen and then sold, I wouldn't be in this state."

"But isn't this house also the most tangible reminder of your grandmother?"

I thought a moment. "No. Gram left me her love, wrapped up in some of my very best childhood memories. I don't need bricks and mortar to remember her. I believe she thought leaving me her house was an act of love, and I did too, but neither of us realized what a weight it would become. Stolen property is stolen property, even when it's several generations later."

"Wow," she breathed, "where would you live?"

"In an apartment, like you. Or, there's a bunch of condos around here and I could probably afford a down payment. That's what I was figuring out when you arrived."

Angela looked at my computer screen. "I'm truly in awe. This sounds so generous."

I shrugged. "I don't think of giving back what was stolen as generous. I just think of it as the right thing to do."

We sat in silence. I heard the refrigerator start to hum, and wondered when it would break down and need replacing.

"Can I switch topics?" she asked, a playful grin sliding across her face.

"Sure, what?"

"Well," she said as though about to make a big announcement. "Do you remember Dr. James Oatman?"

"Of course."

"We've been communicating, and he's invited me to go to an event blessing a piece of Miwok ancestral land up in Marin County. It isn't an actual date, there will be a whole bunch of other Indian people there." But by the way her eyes danced, I suspected this was, if not a date, then a prelude to one.

I raised my eyebrows and she continued. "Over email, he asked a little bit about my background. When he found out I'm part Ute, grew up as a white Californian, and have been learning about the Ute side of me through my grandmother, he started sharing some of his own background, which isn't all Miwok, like people usually think. By then we were talking on the phone. I asked how he got into the work he's doing now, and he told me quite a lot about how he grew up hearing things from elders that seemed to make more sense than what white people said. This morning, he invited me to the event next Saturday."

"Cool." I wasn't sure what to say, since Angela's love life had been a series of disasters as long as I had known her.

"I know what you're thinking, Denise," she said. "This relationship may or may not go beyond friendship, but do you know what? It doesn't matter. As I'm getting to know Jim—" Jim? It was Dr. Oatman a minute ago—"I'm realizing something about myself. All these years, I've been selling myself short, Denise. I've been grabbing at guys, worrying about my biological clock running out, without thinking about who I am and what I actually want. I've realized Jim is the kind of person I could enjoy spending time with, whether romantic or not, because he's smart, he's well-grounded, and he knows himself. That's probably the biggest thing. He isn't out there chasing ladies; he has other, more worthwhile things to do. And do you know what? I also have worthwhile things to do that don't require a man, but things someone like Jim actually finds interesting."

She cocked her head, eyes searching mine for clues that she was making sense. I said, "You mean, like, you had been binging on fast food for years, then happened to have a great home-cooked meal, and now wonder what you saw in fast food? Like that?"

Food analogies seemed to work with us. Angela laughed. "Yeah, I guess like that."

I grabbed her shoulders. "Angela, I've always known you had a lot more going for you than you seemed to think. I guess if it took Jim to knock some sense into your head, then more power to him."

"I know you thought that," she said. "The problem is how I relate to men. I mean, I didn't seem to think, deep down, that I had that much to offer that a guy might find interesting. The fact that Jim finds me interesting changes everything. Regardless of what does or doesn't develop between us, he's given me a different mirror in which to see myself."

Ian's face flashed into my head. Dear Ian, who I'd been hiding things from, who now believed he could not trust me.

I had to be able to offer Ian more than words. I knew what I needed to do.

⍩⍩⍩

THE NEXT MORNING while my students were out having music I dialed the phone number for Paul Rodriguez, a realtor Mr. Jackson had recommended. I was being routed into his voicemail when he picked up the phone. I introduced myself, told him I was looking for a realtor to help me sell my house, and dropped Mr. Jackson's name.

"William Jackson!" Paul exclaimed. "A fine human being if there ever was one. We served together on the board of the Boys and Girls Club years ago, and have stayed in touch. So you're his neighbor."

"Yes," I replied. "And I hope to stay that way, but in a condo that's smaller and less complicated than this house my grandmother willed me before she died."

"Great. I'd like to come meet you at the house so I can take a look at it. I can squeeze you in around five this afternoon; I just had a cancelation. Otherwise we're looking at next week, maybe Wednesday or Thursday."

I told him five would be perfect, and gave him my address.

He arrived promptly. As I ushered him inside, I was struck by something in his manner that reminded me of Mr. Jackson. They looked nothing alike—while Mr. Jackson was thin and wiry, Paul Rodriquez resembled the Pillsbury Doughboy, and while Mr. Jackson had a full head of salt-and-pepper hair, his was thin, receding, and grey. Maybe the resemblance was in his warm smile and self-assured bearing. Since I had never worked with a realtor before, he patiently explained the process to me, from appraisal to closing costs.

By the time he left, I felt as though I had turned a corner. I was no longer debating with myself about whether to sell the house, whether to return what had been stolen from the Utes, or even whether to remain a teacher. My main concerns now were reconciling with Ian and helping my parents come to terms with my actions.

I punched in Ian's phone number. As it rang, I wondered if he would avoid my call.

He didn't. "Denise," he said. A statement, not really a greeting.

"When we last spoke, you said we could talk when I get my priorities figured out," I plunged in. "Well, I've been doing a lot of work and I know where I'm going now."

Silence.

"Tomorrow's Curriculum called for a job interview, but I canceled it. I had been distraught when I applied. But it isn't what I actually want, so I canceled."

More silence. "Ian, are you still there?"

"I'm listening," he replied. He wasn't going to make this easy for me.

"Okay. I'm going to keep teaching, and I'm also going to keep learning new relationships between the Indigenous people and the colonizers, even if I'm a newbie at it. Angela's grandmother not only told me she believes in me, but she's also setting up a collaboration between me and Angela and maybe a couple more teachers from here, and teachers at the school on the rez where her great-grandkids go. But since neither of us has ever really studied American Indian anything, we signed up for an evening course that starts in a couple weeks. When I saw how much my curriculum favors the colonizers and how important what we teach is to how next generations view the world, I thought I needed to fix everything right away. And when I realized I don't have the knowledge to do that, I gave up. Which didn't solve anything. You got me started on a long-term learning process I've realized I need to stick with."

"I'm glad to hear that," he said.

When he didn't elaborate, I continued. "The other thing is that I'm putting this house up for sale, and plan to give the proceeds back to the Ute Nation."

He made a whistling sound. "I didn't think you'd go that far."

"Yeah, well, what I realized is when white people like me actually think about what our ancestors took from the Indian nations, we either blow it off or wallow in guilt. Since I tracked down enough documentation to have a pretty clear idea who took what from whom, I was dealing with more guilt than I admitted to myself. I tried to rationalize that it would be enough to teach the next generations to respect Indian nations' sovereignty and land, and maybe eventually better policies would emerge. And that kind of teaching is something I need to do; it's important. But I'm still sitting here, hanging on to what rightfully isn't mine." I paused. "You're awfully quiet, are you still there?"

"I'm still here, Denise."

"Okay. You see, I was afraid I'd lose everything. Here I am, sitting on the homelands of the Ohlone, in a house paid for by the Utes, at least partially. I was afraid dealing with that would put me out in the street. But then I remembered your friend telling you, 'No one's gonna chuck your mum out into the motorway.' And Mr. Jackson pointed out that even if the basis for buying Gram's house was cashing in on stolen Ute land, other things have gone into it as well, including my own twelve thousand bucks fixing the sewer line. I'll probably never be able to untangle exactly how much of the house came from what sources. But a reasonable estimate I can live with is two-thirds of what I sell it for going back to the people who I know my ancestors stole from, even if they didn't exactly know that's what they were doing."

"You have been doing some serious work," he said. "Where's your ex-boyfriend in all of this?"

That stopped me in my tracks. "Sean?" I asked, puzzled. "Nowhere. I haven't talked to him since we split up. Why?"

"Just checking. Not that long ago, he was in the picture but you were keeping that fact to yourself, so I need to ask."

"Ian, Sean is history, although he is a nice guy and one of these days you might meet him. But my secrets from you are history, too. No more of those."

"That's what I needed to know. Want me to come over?"

Warmth shot through my body. "Yes, I do, very much."

Later, while Ian was in the shower, I summoned Gram. I wanted to make sure she understood why I could not keep her house. I picked up her perfume atomizer. If I needed any object to symbolize her, this piece of glass, still carrying a hint of Shalimar, was it.

"Gram, I know you had no idea of the stress your house would create for me, nor the temptations it would present. But if you were standing in the shoes I inhabit right now, I think you'd make the same decision." Indeed, Gram had been more practical than sentimental. She had tried to live life honestly, as best she could, and she had always valued relationships with people over things.

"I also need to thank you for telling me that white child story," I continued. "Family stories passed down become distorted along the way. But in passing yours on to me, you prompted me to uncover a much more profound story about this country, and about my opportunity to help right some wrongs. We've been like the iceplant Mr. Jackson uproots. But I'm learning we don't have to be invasive or predatory. You always believed in me, Gram, and your belief gives me strength to move forward."

Actually, it was three elders—Gram, Mrs. Walker, and Mr. Jackson— helping me move forward. I whispered another thanks to all three.

I replaced the atomizer on the dresser as I heard the shower shut off. Then I dove into bed to wait for Ian.

I SLEPT POORLY the following Friday night despite Ian's soothing presence. I obsessed over my relationship with my parents, whom we would be visiting the next day. How could I learn to stand my ground with them without looking for agreement, but also without sacrificing our relationship? They too seemed to be struggling, although in their case, it was to make sense of their increasingly assertive only child.

Just two days earlier, when I talked to Mom about visiting them this weekend, her voice had sounded tentative.

"Yes, of course you can come, we'll be here." Then with reference to Ian, "What did you say his name was, again?"

I told her.

"Ian," she repeated. "Yes, of course. And you met him at the university, you said?"

"Yes. He's a guest professor there."

"Well, bring him along. By the way, did you get that job working with Sean?" she asked. "You weren't sure if they'd call you when you were here a couple of weeks ago." I pictured her trying to figure out how Ian would deal with me working with my ex in San Francisco.

"No," I said. "I decided that job wasn't for me. I'll be staying right where I've been, teaching at Milford."

"Oh. Well, maybe another opportunity will come up," she said.

I didn't pursue that. Maybe she imagined me moving up into the corporate world, or into school administration. Maybe my complaints about teaching led her to believe I was trying to escape. And for a time, she would have been right.

Saturday morning as we drove, I wrestled out loud with my struggle to reconcile my relationship with my parents with my conviction that my family's welfare rests on historical injustices. I told Ian about the Colorado records I brought along and the strategy I intended to use with my folks: I would present them with my paper trail and invite them to make sense of it for themselves.

"How do you think they'll react?" he asked. "I don't know them, but that doesn't sound like a great idea."

"Maybe they'll at least see where I'm coming from. That's the hope. At least your parents might have anticipated your critique of the ancestors and not blown a gasket like mine did," I said.

"I wouldn't put it quite like that," he replied. "But our Waitangi Tribunal has been in operation for about forty years and periodically issues reports, so a lot of New Zealanders are at least aware of it. Here, you've got violations against heaps of treaties with heaps of different tribes, and almost no consciousness about any of it among the average non-Indian American."

"True."

206

"But even with the Waitangi Treaty, when I approached Mum and Dad with my newly found consciousness about our colonizer history, well, at first it was like I had suddenly switched sides. It was only later, after my revisionist interpretation settled in, that they had this other public discourse about land claims that backed me up. They hadn't paid much attention to it, but it was there."

I sighed. I already knew my parents knew nothing about the Utes and probably couldn't name five California tribes, including the one closest to their home. To them, Miwok—Miwok Village, actually—is a cute little town in the Sierras. The fact that over three thousand Miwok people still live in California, and Mom and Dad have probably spoken with some of them without realizing it—well, that would come as a surprise.

Ian continued. "My parents also know quite a number of Māori people. Some of our neighbors when I was growing up were Māori, Māori kids went to the schools I attended, a couple of clerks in stores we patronized were Māori. I think it was easier for Mum and Dad to put a human face on treaty claims than I sense is the case here. That doesn't mean they didn't give me plenty of grief. They did, but they couldn't deny what I was saying. As I said, what I think bothered them most was that I had switched sides."

I wondered why this issue had to be a matter of which side you were on. Or, rather, whose side. I thought about what it meant to grow up learning to see everything in terms of good guys and bad guys. That was certainly how superhero and space alien movies portrayed the world. What if I were to join the Megatron in the *Transformers* movies? As the bad guy, he was always portrayed as a destructive monster, but what if he was actually just defending himself?

"They'll surely have a cow when I tell them I'm not only selling Gram's house, but turning over a big chunk of the proceeds to the Ute Nation," I said. "Last time I was here I assured them I wasn't planning on selling it, and now here I am with a different story. They'll probably think I've flipped out. I just hope they don't attribute any of that to your nefarious influence." I reached for his hand and squeezed it.

"We Kiwis are notorious for corrupting innocent damsels," he joked. I didn't mention the fact that my parents might think exactly that. Good chance they would blame him for converting me to an un-American way of looking at the world. They might even blame him for luring me away from Sean over the summer.

I slowed the car. "The blue one's my parents' house," I pointed out as I parked at the curb. "I grew up there," I added, reflecting on not having regarded the place as home for years.

Whatever suspicions Mom and Dad harbored about Ian, they kept to themselves as they dutifully rolled out the welcome mat. In addition, Ian's accent and relaxed manner seemed to charm Mom. After introductions, she quizzed him about why he was in the U.S., why he left New Zealand, what New Zealand is like—it felt to me like an interrogation, but he rode right along with it.

"Such a beautiful country, I understand," Mom gushed. "I saw *Lord of the Rings* three times." It was probably the only movie she had seen in a couple of years. Besides, the movie was pure fantasy, and most of New Zealand isn't like that, at least as far as I knew.

"Mom—" I began. But Ian touched my arm to snuff out my reply.

"New Zealanders love *Lord of the Rings*," he said. "Course, we don't see many hobbits running around, but a lot of us, when we watch it, can identify someone we know as an extra."

It wasn't until after lunch that I told them my main concern. By then, I sensed my parents knew I had come with an agenda. I dove in: "Mom, Dad. When I was here in July, I know I said some things about our ancestors that upset you. I really didn't mean to do that. But in case you'd like to look at it, I brought along the evidence I collected while I was in Steamboat Springs."

Mom's back stiffened at the word "evidence," a term I immediately regretted using. Ian and Angela were probably right that this approach would feel like a confrontation, but here we were. Maybe I shouldn't have brought Ian along, but since he had been through something similar with his parents, I thought his presence might help.

"So what is it you have?" Dad asked suspiciously, eyeing my backpack.

I opened it and dumped onto the table a jumble of documents, copies of records, and notes on index cards. Mom picked up a scrap of paper, perplexity wrinkling her brow. "Are you going to explain what all this is?" she asked, laying it back down as though it gave off a tainted smell.

"Well, I didn't want to impose my conclusions," I said.

"Honey, you can at least tell us what these things are," Dad said. "You don't have to turn them into a story, but at least clue us in on what we're looking at."

Mom picked up a stapled bundle, looking puzzled. I explained, "Those are copies of newspaper articles documenting property in Steamboat Springs that Orville bought."

Her eyebrows rose as her mouth assumed a rigid line. She set down the bundle and picked up the chapter I had photocopied from Powell's *Steamboat Springs: The First Forty Years.*

"You can see how white people thought about the Utes by reading that," I said.

She scanned the first paragraph, then set it back down. "I fail to see what that has to do with things now. I can see where you'd be incensed reading this, but it was published in, when was it? Is that 1972 written at the top?"

Dad had picked up the paragraph-long biography of Orville. He chuckled. "Great-great-grandpa went from running the bath house and pool hall to being Justice of the Peace. Looks like the qualifications for JP weren't very high."

I glanced at Ian, wondering what he was thinking. His face seemed to say my parents were reacting as he'd expected. I wasn't sure what to do. I fiddled with the hem of my T-shirt. I needed to encourage them to at least read some of the material before telling them I was in the process of selling Gram's house. I couldn't keep that a secret from them, even if I wanted to. I bit a hangnail.

Dad was pawing through my notes on index cards, while Mom stepped back, exasperation settling into her face. Finally, Dad said, "Honey, I don't know what you expected us to make of all this, but I'm not seeing what you seem to see."

"Okay," I said, picking up the biography of Orville. "Here's how I know they homesteaded, and when. It was right as the Utes were being expelled from Colorado. Surveyors came in and divided up the land into homestead plots to give to white people for almost nothing. Orville kept the homestead for six or seven years, long enough to be granted title to the land, then apparently sold it for a profit to buy these lots in Steamboat Springs." I pointed to the stapled bundle of papers.

Mom said, "A lot of people were doing that at the time. Probably most people we know have someone in the family tree who homesteaded. Is there something wrong with that?"

"What it means is that a lot of what we have now came at the expense of the people who already lived there." I tried not to sound argumentative, but could hear a combative tone seeping into my voice. "Homesteading for white people—getting a home for free, basically—left Indian people homeless. That's what's wrong with it."

"So what are you proposing, that we all go back to Europe?" she shot at me.

Dad flashed an annoyed grin. "That'll be tough. You'll have to mail your right leg to England, your arms to Sweden, your torso to France—"

"This isn't funny." I could almost see smoke rising from Mom. She turned to Ian, hoping to find an ally. "Ian, Denise usually has a level head. Somehow she got this bee in her bonnet that we descend from racists, or something like that."

"Well, actually, we have the same situation in New Zealand," he said. "I grew up assuming my Scottish ancestors hadn't displaced anyone. It took some Māori mates to get me to look into the truth of what happened."

"Why?" The sharpness in Dad's voice startled me. "That's generations ago. So our ancestors weren't perfect, but nobody is. I can't see the point of digging up this old stuff, especially when it leads you to disrespect the people you come from."

"It was the policies that were wrong, Dad," I said. "You're right, our ancestors were just doing what other white people were doing at the time. But the policies—policies they didn't create, by the way—those policies gave them other people's land. And no one ever gave it back."

Two sets of eyes shifted from me to Ian. Mom asked, "Is this something you put her up to?"

"Mom!" I exclaimed. "I already told you. What got me started was the story about Gram's mother being the first white child born in Colorado. I hadn't even met Ian yet when Angela and I went there."

She scowled. "This is Angela's doing?"

"No, Mom. But Angela's grandmother does descend from the Utes who lost their land to people like our ancestors," I said, then added, "You'd probably like Mrs. Walker if you met her."

"Where does Angela's grandmother live now?" Dad asked.

"In Colorado Springs, like I told you. In a house." I wondered if they thought she lived in a teepee.

Mom's eyes jumped from my face to Ian's and back to mine. "So if she lives in a house like we do, what am I missing? She isn't homeless like you just said. You seem angry and I don't follow what you're angry about."

Dad added, "Look, sweetie. I'll grant you that unfair things happened a long time ago. And our ancestors might have partaken. But they were a product of their time. I don't see the point in dredging up this stuff from the past and making yourself feel guilty over things you had nothing to do with. Can't we just forget it and move on?"

I studied the floor as my mind whirred. "Mom, Dad. Land was stolen. I intend to give back the little piece of it I have."

Mom looked lost. "But you don't own land in Colorado. Do you?"

"No," I said. "That got sold eons ago. What I have came from the proceeds of selling it. Gram never would have bought her house if she hadn't inherited that chunk of money from her mother. Part of the house should rightfully belong to the Ute Nation, so that's what I intend to give back."

"What would they want with part of a house in California?" Mom asked, clearly baffled.

Dad had followed what I was saying, though, and I could practically see steam coming out his ears. "You are doing no such thing. I simply will not allow you to sell my mother's hard-earned house and then give away the proceeds in order to, what, make you feel less guilty about something you didn't even do, is that it?"

"I'm not giving anything away," I replied. "I'm simply returning what was taken, although in a different form because, as you point out, Mom, I don't own any property in Colorado. But this isn't charity, it's honesty. Like, if one of your neighbors dropped a twenty behind the couch and you found it and knew where it came from, what would you do? Keep it?"

"That's not the same thing at all, and you know it," Dad retorted.

"But it is," I insisted.

"My mother must be turning over in her grave," Dad spat.

"I don't think she is," I said quietly. "I think she would get what I'm doing and why I'm doing it. You and she always taught me to be honest and not to take advantage of other people. You've been incredible role models for me in living those values. I might be applying them differently

211

from how you would, but they're values all three of us hold dear. And Gram did too."

That was true. This was the first time I had verbalized, even to myself, that rather than acting in a way that was contrary to my parents' values, I was honoring those values. I was just doing so in a very different way than they would, at least right now.

"Mom and Dad, I want to take you to Colorado one of these days to meet Mrs. Walker. Just think about it."

As I made this suggestion, a voice in the back of my head reminded me that I still hadn't even thought to ask my parents about their upcoming cruise. I needed to shift the conversation toward something they were excited about, but not before leaving us in a better place, if that were possible.

I scooped the documents into my backpack. Poor Ian! I glanced at him standing off to the side. He winked back at me.

"I'm sorry to have put all of you through all of this, but I have to stand on what I believe. I still love you both, even if it might not feel like that." My voice quavered. Tears weren't far.

In typical Mom fashion, she turned to Ian and changed the subject. "Can I get you a glass of lemonade?"

"Sure, thanks," he replied. Ian doesn't drink lemonade because of all the sugar in it. But sugar, shmugar, he was doing what he could to calm the waters.

Dad said to him, "Sorry you drove all the way up here just for this."

Ian smiled wryly while Dad's face screamed that he and Ian could have met under better circumstances. Mom asked him a couple more questions about New Zealand while he drank the lemonade she brought him. She hadn't offered me anything.

Even as I asked them about the cruise they were about to take, my parents seemed to regard me as if I had become a two-headed cow, or maybe a fish with legs rather than fins. A freak they didn't want to disown, but couldn't match up with anything they recognized. While my relationship with Mom forever had its bumps, Dad had been my cushion, the one to pick me up when I fell, the one I could lean on, the one who could turn tears into laughter. Was that all gone? Could it be revived, but on new terms? I wasn't sure, but I vowed to keep trying.

As Ian pulled the car onto the freeway, I began to sob. My parents hadn't tossed me out of their home this time, and they hadn't lectured me about my apparent disrespect for my elders. But their anger, followed by politeness, felt worse. I thought about Ian's remark about having switched sides. In their eyes, that's what I had done, and for no reason that made the remotest sense to them. I wondered what might happen if I took them to either Utah or Colorado so they could meet real people who, like us, were also products of history. But the Ute people descended from those who had lost rather than gained through racist policies not of their making. Might my parents then begin to see what I now saw?

Ian laid his right hand on my thigh while his left gripped the steering wheel. "You going to be okay?" he asked.

"I suppose," I said, reaching for another tissue. "Ian, I'm realizing that I used to blame that first white child story for launching me onto a path that's become way difficult. But what's happened is that my perspective has shifted. The idea of someone being first? It sounds like a new beginning, a fresh start, which is the whole glorification of settler colonialism. And the idea of innocence that people of European descent attach to 'white,' well, the story makes it seem like there was a brand-new beginning, like history started at that moment. But it didn't. There were whole histories going on before that moment, the Indigenous peoples' histories and the colonizers' histories, and they collided. Angela was always leery of the first white child story, right from the beginning, and her grandmother dismissed it entirely. I finally recognize the collision it represents, and now I can't un-see that, you know? Even if my parents don't."

He squeezed my thigh, then returned his hand to the steering wheel. "You're on a journey, my love. There's no final destination to this stuff, but you're a lot farther along that journey than your parents are at the moment. Let your love for them keep the lines of communication open."

"I'll never have the same relationship with them that I used to have, though," I said from a deep well of sadness. "I know our relationship needs to accommodate me making my own decisions, but I miss the easier one I had with them as a child."

"I imagine you do," he replied. "But you'll work out a new way of relating."

Chapter Fourteen

Mending

I STARED OUT the window as the rental car turned southeast off Interstate 80, en route to the Uintah-Ouray Reservation in Utah. My eyes were fixed on the jagged mountains, our surroundings already white with snow. Thankfully, today's sky was clear.

Angela, driving, was engaging Ian in a stream of conversation about American Thanksgivings. "When I was growing up, one of my elementary school classes made these awful headbands with paper feathers. I can't believe I actually wore one of them. Some kids played Indians and others played Pilgrims."

"People don't still do that, yeah?" he asked.

"Some still do," she replied. "Last time I tried getting another teacher to cut the Indians and Pilgrims crap, she refused because she thought kids need to learn positive stories about white people and Indians. I can't wait to tell her next week what we did this weekend. That'll give her a different kind of positive story! You don't have anything like Thanksgiving in New Zealand, do you?"

"Not unless there's an American in the family or living next door," he laughed.

I smiled to myself. Angela was right. We would be spending this Thanksgiving weekend very differently than most people I knew. Rather than sitting around the table stuffing ourselves with turkey or enacting some fantasy about white–Indian relationships in the past, we would be participating in the Utes' annual Thanksgiving powwow. Tomorrow morning, we planned to meet with members of the Tribal Council to whom I was returning stolen property. Then we would go to Mrs. Walker's son's home, where Angela would meet some relatives for the first time. After that, we all planned to go over to the high school where a huge powwow takes place every year. I couldn't wait. I had heard that this four-day event draws Indian people from all over, even from adjacent states.

215

Just a year ago, today would have been unimaginable to me. Angela, Sean and I had gone to my parents' house for Thanksgiving. Driving home by way of Berkeley, it hadn't occurred to us to stop at what I now knew as the Emeryville Shellmound Memorial, just a few miles south of the West Berkeley Shellmound. Even if we had stopped, I would have thought of it in relationship only to the past, rather than linking it to Ohlone people here and now.

Since then, I had learned that we cannot separate the past from the present, and we should not paper over the past with cheery (and mostly fictitious) stories. Nor should we regard the present as determined by the past. Of course, we can't change history.

But we can reach back into history, grab hold of something, and give it a sharp turn. While we can't bring back the people who were slaughtered, the knowledge that was destroyed, the lives that were ruined, all of us can learn to mend some things, reset them, enable ourselves to move in a different direction.

My mind replayed my parents' reaction when I told them how I was spending this holiday weekend.

"I just can't believe you're actually giving away your inheritance to the Indians," Mom had said. I hadn't realized what little regard she had for Indian people until then. "Just what do you think they'll do with all this money you're giving them? Build casinos?"

"Mom, I'm returning stolen property," I said for the umpteenth time. "I'm not giving away anything. How the tribe decides to use it is their call, not mine." As I said this, I made a mental correction. The word "property" carries quite a different implication from the word "land." Property is something over which you claim ownership. You place yourself and your wishes over property, you buy it and sell it for profit. Land, on the other hand, is the mother that sustains life. Land is home, land provides for us, land grounds us. Turning land into property trivializes it and ignores the power of nature. That way of thinking throws us way off balance, a lesson I was beginning to learn.

"We know you see it that way, honey," Dad was saying. "We just wish you wouldn't rush into this. Give yourself a few more months to think about it. You don't want to do something you'll regret later."

"Why don't you bring Ian to join us Thanksgiving?" Mom asked. "I don't understand why you have to go away on that particular weekend."

"Mom. Dad. First off, I'm not the first white person to return stolen land. Have you seen this newspaper article?" The previous month, several news outlets had featured a man in Sonoma County who was returning to the Kaisha band of Pomo Indians 700 acres along the California coast that his family had farmed for almost a century. If I had any doubts about what I was doing, this story squashed them. I printed a copy of the article to show Mom and Dad. They glanced at it, then dropped it on the table, just like they had done earlier with the documents I had sleuthed in Steamboat Springs.

"Second," I continued, "I picked Thanksgiving weekend because we have four days off work. I could have waited until after Christmas, but we want to start working with some teachers then. I really wish you'd change your minds and come with me to Utah." I had tried to talk them into joining us, but they didn't seem ready yet.

Mom slumped into a chair, arms folded, eyes trained firmly on the floor. Dad shook his head, seeming to search for words. He finally said, "Denise, Thanksgiving is a time for honoring family. I know you aren't trying to dishonor your mother and me, and I know you hoped we'd come along with you. But it still feels like you're deliberately dishonoring my mother and my grandparents."

"Dad, I honestly believe Gram would support what I'm doing," I replied. "And I think it's possible for me to respect my great-grandparents while, at the same time, believing what they did was wrong, even if it was commonly done. What was really wrong were the policies of removing Indian people so white people could claim their land, but white people didn't have to go along with those policies. And I don't think respect means we have to pretend everything someone did was right. Besides, you've even referred to your grandfather as 'no good' because he eventually abandoned the family. Does that mean you don't respect him?"

"Abandoning the family is different," Dad said.

"Different, how?" I asked.

Dad and I stared at each other in silence while Mom studied the floor. Then I said, "I'll bring Ian at Christmas. If that's okay."

They just nodded.

"And maybe next summer you'll take a trip with us to Utah," I added.

How would other white people react to me returning what my ancestors had stolen? I hoped a few might want to do the same, but suspected many others would think I was nuts. So far Jessica was the only person at Milford I had talked with, mainly because she and I were now working with a local Ohlone elder who was interested in helping us bring Ohlone knowledge into our fourth- and fifth-grade classrooms. I would like to say the other fourth-grade teachers were also interested, but after glancing through my Gold Rush project, they bowed out, although one of them wondered if the elder we were working with might come in as a guest speaker. Maybe I could prod them at least to start using the California Indian resources on Sacramento State University's website.

When I had told Jessica about my decision to repatriate, I realized the issue was even more complicated than I had thought initially.

"Wow, that's amazing," she said. Then she wrinkled her brow and asked, "How did you know who to return it to? I mean, you didn't know exactly who had been using that piece of land before the white people took it, did you? Do you just show up at a tribal office and say, 'Hey folks, here I am with some land to return'?"

"If I didn't know Mrs. Walker, I'm actually not sure who I would have gone to. She knows the people, the internal politics, all that. I imagine it's the tribal council you meet with. That's who I'll be meeting with. But that's a good question."

She studied her hands, then said, "What if you know exactly how many acres your ancestors homesteaded, and can even locate them on a map, but the next generation squandered everything? I mean, the idea of returning stolen land sounds good, but what if, as far as you know, there's nothing left by the time it gets to you?"

I recalled Angela having come to a similar conclusion when attempting to trace what she had inherited from her ancestors' homestead on Ponca lands. I asked Jessica if she was referring to her family history.

"Yeah," she replied. "See, I have the actual homestead documents in Illinois, or a copy of them, and a map showing where the farm was. And a newspaper article talking about the next generation inheriting those acres, then selling them to buy something grander in Iowa. But what they bought turned out to be swampland. A land speculator basically ripped them off."

"How awful. I guess you can't return what you don't have," I said. "Or what you can't trace because the records just aren't available. But I've learned of other things we can do."

"Such as?"

"Well, re-educating the next generation. They'll be voters."

"Of course," she agreed.

"But I don't think we give ourselves credit for how much power we have as teachers. And I've also realized that we need to educate ourselves first. Angela and I are taking an American Indian History class right now through Adult Ed. It meets one evening a week, and I'm learning a ton. You should join us next semester," I suggested.

"I'd like that," she said. "Send me the information for spring when it comes out."

"I will. Oh, and some of the Indian educators from around the state are talking about having a California Indian education summit next fall in conjunction with Indigenous Peoples' Day. If that happens, we'll have to go."

"I'm in," she said. "Keep me in whatever loop you have going."

"I will. In the meantime," I continued, "I've discovered various organizations and buy-back systems working on the return of land to tribes. And of course our support of local Indian activists is important, like when we joined the shellmound walk put on by Indian People Organizing for Change."

"But it just seems like the government should be the main one to return land," she said. "After all, it was government policies that enabled land to be taken in the first place. Reversing the damage done by those policies shouldn't have to depend on individual acts here and there."

"Well, yeah," I agreed as I wondered how many people in Washington D.C. were inclined to return land to tribes. "I guess that's why we need to reeducate the next generation. And ourselves."

Jessica, along with me, Angela, and one of Angela's colleagues, teamed up to work with teachers in the elementary school Mrs. Walker had been communicating with. We had tried a couple of virtual meetings using Google Hangouts, but spent more time futzing with the technology than actually talking about our work. We planned to meet face-to-face here in Utah over the winter holidays to begin thinking together about what a decolonized curriculum might look like, or at least the best we could do as non-Ute and non-Ohlone teachers collaborating with elders.

I thought briefly about Cynthia Jorgenson—then dismissed her from my mind. What could she, and others like her, do to me if I refused to submit to their ideas about curriculum and teaching? They could threaten me with dismissal, but how many schools actually want to dismiss teachers whose students are doing relatively well on the mandated tests, as mine were? I suspected they would do even better if I followed what I knew about engaging young people in meaningful learning, and stopped trying to follow other people's orders. I thought back to the activity Ian had challenged me with when he asked who I work for. He put the kids at the top of the list. I was learning to do the same.

I watched the back of Ian's head as he responded to something Angela was saying. As rocky as Christmas promised to be, he had accepted my parents' invitation "with pleasure."

Ian. I had never imagined how right it could feel to be with someone – except maybe Angela, and Gram. Somehow, I felt as though I had known Ian my entire life. Being with him felt like an ongoing mixture of surprise and familiarity. Take last night. While cooking dinner in his apartment, he had me in stitches with stories of car repair disasters. He was okay portraying himself as clueless about auto mechanisms, an area most guys at least pretend to know something about. He was comfortable in his own skin. As I listened to him, he reminded me of someone. Was it Dad? But Ian didn't look at all like Dad, and Dad liked to tinker on cars. A cousin, perhaps?

Or perhaps it was me who was finally becoming comfortable in my own skin. With Ian, I relaxed into myself. I didn't impose grandiose expectations on the relationship, as I had with Peter. Nor did I guard myself from diving in too deep emotionally, as I had with Sean. And I didn't try to figure out what Ian wanted because he seemed most happy with the unvarnished me. Our relationship felt natural.

Or maybe it was that I had grown into simply liking myself better, and Ian was just a beneficiary.

"We're here," Angela announced as she turned the car toward the motel registration office. She parked, we grabbed our bags and entered.

Suddenly Angela, bounding ahead of me, squealed, "Grandma!" We hadn't expected a reception, but now Mrs. Walker was being crushed by Angela's embrace. They were flanked by an older Indian man who looked a bit like Angela, and an Indian woman about my age.

"Denise, welcome," said Mrs. Walker as she took one of my hands. "And you must be Ian. Welcome." Then she stepped back and introduced us to Angela's uncle and his youngest daughter—Angela's cousin—a first-year teacher in the school we would be meeting with on Friday. Our work of mending and resetting history had begun.

৺৺৺

AS WE LEFT the Tribal Council chambers the next morning, I felt elated. Angela wrapped an arm around me and whispered into my ear, "I'm so proud of you."

The meeting itself, although short, moved me. After introductions, one of the Tribal Council members gave me a certificate of thanks, and a young woman took photos. Another gave me a beautiful blanket; more photos. A third member gave me a book about the tribe, published locally several years previously. Then, although they had heard my story from Mrs. Walker, the Tribal Council members asked me to tell it in my own words. So I told them about my journey that the first white child story had launched. They smiled warmly and nodded as I talked. When I finished, they thanked me again, and we stood together for more photos.

A young white man sitting in a corner turned out to be the tribe's financial officer. He gave me information to take to the bank to complete the financial transfer. The Indian woman taking photos worked for the *Bulletin*, a bi-weekly newspaper that would run an article about me. Then, since it was Thanksgiving morning, the meeting adjourned. Later at the powwow, the Tribal Council Chair would introduce me to the tribe and invite me to say a few words.

My eyes watered as a profound sense of relief settled over me. I had been carrying around a heavy load of guilt since I realized the origins of my house. Actually, the guilt began many years earlier when I realized Indian people didn't just disappear, but white people like my ancestors had brutalized them in order to take their land. I had shoved guilt away by telling myself I had no responsibility since I had done nothing. Now, on this day of Thanksgiving, I had finally confronted the past. By acting, I had initiated a process of mending history.

Author's Note

WHAT WOULD IT mean to take seriously being a descendant of the colonizers of Indigenous peoples? I wrestled with this question as I researched my family's own history of taking land from several of the North American tribes. In many cases, the theft happened so many generations ago that I have not been able to trace a direct impact on myself. But in one case – the one that formed the basis for this novel -- I was able to trace an inheritance to homesteading on what had been Ute peoples' homeland. I did not find the pieces documenting that link all at once. And when I did, coming to terms with their full weight took some time. But in September 2017, I traveled to the Ute Nation in Utah, where I met with members of the Tribal Council to return what my ancestors had stolen – not the land itself, since that had been sold before I was born, but my share of money that derived from selling the land. The hospitality of people I met during that visit and a subsequent one was truly humbling.

This novel is based on that experience. As with all novels, much is the product of my imagination. The characters are all fictitious; any resemblance between them and real people derives only from impressions real people have made on me. I set *The Inheritance* in 2015 so that it flows from my first novel, *White Bread*, which takes place in the same elementary school and includes a couple of the same characters. But the homesteading story, and the process of digging out that story, parallels my own family history research very closely. I tried to provide enough detail about how I did that research so that readers, should they choose, can pursue similar lines of inquiry with respect to their own families.

To develop my knowledge of Ute history and culture, I consulted the following: Virginia McConnell Simmons' *The Ute Indians of Utah, Colorado, and New Mexico* (University Press of Colorado, 2000), Clifford Duncan's article "The Northern Utes of Utah," in *A History of Utah's American Indians*, edited by Forrest S. Cuch (Utah State Division of Indian Affairs, 2003), Fred A. Conetah's *A History of the Northern Ute People* (Unitah-Ouray Ute Tribe, 1982), and Peter E. Decker's *The Utes must go!* (Fulcrum

Publishing, 2004). To expand my knowledge of Ohlone history, I consulted Deborah Miranda's *Bad Indians: A tribal memoir* (Heyday Press, 2013), Linda Yamane's *A Gathering of Voice: The Native Peoples of the Central California Coast* (Santa Cruz County History Journal, 2002), Lowell John Bean's *The Ohlone Past and Present* (Ballena Press, 1994), Les Field's chapter "Mapping Erasure" in Amy E. Den Ouden and Jean M. O'Brien's *Recognition, Sovereignty, Struggles, and Indigenous Rights in the United States* (University of North Carolina Press, 2013), Lynn H. Gamble's *First Coastal Californians* (School for Advanced Research Press, 2015), and Thomas C. Blackburn and Kat Anderson's *Before the Wilderness: Environmental Management by Native Californians* (Ballena Press, 1993).

For knowledge of Steamboat Springs and the Yampa Valley, I visited the area and spent time in historical archives there, I also consulted Lee A. Powell's *Steamboat Springs: The first forty years* (self-published, 1972), James H. Crawford's *1889 Copybook: Business letters written by James H. Crawford during 1889 - 1892 Steamboat Springs, Colorado*, edited by James Logan Crawford in 2015, and numerous newspaper articles published in the *Steamboat Pilot* during the 1800s.

I owe a deep debt of gratitude to many people who helped me along the way. Ronit Wagman's editorial advice significantly improved the structure and flow of the story. I am indebted to several critical friends who read all or parts of earlier drafts, offering many helpful suggestions: Russell Bishop, Rowan Bishop, Rose Borunda, Larry Cesspooch, Clarissa Conn, Jeanette Haynes Writer, James Jupp, Joe Larkin, John Maddaus, Luanna Meyer, Leslie Patiño, and Dorothy Vriend. I am also grateful to Valerie-Jean Rivera for sharing insights about the Ohlone Costanoan Esselen and pointing me toward excellent sources to read. Kris Hellén did an exceptional job proofreading.

Finally, to Indigenous colleagues on both Turtle Island (North America) and in Aotearoa New Zealand, thank you for gently pushing me over the years to look into my own history and take some responsibility for its consequences.

About the Author

CHRISTINE SLEETER is Professor Emerita in the College of Professional Studies at California State University Monterey Bay, where she was a founding faculty member. She is an internationally recognized leader in social justice multicultural education, ethnic studies, and teacher education, and is author of numerous non-fiction books in those areas. Her work has been translated into several languages. *White Bread*, published in 2015, is her first work of fiction. She currently resides in Monterey, California. For more information, please visit www.christinesleeter.org.